GLASTONBURY TOR

GLASTONBURY TOR

LeAnne Hardy

Kregel
Publications

Glastonbury Tor

© 2006 by LeAnne Hardy

Published by Kregel Publications, a division of Kregel, Inc., P.O. Box 2607, Grand Rapids, MI 49501.

Other than the historical characters and events mentioned in the afterword, the persons and events portrayed in this work are the creations of the author, and any resemblance to persons living or dead is purely coincidental.

Mass quotations are from *Latin-English Booklet Missal: For Praying the Traditional Mass, Third Edition* (Coalition in Support of Ecclesia Dei, 2000).

Scripture taken from the 1526 edition of William Tyndale's translation of the New Testament.

Library of Congress Cataloging-in-Publication Data
Hardy, LeAnne.
  Glastonbury Tor: a novel / by LeAnne Hardy.
    p. cm.
1. Catholic Church—Fiction. 2. Glastonbury Tor
(England)—Fiction. 3. Great Britain—History—Henry
VIII, 1509–1547—Fiction. I. Title.
PS3608.A728G63   2006
813'.6—dc22   2006021228

ISBN 0-8254-2789-4

Printed in the United States of America

06 07 08 09 10 / 5 4 3 2 1

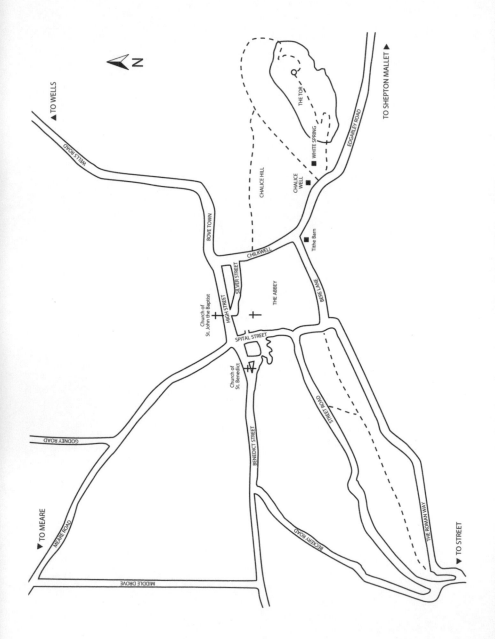

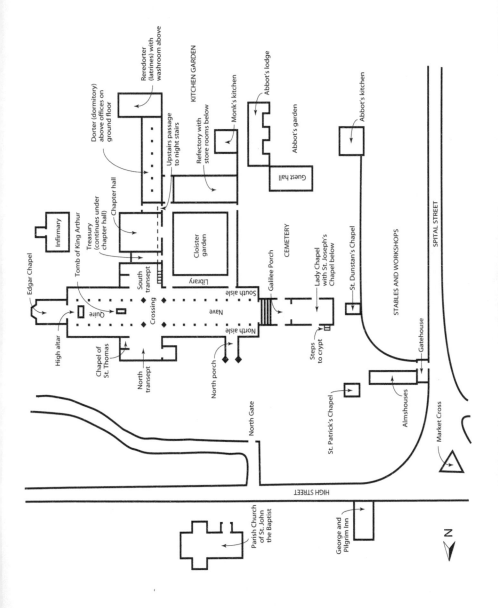

Reredorter (latrines) with washroom above

Dorter (dormitory) above offices on ground floor

KITCHEN GARDEN

Upstairs passage to night stairs

Chapter hall

Refectory with store rooms below

Monk's kitchen

Abbot's lodge

Abbot's garden

Guest hall

Abbot's kitchen

Infirmary

Treasury (continues under chapter hall)

Tomb of King Arthur

Edgar Chapel

Cloister garden

Library

South transept

High altar

Quire

Crossing

Nave

South aisle

North aisle

Galilee Porch

CEMETERY

Lady Chapel with St. Joseph's Chapel below

St. Dunstan's Chapel

STABLES AND WORKSHOPS

SPITAL STREET

Chapel of St. Thomas

North transept

North porch

Steps to crypt

St. Patrick's Chapel

Almshouses

Gatehouse

Market Cross

North Gate

HIGH STREET

Parish Church of St. John the Baptist

George and Pilgrim Inn

N

PROLOGUE

WHEN SAINT COLLEN, SON OF Pedrwn, son of Coleddog, of the court of King Arthur returned to Britain after vanquishing Bras the Pagan, he was made abbot of Glaston on the Isle of Avalon. Now Glaston was the holiest place in all Britain for it was said that Jesu himself walked its sacred hills when he came as a Child with his Uncle Joseph of Arimathea, the tin merchant. It was to Glaston that Saint Joseph returned many years later, bearing the Christ's own cup, which Joseph had filled with the blessed Savior's blood at the very cross.

Five years Saint Collen served as abbot in Glastonbury, but the monks were a lazy and worldly lot who tried his patience until he left them. After traveling the length and breadth of the land, preaching the Good News of the Christ, he retired to live as a hermit in a rude shelter at the base of the great hill of Glastonbury, called in the ancient tongue, "the Tor."

As Saint Collen sat one day in his booth of withies, hid among the brush and brambles of the great hill, he heard two peasants passing on the road below.

"Neath lies the Hall of Faeries," said one.

"Aye," answered the other, with a fearful glance toward the summit. "There reigns Gwyn son of Nudd who rides forth with his Wild Hunt to claim the souls of the dead."

9

"Hold your peace," said the hermit, putting his head out of his boothie. "Gwyn ap Nudd is a demon and king of all that is evil."

"Best hold your own peace, Granfy," said the first speaker with a toothless grin. "Or he may call ye to account for your words."

That very night a messenger, cloaked in garments red as blood and white as frost, appeared at the hermitage. "Gwyn ap Nudd bids you come and speak with him on the Tor," the messenger said.

"I will not come," replied the hermit.

The following night a cold wind blew through the withies of the shelter. Again the messenger called at the entry. "Gwyn ap Nudd bids you come to him and not tarry."

"I will not come," the stalwart replied.

The third night, a storm raged about the mountain, splitting the sky with fire and shaking the very rock under the old man's shelter.

"Gwyn ap Nudd says come!" roared the voice of the messenger above the rush of wind and crash of thunder. "Refuse, and this Isle of Avalon will sink forever beneath the waves."

At this, Saint Collen gathered his courage and a flask of holy water and followed the messenger.

When he came to the top of the Tor, he saw a castle, more fair than any built by man. Its courts were arrayed with the best-appointed troops, and minstrels made every kind of music of voice and string. Comely youths sat upon fine steeds and maidens danced sprightly and light of foot.

On a golden throne at the end of the great hall sat Gwyn ap Nudd.

"You are most welcome, my friend," the Horned King said. "Sit and feast with us. Whatever food or drink your heart desires, you have but to speak, and it will be yours. My young men and maidens stand ready to provide you with every luxury of courtesy and service."

But Saint Collen knew the food was not real, and if he ate, he would later find that he had stuffed his belly with leaves and grass and vile, unclean things. He drew out his flask, and scattered the holy water about the hall and upon the heads of all the assembly, whereupon they vanished from his sight, so there was neither castle, nor troops, nor men, nor maidens, nor music, nor song, nor steeds, nor youths, nor banquet, nor the appearance of anything whatever except the green hillside and mists of night.

And so the heathen spirits were banished from the land for a thousand years.

PART 1

THE TOR

CHAPTER 1

I AM A COWARD.

Were I not, I would have died this morning on the Tor with the others, but I fled and hid. The abbot told me I should be gone to Wales by now, but I hadn't the courage even for that. My father spoke truer than he knew. He said I would never amount to anything as a monk, and he was right.

I close my eyes and mutter the prayers of protection for the dying.

> . . . From the ancient enemy: free and defend their souls, O Lord. . . .

Across the moors three gallows loom atop the Tor. Three bodies swing in the cold November dawn. I draw my cloak around me. The bundle that is my treasure presses against my side, safely wrapped in the wool of my old habit. I try again to pray, but it is the warm baritone of the priest in my old parish in Wales that fills my mind. More than a year has passed since he chanted those prayers for my mother. The pain still runs deep, and it is for her that I weep.

～

... From the ancient enemy: free and defend her soul, O
Lord. . . .

The voice of Father David rose and fell. My mother stirred faintly
and drew a ragged breath, her once golden hair strewn on the pillow
like so much lifeless straw.

... From the stratagems and snares of the Devil: free and
defend her soul, O Lord. . . .

I knelt in the rushes on the floor, joining my voice with the priest's
in the refrain.

"Free and defend her soul, O Lord."

It numbed my grief-stricken mind like pounding rain. If I had not
left her that night. . . . If only I had raised a hand to stop him. Incense
masked the odors of blood and illness, and my stomach felt empty
and hollow, as indeed it was. The light of a single candle flickered
on the gold threads of the Holy Grail in the tapestry my mother had
hung against the half-timbered walls of her room. She had woven it
with her own hands and brought it to this house some twenty-three
years ago when her father arranged her marriage to Sir Stephen Hay.

... From the onslaught of malignant spirits: free and defend
her soul, O Lord. . . .

The murmuring voice of the priest gave little comfort.

. . . From fear of enemies: free and defend her soul, O
Lord. . . .

At least in death she would be free of him—Sir Stephen, who
showed more tenderness for his horses and hounds than for her who
managed his household and bore him sons. Seventeen years ago when
I was born and nearly killed her in the birthing, the doctors had said
she'd stand no more children. He had other women. The tales of his
lechery surpassed even those of his father.

But he came to her one winter's night when the snow lay on the high hills. I was huddled close to the warm brazier on my stool, leaning against her knees while I read to her from a romance of King Arthur. Llwyd, the harper, strummed lightly on his instrument.

"King Arthur lies at Glastonbury, *Collen,*" my mother reminded me, twirling the end of her long braid, as golden then as when she was young. She used the Welsh form of my name. The soft dentals sounded so much gentler than my father's clipped English "Colin."

A cold rain had fallen all day and trapped him indoors. His step sounded on the stair, and more than once he lurched unsteadily against the staircase wall.

"A man has a right to his wife," he declared as he entered, thrusting his grizzled head forward on his thick neck in challenge.

"My lord." My mother lowered her eyes submissively, but not before I caught the startled fear of a cornered rabbit in them. Her hands trembled, and she clasped them tightly in her lap.

"Father!" I scrambled to my feet. "What do you intend?"

He laughed coarsely. "Time you learned, boy! You're near a man, or would be if you didn't spend your days with women and harpers." He sneered at Llwyd, grasped my mother, and dragged her to her feet.

She gave a little cry before he smothered it with his mouth on hers. Brigit, the waiting woman who had nursed my mother from infancy and me after her, backed into the shadows of a corner, clasping her embroidery to her breast.

I started forward, but Llwyd gripped my shoulder and jerked me back.

"Sir Stephen," he began, "I hardly think . . . The lady is delicate."

Sir Stephen thrust her away from him and turned smoldering eyes on us. "Don't think I don't know what goes on between you two." He took a menacing step in our direction, and I shrank against Llwyd's thin form. "Your looks, your touch, your ingratiating ways."

The minstrel paled, but stood his ground. "I assure you, Sir Stephen, nothing improper has ever . . ." My father drew back his beefy hand to strike.

"Llwyd . . ." My mother's voice was quiet but insistent. Even my father paused. "Best leave us now. I shall not be needing you any more this evening, Brigit. *Collen,* come kiss me good night. You should have been in bed long ago." Whatever her fears, she mastered them. She sat on the bed where my father had thrown her. Her face was void of color, but her voice lost none of its commanding dignity.

"But, Mother!"

She raised her chin in the proud tilt I knew so well, and I could not cross her.

Llwyd's body stiffened behind me as he hesitated. His fingers dug into my shoulder. The moment passed; he would not cross her either. "Yes, my lady. Sir Stephen, good night." He pushed me forward, and I bent and kissed my mother. Her lips felt warm although the fingers that touched my hand were icy cold.

"Good night, *Collen.*"

I swallowed hard and found voice to form the words. "Good night, Mother."

That was near the Feast of Saint Valentine, when the nights were long and cold. Summer had come and gone. Now it was autumn—too soon for the babe, too late for the woman who bore her. The midwife carried away the stillborn girl early that morning, and for a few hours we thought my mother might live. Now it was clear she would not.

Sir Stephen had gone riding with his hounds before his infant daughter's body was cold. I thought Brigit, the waiting woman, might try to defend him with some pap about his way of dealing with sorrow. But even she, faithful servant that she was, pursed her lips in silent rage.

My father cared nothing for the tiny child that had never drawn breath, as he cared nothing for me. He preferred my brother Walter's tolerance for ale and skill with a sword to my love of books and way with a pen. It was good that Walter was the heir, for I wasn't man enough for their company and never would be no matter how much I tried.

Pater Noster, qui es in caelis. . . .

The litany ended, and we recited the Lord's Prayer. "Our Father, which art in heaven, hallowed be Thy name." My lady mother no longer stirred. Although her breast still moved in faint, feeble breaths, she was past hearing.

The prayers ended, Brigit saw the priest to the door. She was weeping. Walter's voice echoed through the hall below. My elder brother by five years, he had come with the others of the household to pay their respects and to hear my mother's last wishes. I saw the nervous twitching of his powerful hands and the cold sweat on his brow. He held back from kissing her as though her very touch would bleed his life away. For all his strength and manliness, he had a horror of death. He escaped to the hall as soon as he might. But unlike our father he fled no farther, for he did love her.

My eyelids felt strangely heavy. Twice I jerked my head from where it had fallen forward against the coverlet. If I slept, I might lose her forever. But the room was close and airless, and my consciousness drifted.

I seemed to be in a cavern, its passage narrow and low. The splash of falling water echoed on every side, and a stream ran at my feet. The walls ahead glimmered lacy white in the light of hidden torches. My fingers ached with cold as I braced myself against the wet walls.

The passage opened into a great hall, crowded with pillars of pure white stone. Some hung from the ceiling; some rose from the floor and some met in delicate columns, too insubstantial to hold the weight of the earth above.

Were these the gates of purgatory, where I would join my mother? Or was this the enchanted kingdom of the Faire Folk of which Brigit spoke?

Far in the distance, I heard the baying of hounds and the call of a hunting horn. They echoed inside the cavern of my dream, resounding from the bowels of the earth, rising from an opening in the rock face on the far side of the hall. The clatter of hooves rang after them from the depths.

The stone beneath my feet shook, as from the din of horsemen, until the faery pillars began to sway. One dropped from the ceiling and shattered into a thousand pieces on the floor. Trembling with cold and damp and fear, I took shelter behind a curtain of stone. I chanted the names of Jesu and clutched the silver cross that hung on a ribbon around my neck. A sliver of flying stone stung my cheek. When I took my hand away, the palm was marked with blood.

Torches fell and were extinguished. The noise of the approaching hunt reverberated in the chamber. I daren't look and I daren't look away as a pack of phantom hounds burst from the passage. Their fur shone silvery white as the light of a full moon. Their eyes gleamed red like the coals of a dying fire.

I covered my ears to block the sound of my own scream. With a deafening rumble a rider on a horse as black as a moonless night thundered into the hall. He wore a blood-red cloak, and his head was that of a stag with a five-point brace of antlers—Gwyn ap Nudd, White Son of Night—come to seek the souls of the dead.

"No! You shall not have her!" I cried.

"*Collen,* awake." It was Brigit, not the Horned King, who touched my arm. What seemed a loud cry asleep was only a dull moan awake. The faint baying of hounds sounded in the distance.

Brigit brushed aside the heavy cloth that hung over the leaded glass of the window and looked into the darkness. "Your father is returning."

She turned and patted my mother's damp face with a soft cloth. "It will not be long now."

Indeed, the sound of the lady's breathing had changed. There were long pauses between each labored breath. I knelt by her bed and took her hand. It was cool and pale blue like ice.

"Mother," I whispered. I leaned my head against the coverlet and breathed the spicy scent of the herbs used to poultice her. "Why has he done this to you?" My mind was filled with the Horned King of my dream. My shoulders stiffened.

◆

My earliest memory of my father was of being carried to the hall at Michaelmas. Torches cast weird shadows on the revelers, and the air was thick with wood smoke. My father must have been well into his cups. Meat juices dripped like blood from his beard and fingers. He leered at me. A pair of antlers nailed to the wall behind him appeared to my childish eyes to project from his head. I recognized him at once as Gwyn ap Nudd of Brigit's nursery tales. I screamed in terror and struggled to escape my nursemaid's grasp.

"What? The boy afraid?" my father roared. "Curse him for a fool and a coward!" He hurled the cup at Brigit who dropped me in the scramble. I tried to hide under the table but overturned a trestle. The boards collapsed on me, spilling their burden of wine cups and platters of food. Hounds leaped at the fallen meat. I screamed the louder until Llwyd swept me up and carried me to my mother.

Was it that day my father learned to despise me?

I was seven before Walter put me straight that our father was not god of the underworld.

"Only a mortal man," I reminded myself, watching the life fade from my mother. "Someday he, too, will die. May no priest be near to chant the prayers, no absolution to pluck him from the flames of hell. I will not tremble before him again."

A shudder went through my mother's thin frame. I clasped her hand in both of mine, desperate to hold her in this world. The baying of hounds and clatter of hooves sounded in the yard. My father was home.

Brigit once more dabbed the tiny drops of sweat from her lady's face. My mother's breath caught. Time seemed to hesitate. The air slipped out in one long sigh. Brigit began again to weep.

Not I. No tears would fall. Their flood pressed against my chest like water against a mill dam near to bursting. My father's voice boomed through the hall, calling for wine. Had he no respect even now?

Brigit gently pried my fingers from their crushing grip on my mother's hand. *"Collen."*

I stood, shaking my head to clear the last of my dream. A knot at the back of my neck thrust tight fingers around my skull. The heat of the room stifled me. My vision was blurred and dark, and Brigit's voice seemed to come from that far off cavern. The stag's head loomed in my mind's eye. He would not have her.

I stumbled against the walls of the narrow stairway and into the hall below. Walter stood by the stone fireplace, as tall and broad-chested as our father beside him. He looked up. I could see in his eyes that he guessed the news.

Sir Stephen bellowed for more wine. His words were slurred. He had obviously drunk elsewhere. A servant scurried from the buttery with a brimming cup.

Walter's sword belt hung from the arm of his chair. The polished hilt glittered in the firelight. It angled toward me in silent invitation. I lunged for it and drew the blade awkwardly from its sheath. It felt heavy and unnatural in my hand.

"You killed her!" I gripped the sword in a ready position and took the stance I had been taught. I would never have Walter's strength or skill, but my anger would make up for that.

Sir Stephen was just reaching for the cup of wine. He stopped and stared at me, his eyes suddenly clear of drink.

Walter spoke evenly. "Colin, don't be a fool!"

My father's face relaxed in a smile. "No, Walter." He laid a hand on Walter's arm. "Perhaps your brother has found his manhood after all." He lifted the cup in a mocking toast.

I lunged for him. He jerked back, and my thrusting sword passed between him and Walter. The cup of wine spilled red as blood down his doublet. His amusement turned to anger, and he sputtered his contempt. I shouted and thrust again. My father whirled away, but his sleeve was stained with a red that wasn't wine.

His own sword hung on the wall behind him. Had the trestle table been put away, I would have had him before he found the weapon. I thrust the table aside with a strength I hadn't known I possessed. One corner bashed a hole in the clay plaster of the wattle wall as the boards clattered about.

Before I could clamber over them Sir Stephen had his sword down and faced me. He carried twice my weight and had thirty years' experience on me. All I had was the passion of my hate.

"Colin, stop this foolishness." A tremor in Walter's voice betrayed his fear.

I didn't take my eyes from my father's face. The veins in his swollen neck stood out like purple cords. His eyes showed full circles of bloodshot white around deep blue centers, and I thrust again. It was the foolish lunge of a beginner. I stumbled on one of the fallen boards and nearly fell on my father's blade. He twisted it away and only nicked my sword arm just above the wrist.

I dropped the sword and grasped my arm to stop the spurting blood.

My father's anger dissolved in harsh laughter. He stepped over the boards into the center of the room.

"Come, boy! If that's all you can do, I'd better find a worthier sword master to teach you." He beckoned me closer, his eyes merry with derision. "Or pack you off to the monks like your mother wanted."

The reminder of my mother lying still and lifeless on the bed upstairs spurred me on. Behind my father's head the stag antlers hung from the wall. I knew the likeness to Gwynn ap Nudd was an illusion, but I sprang like a madman from my crouch on the floor. I grasped the sword in my bloody hand and thrust it toward his middle with all my strength. The quilted fabric of his doublet resisted, then gave way as the sword slid into his side.

My father's eyes showed startled shock. Not only had the blade found his innards, but his worthless son had done the unfathomable—what he'd never thought me man enough to do.

Gorge rose in my throat, and I thought I would surely choke. Walter eased Sir Stephen to the ground. Voices called for someone to go for the physician. The room swirled. The heat and smoke of the fire suffocated me. I let the bloodied sword slip from my hand and clatter on the floor.

There was nothing in my stomach to vomit but its own bile. I left that outside the door as I fled for sanctuary to the parish church.

CHAPTER 2

I THREW MYSELF FACEDOWN on the cold tiles of the church floor. There was no light but the candles that flickered before the carved statue of Our Lady. If I hadn't known that powerful prayers prevented them from entering this holy place, I would have feared that demons lurked in the dark corners to steal my soul.

What have I done? I thought. *Is there a worse sinner than one who kills his own father?* I shivered with terror at what I had become. But it was my father who had made me so. His derision and lust had turned my hand against him.

I stretched my arms wide in imitation of the ivory Christ pinned to a silver cross on the altar. The wound on my arm pulled open, and I felt the blood begin to seep from it into the bandage I had fashioned from a strip of my shirt. I didn't care. The cold hardness of the floor made me tremble. If I lay here long enough . . . if my penance were great enough, might I yet escape the fires of hell?

How could God forgive me or accept penance? I was not even sorry for my crime.

Yet if I did not repent—if I were damned to hell for all eternity—I would never again see my beloved mother. I wailed like one of the souls of the damned that cried out from the painting covering the west wall of the church. I banged my head against the clay tiles until blood ran into my eyes as Christ's blood ran from his crown of thorns.

Even if I could not repent, perhaps I could pay for my sin with enough suffering that God would overlook it.

The heavy wooden door of the church creaked on its hinges. I clutched at the altar lest I be dragged from it to my death. But nothing entered except the wind, carrying a few dry leaves that skittered across the floor.

I closed my eyes and sought to steady my breathing. I had seen a hanging once. A boy younger than I. He'd stolen two of my father's ponies. They hanged him at a crossroads as a reminder to all who passed of the consequences of crime. His face was blue and swollen. His eyes bulged. Is that what they would do to me for killing my father—hang me?

The sky was beginning to show light beyond the glazing of the windows when Father David came to say Prime. He entered through the side door and shuffled back and forth across the front of the chapel, lighting candles, before he saw me.

"Colin? Is that you?" he asked. "Why are you here?"

I was curled into a ball at the base of the altar. I unfolded my stiff body and showed my contorted face. The salt left by my tears and the dry blood from my forehead cracked as I began my confession.

"Father, I have sinned."

❧

Walter came an hour later. His face was pale and dark circles rimmed his eyes. His mouth was set in a hard line. "Brigit thought I'd find you here," he said.

I sat trembling on the altar steps while the priest finished dabbing the blood from my face with a damp cloth.

Walter's eyes stared coldly. "You've done it now, you fool," he said as the priest quietly rinsed the soiled cloth in a bowl of water. My arm throbbed beneath a fresh bandage. "Father is furious—threatening to disinherit you. He'll have you soundly beaten if he finds you."

My body was numb. My brain was foggy with lack of sleep. Walter's shape seemed to sway in front of me.

"Father?" I fumbled to grasp the meaning. "He isn't dead?"

"No, he's not dead, though he might have bled out if we hadn't tended him quick. The physic says he'll be right unless it festers. But he's angry as a stuck bull."

Tension drained out of me like wine from a burst skin. I wished for some place to empty my bowels. He wasn't dead. I hadn't killed him, although I was no less guilty of trying. No words came, only slow, ragged breaths.

"Brigit has been up all night with his demands, else she would have been here herself to look for you. She has hardly had time to prepare our lady mother for burial." His hardness seemed to melt when he spoke of our mother. "Colin, how could you do this?"

"Need you ask?" My voice was hard and bitter. "Were it not for him, our mother would still live." Walter's silence told me he knew it was true.

"But to draw a sword on him while her body was still warm. . . . It's—not like you." He looked around at the tiny parish church. "This is where you belong. This is where Mother wanted to see you. In the church."

I shuddered. However I might justify my act, I knew my mother would not have had it so.

"You must leave," Walter went on, coming to a decision. "You must be gone before he heals enough to rise from his bed." He pulled a ring from his hand. It was an amethyst given him by our father at his knighting. "This will show you to be the son of Sir Stephen Hay. Take it to John Thorne, Father's cousin at Glastonbury Abbey. He'll find a place for you."

I took the ring and stared dully at it. I had envied Walter Father's love when he received it. Now I wanted to fling it away. Instead I slid it on the black ribbon around my neck where it clinked against the silver cross our mother had given me for my twelfth birthday.

"They're closing the smaller monasteries," Father David said slowly. "But surely—Glastonbury is the oldest house in all of Britain, and one of the largest." He laid a hand on my shoulder. "You have the gift for learning, Colin. The monks of Glastonbury can teach you far more than I ever could." Father David made exile to Glastonbury seem as pleasant as study with the masters at Oxford.

"I brought your cloak," Walter said. "And a few things Brigit thought you would want."

So my exile was to begin immediately. *Better to leave the church for a monastery than for the gallows.*

I stood slowly. My limbs ached with stiffness from my night on the floor. Walter embraced me roughly. He was less like our father than he sometimes seemed.

He thrust a purse at me. "You'll need to make a gift to the Abbey for their hospitality."

I weighed the purse in my hand. It would take more than money to pay for my sin. I followed Walter through the arched door of the church and into the pale light of the new day.

CHAPTER 3

BY EVENING I HAD REACHED the banks of the Severn. The next morning I arranged passage across the broad estuary to the Somerset Levels. I left behind the mists that hung over the water and emerged into one of those rare late summer days when the sun shines like molten gold and the sky is blue from one edge of the world to the other. It was hard to feel any guilt for what I had done. I was free of my father's demands and criticisms. No longer would he make me feel a worm beside my brother. My heart felt almost light.

My horse had been left at home. If Father were to disown me, I wanted to give him no excuse to accuse me of theft. Besides, it seemed more fitting to do my penance on foot. But Glastonbury was fifteen miles from the sea. I was tired from the unaccustomed exercise of the day before, and the crossing of the Severn had taken longer than I'd expected. I had made no vow to walk, so when a farmer offered me a ride in a cart smelling of apples, I accepted gladly.

He introduced himself as Wilfrith Thatcher. I gave my name, and although he eyed the scab forming on my forehead after its contact with the church floor, I offered no explanation, and he asked no question. My sleeve hid the wound on my arm.

Wilfrith Thatcher's homespun shirt was clean for a laboring man, although it showed wear at the wrists and elbows. He pointed out the sea walls and the canals, maintained by the monks for hundreds of years to drain off water from the bogs surrounding the Isle of Avalon, as Glastonbury was once called.

"Them sea walls be one of the few good things the monastery does," Wilfrith complained. "Useless lot, the monks."

I held my peace.

"Prayer, charity, and hospitality—them's the duties of the clergy." He went on, "'Stead, they mind to their Matins and tend to their full bellies. No fastin' for the likes of them."

I squirmed on the hard wooden seat. My own belly was comfortable, thanks to Brigit's forethought.

Wilfrith clucked impatiently to the horse. "'Tidn't like the old days. They takes our tithes, and what do they give, I be askin' ye? Even their charity be grudged, as though a poor man was takin' their last crust."

Wilfrith warmed to his enumeration of the sins of the monastery.

"And the women . . ." He gave me a sidelong glance as though evaluating my youth. "Well, thank God and Our Lady, we haven't them problems here. Glassonb'ry's a respectable house. Abbot Whiting sees to that, and Abbot Beere afore him."

I had no experience of girls and was half afraid of the few I'd met. The changes in my own body frightened me with the feelings they stirred. At least I wouldn't have to face that problem at the abbey.

"The church needs a good knockin' about, it does," declared the farmer. "Tha's the simple truth, and the monasteries need it more than most. Tha's why our Henry is breakin' them up. These little houses what do nothin' but feed off the land and let the monks idle the day away. Close them down, why not? Won't hurt nobody. Do a sight of good, I 'spec. Too much wealth for their own good or the good of hardworkin' Englishmen."

Considering what I'd heard from Father David, I suspected King Henry was thinking less about hard-working Englishmen and more about the royal purse. His fondness for tournaments and lavish palaces was the subject of gossip even in our Welsh valley. Between his divorce of Queen Catherine and his dallying with the Lutherans, there was talk of war with Europe.

Wilfrith glanced at me and dug his elbow in my side. "Ye knows

what they says, lad." He chuckled. "If the abbot of Glassonb'ry mar-
ried the abbess of Shrewsbury, they'd have more land than the king of
England!" He laughed coarsely and slapped his thigh.

My cheeks grew red at the lewd idea of an abbot and an abbess
marrying. They had both taken vows of chastity, obedience and pov-
erty. The farmer broke off his laugh and cleared his throat loudly.

He was thoughtful for a minute. "Henry rightly broke with Rome.
What do popes know about our ways? Better an English church with
an English head. Henry'll straighten it out, mind me words. Give us
our due and no thievin' pope carryin' off our tithes to fill his own
cup."

The flat moors of Somerset looked strange to my eyes, accustomed
as they were to the hills of south Wales. Where the marshes had been
drained soil was rich. The fields were green and the orchards heavy
with ripening fruit. Wilfrith was in no hurry, and the sun was warm. I
had hardly slept since my vigil by my mother's deathbed. In the peaceful afternoon, it seemed that my troubles had been left on the far side
of the Severn, and my head drooped on my chest.

When I awoke, a strange conical hill could be seen in the distance,
rising above the plain. Its irregular sides showed like steps against the
clear blue sky. A stone tower on the top pointed like a finger toward
heaven.

"Ye're awake." The farmer chuckled deep in his throat. "I put ye to
sleep with me chatterin'."

He followed my gaze. "Tha's the Tor."

I knew that *tor* was the ancient Celtic word for "hill," but this
hill, rising alone above the surrounding moor, was like none I'd ever
seen. Wilfrith gazed at the scene with pride of place. "And tha's Saint
Michael's Church at the top, or what be left to it. Most come down
long ago when the earth moved. Small wonder with the gates of
Annwn beneath it."

The old man chuckled, but I crossed my fingers in a sign against
evil and looked at him sharply. "How do you mean?"

"Don't ye fret, boy. 'Tis but an old story in these parts." But he
crossed himself for good measure. "Even Gwyn hisself couldn't bring
down Saint Michael. He's still there."

The tower stood bravely against the sky. No doubt the fires of pagan festivals had lighted the peak long ago. There were always such stories of isolated hills, and this was no ordinary hill. If it wasn't the gate to the underworld, it would be a good place to build one.

"Pater Noster, qui es in caelis. . . ." I crossed myself, and said a prayer under my breath.

We rolled into a tiny village. A string of cottages faced a grassy common with the manor farm beyond. A large pool edged with the tall grasses used for thatching spread for miles over the moor. Swans and ducks, settling for the night, disturbed the deepening blue of the evening sky reflected on its surface.

"Meare Pool," Wilfrith explained as the horse stopped on his own at the first cottage in the row. "They calls the village Meare as well. Abbey land." A pile of thatching grass lay drying in the yard, and apple trees clustered close in the garth.

"This be far as I go, lad. Glassonb'ry be there under the Tor." He pointed to where the tower of Saint Michael's glowed orange in the setting sun. "Ye're welcome to stay the night. Me daughter Matilda'll have the stew on the fire. But I'll wager a gentleman like yourself'd sooner stay at the manor house."

I hesitated. Wilfrith's house was little more than a hut, but I didn't relish the idea of explaining my presence at the manor. Besides, I found myself reluctant to part from this earthy farmer.

A sturdy woman of little more than twenty stood in the doorway. Her hair was covered with a gray wimple, but the roundness of her eyes and straight line of her nose told me she must be Wilfrith's daughter Matilda. "Well, ye're home at last. I wondered if ye'd fallen in the rhyne and drowned." The twinkle in her clear eyes belied the harshness of her words. "Little Wil's been pesterin' me all the day, since his Granfy wouldn't take him along."

"Granfy!" A small boy charged around the corner and into his grandfather's arms. Wilfrith swooped him into the air over his head and shook the boy until the giggles spilled out, then set him on his feet again.

"Come and wash," the woman invited, "and bring your guest."

I had lingered over collecting my pack, wondering what difference a day could make. Her warm invitation convinced me. "I'd happily stay the night . . . if it's no trouble." I clutched my bag in front of me trying to look as meek as a gentleman's son could.

"Ye heard the woman." Wilfrith slapped my back. "Come, wash. Don't see no point to it, but Tildy is fierce for a man to come to table washed."

A tall, muscular young man with thick fair curls was already at the washbowl. He grabbed a piece of coarse sacking to dry his face and arms as we entered.

"This be Tildy's husband, Nicholas," Wilfrith introduced him. "And that be me daughter Alice."

A slender girl bounded from the hearth and embraced her father. I guessed her to be a little younger than I. Long yellow braids trailed behind her, and I envied the pride I saw in her father's eyes.

"This here be Colin," Wilfrith said. I nodded awkwardly.

"Did ye bring the dyed thread I wanted, Father?" Alice asked. Wilfrith drew a packet from the breast of his tunic. Alice whirled away with it. "Blue! 'Tis perfect!"

"Now ye can make yourself a hood like a fine lady of court, eh?" Matilda shook her head. "Girls' heads be full of fashion. Queen Jane's the one Alice favors. . . . God rest her soul." She crossed herself. Queen Jane, King Henry's third wife, had died the previous autumn.

"Least Queen Jane was English," Alice retorted. "Not Spanish like Catherine or a Frenchy like that—woman."

"Alice," her father warned. "Hold your tongue." He looked at her sternly, and I suspected she had been about to use another word that had commonly been applied to the king's second wife, Anne Boleyn.

I couldn't resist the temptation to tease. "I've heard the chancellor is arranging a marriage with a German princess now."

"Fah! But 'twas the Englishwoman what gave the king a son!" Alice tossed a braid over her shoulder.

"True," I admitted. Jane Seymour died after birthing an infant boy. With the succession assured, there would be no return to civil war or the rule of a foreign consort over the little princess Elizabeth. The small, flame-haired daughter of Anne Boleyn had been banished from the court, as her half-sister Mary had been before her. I doubted we'd hear more of either of them. Too bad for gossiping tongues like Alice's.

Wilfrith put a hand on my shoulder. "Colin be bound for Glassonb'ry."

"For the fair?" Matilda asked. Nicholas drew two trestles into the middle of the room. Alice tucked her packet into her bodice and examined me from my dark curly head to my square shoulders and skinny legs. Her eyes were intensely blue, and I couldn't help thinking how nice they would look with a blue embroidered hood.

"Are ye goin' to Glassonb'ry for the fair then?" Matilda repeated.

I glanced at Wilfrith. It would be wrong to deceive them. "No, Mistress Thatcher. I have a relative at the monastery. I'm going to him. I intend to be a monk."

Nicholas's back froze over the board he was laying on the trestles for a table. He looked hard at me before settling the board and straightening his back. "A monk, eh?"

Matilda plucked nervously at her apron. The easy manner with which she had greeted me was gone.

Wilfrith self-consciously rubbed the stubble on his chin with a dry hand. "Don't suppose ye appreciated me thoughts on the clercs back along," he said slowly.

"I was glad of your thoughts." I swallowed deliberately. "You made me think. I like to think. I know not all monks are what they should be . . . but then . . . neither am I. My desire is to be a scholar. Father David says there are books at Glastonbury."

"A fine lad as yourself could go to university," Nicholas suggested warily. "Be books there, too, I hear."

I hesitated. "Perhaps."

If only I had gone to Oxford two years ago, when Father David suggested it to my father . . .

"I'd go to university," Alice broke in wistfully as she set the trencher of stew firmly in the middle of the table.

Matilda put her hands on her hips and laughed. "And how much church-tongue Latin would a lass need in such a place? Nicholas be daft for teachin' ye letters as 'tis."

"You know your letters?" I asked with interest.

"Course I do." She tipped her nose in the air. "I can read as good as anyone."

"You read?" I was astounded. Although my mother had read a little, I knew no village women who could and few men.

Nicholas gave her a wary look, and Matilda clutched at Alice's hand.

The girl rushed on: "There be books about. People read things, and pass them on. And they're in our own tongue, not your silly old Latin." Her face flushed as if she realized she may have said more than she should. She turned away and worked with the fire although I couldn't see that anything needed doing. There was a tension in the room that I didn't understand.

Little Wil took my hand and led me to a stool. "Sit by me."

When Wilfrith had recited the blessing, we dipped fresh nutty barley bread into the thin stew. It was simple fare but well-seasoned. I broke the silence with a compliment, but Matilda only nodded and kept her eyes lowered.

Wil leaned against me and touched the mark on my forehead. His small face was full of concern. "Do it hurt?"

"Only a little," I replied. I had nearly forgotten the scrape. The hidden wound beneath my sleeve hurt more.

"I gotta sore." The little boy twisted his elbow around to show me a healing scab just out of sight. Alice's laughter rang from the other side of the table.

"Well, I have!" retorted the child in indignation.

Wilfrith wiped the bottom of the trencher with his last piece of bread and stood.

Wil looked up expectantly. "We read the Holy Writ?"

Matilda gasped and turned a fearful glance on me. Wilfrith cleared his throat and looked sternly at Nicholas. I wondered what the child could be talking about. Surely they couldn't have a Bible, although I had heard of Lutheran sea captains smuggling in the forbidden book from Protestant printers across the Channel. Only heretics read the Bible in English. People had been burned at the stake for owning one.

Only Nicholas remained calm. "Not tonight, Wil."

"But Father, ye said tonight we'd read about tearin' up the roof."
He turned to me. "Last night we read about—"

"Wil!" His father's voice was firm. "I told ye not to speak of this."

". . . Outside the house, Father—ye said not to speak of it outside
the house. This be inside." The little boy began to whimper and buried his face in my side.

My arm went protectively around him even though his father had
made no threat. My own hands had gone cold. My heart pounded
against the wall of my chest. How could I report them when they had
been so kind to me? Yet not to report them was a crime. The Bible
must be read in Latin and interpreted by priests.

If unlearned men read it for themselves, they would fall into all sorts
of errors. Even now the Lutherite heresy was sweeping Europe, tearing
people from the true church. Of course, King Henry had already torn
us away from the true church. Not the true church, he said, only the
pope. Ours was the true church. An English church with an English
head—Henry—but still the true church. It was all very confusing.

But one thing was sure and agreed upon by all proper folk: No
English heretic Bibles were supposed to be read at the firesides of
Meare.

"I told ye no good'd come of this." Wilfrith's harsh voice intruded
on my thoughts. "Teachin' girls to read and bringin' new ideas into
this house."

"Father—" Alice clutched her hands in her lap and looked beseechingly at him.

"If your mother was alive—" His words cut my heart like the edge
of a sword.

"If she was alive, she'd be glad of me to read," Alice retorted.

And why not? I savored the forbidden but delicious sense of tasting
a stolen apple. Of course, women's minds were not as strong as men's,
but if they were able. . . . And by that road, if the English church
could be the true church, why not an English Bible? I'd never considered it before. The very thought was a crime. But I'd just tried to kill
a man, and this offense didn't seem much worse.

"If you please . . ." My mouth blurted the words before my thoughts
could catch up. "I would like to hear Alice read."

Matilda gasped. "Not Alice." Her face was pale as milk as she put her arm around her younger sister. "Don't let her be the one."

Alice looked defiantly at me and then at her father.

Wilfrith glared at Nicholas. He grumbled under his breath. "Why I let that girl learn—"

"There's no law that I have ever heard, that a woman can't learn letters," I said carefully. "And if I don't see the title of the book, I doubt I'll know what it is . . . especially if I never heard the like in English tongue."

Nicholas laid a hand on his father-in-law's arm. I could feel Matilda relax only a little on the far side of the table. The two men exchanged a look. Nicholas smiled and nodded slightly.

"Shut your eyes," Wil commanded. He crawled onto my lap and covered my eyes with his small hands.

Alice giggled nervously. I could hear Wilfrith wrestle with the heavy lid of a chest or box and rustle among the things inside. I tried not to listen. I didn't want to guess where the book might be hidden.

"Now ye can look." Wil took his hands away from my face as his grandfather placed the volume on the table. The boy settled himself on my knee, his small back warm and soft against my chest, his hands folded reverently in his lap. By participating in this reading, I would be as guilty as they. I could not reveal their secret without betraying myself. What I would do at next confession, I wasn't sure, but I would never speak of this. I'd pray that the Judge of all mankind would understand.

Wilfrith caressed the book lovingly before he pushed it across the table to his younger daughter. "I cassn't read." His voice was full of regret. "But I be in pangs of hunger for the words of God."

Alice found the place marked by a thin weaving of wool. Matilda kept her arm on Alice's back. Her eyes narrowed and burrowed into my face as though daring me to report them.

Alice looked around defiantly. "I for one choose to trust in God, so I tell ye plainly: This be the gospel according to Saint Luke in the fifth part of his writin'," the girl began. Her words were confident but her voice strained.

And it happened on a certayne daye that he taught: and ther
sate the . . .

Nicholas looked over her shoulder. "Pharisees," he prompted.

. . . *Phair-sees* . . . and docturs of law which were come out of
all ye tounes of Galile Iurie and Hierusalem. . . .

She read well and only stumbled a little on the foreign words. The
story told of men bringing a paralyzed friend to Jesus and finding the
house too crowded to enter. They tore a hole in the roof and let the
man down to the Master on a sleeping mat. I found myself staring at
the thatch over our heads, half expecting a hole to appear, so real was
the story in my native tongue. The characters had never seemed so
alive in Latin.

Alice's voice was clear and pleasant.

When he sawe their fayth he sayde vnto him: "man thy synnes
are forgeven thee."

What sins could a paralyzed man commit? Surely he had not stuck
a blade in the side of his father. Yet the Pharisees complained. No
doubt they were the sort to complain about a family reading the holy
words around a table in a language they could understand. Seems
Jesus had no patience with such.

Alice grew more confident as she read. Nicholas seldom had to tell
her a word. Her voice was loud and dramatic.

"What thinke ye in youre hertes?"

Wil leaned forward on my lap, shivering with excitement.

"I saye to thee, 'aryse, take vp thy beed, and go home to thy
housse.'"

A small giggle escaped the boy, who seemed as amazed as those
who witnessed the miracle fifteen hundred years ago.

"Let us pray," said Nicholas as the reading came to an end. Alice
closed the book and gave me a defiant look. I answered with a reassuring smile and joined them on my knees by the table.

I prepared myself to say the usual *Pater noster* and *Aves,* but Nicholas
began with words of his own making, powerful words of love and
praise to God for *Jesu Christe.* I wondered why the Father or the Son
would condemn as sin deserving hellfire what we had read, or its ending with heartfelt praise to our Lord. Even Wil joined devoutly when
we all ended with the *Pater.* But the words were in English—*"Our
Father, who art in Heaven."*

As I spread the tick and sacks Matilda gave me that night for a
bed by the hearth, I remembered my earlier thought. What difference
could a day make? It had made a difference.

I knew it had.

CHAPTER 4

TWO DAYS LATER I COMPLETED the last miles of my journey. Wilfrith and Nicholas were going in to thatch some booths for the coming Glastonbury fair, and I used that as my excuse to linger in Meare. I watched the men prepare the thatching grass and kept young Wil out of their way. He seemed to have adopted me as elder brother. No one brought out or mentioned the forbidden Bible again. After dinner, the little boy grew strangely quiet and kept his eyes fixed on the table. Even Alice turned away when I gave her an inquiring look.

Wisps of cloud laced the Tor with the Tower of Saint Michael at its top when we started out the third morning. Instead of growing larger as we approached Glastonbury, they seemed to shrink and disappear behind the smaller hills. The streets of the town bustled with visitors arriving for the next day's fair.

"Whoa." Wilfrith stopped the cart of thatching grass in one of the broad streets that led off from the market square.

"Abbey be there." Nicholas pointed to a high, arched gateway, a short distance up the street. A black-robed monk approached beside the wall that bordered the abbey grounds. His hands were thrust into his wide sleeves, and his face wore a sour, pinched frown. I shuddered.

Nicholas gave me a long searching look. I had no doubt that the secret of the hidden Bible was still on his mind. His eyes framed the question that went unasked: Would the bailiff be coming to their door because they had trusted one with such close connections to the monastery?

Wilfrith waited, the reins in his hand, and his eyes fixed on the horse's rump. He wore an air of resignation to whatever life would send.

"Thank you for opening your hearth to a stranger." I hoped my smile was reassuring as I shook Nicholas's hand. "May I take my leave as a friend worthy of your trust. Fare well, Master Thatcher." I waved at Wilfrith, who returned my parting. "My thanks to you." Their cart rumbled over the cobblestones in the direction of the fair field.

The monk lingered at the gate, his eyes fixed on the departing cart. A half dozen such carts were in sight. I wondered why this one interested him so. He had the stoop of a scholar who spent long hours bent over his books, and his face was as pasty gray as the shaggy, silver hair that circled the shaved tonsure on his head. He turned dark, intense eyes upon me and seemed to look through my doublet and tunic and into my heart. He appeared no more pleased with what he found there than my father had been. I ignored the trembling that had started in my knees and refused to look away. The monk gazed steadily for a few moments, then turned and glided through the abbey gate.

I took a last look toward the market square, surrounded by half-timbered buildings and impressive stone facades. If I lingered, I might lose my resolve to withdraw from this world in search of salvation. I took a deep breath and plunged through the crowd toward the abbey gate.

The hubbub of the streets seemed to fade to a murmur in its shadow. A lane led from the gatehouse past a row of almshouses. The monk from the street strode purposefully across a short stretch of lawn toward the abbey church, rising stone upon stone, laced with leaded glass, until it reached the sky.

"Impressive, idn't it?" broke in a voice beside me. I turned to find the abbey porter at my elbow. "Tha's the Lady Chapel." He pointed to the delicately proportioned west end in front of us. "Built over the old church, the one Saint Joe 'Mathea hisself built. His chapel be in the crypt."

The man squinted his eyes and seemed distracted by something moving on the roof of the almshouses just above our heads. "What in creation—?"

The thing was white, but too large and ungainly for a swan. It poked at the drain that led off the slate roof from a stone gargoyle. I stared, fascinated.

"Whoa!" With a shout, the hummock turned into the form of a man who flailed arms and flapped his white cassock in vain for balance as he slid off the roof. Thankfully it was not much higher than my head at this point, but he fell in a crumpled heap on the cobbled path.

The porter sprinted to him with me at his heels. "Brother Roger! What ye be doin' on the roof? Ye're a novice monk now, not the abbey handyman."

The young man on the ground looked no older than Walter. He shook a head of flaming red hair as if to clear away the stars that still floated before his eyes. "Widow Archer . . . complained of water backing up into her room last rain. I checked the drains." He held up a bit of broken slate with a grin as bright as his hair. "This was blocking it."

"'Tis no concern of yours." The porter shook his head good-naturedly and pushed away the broken slate. "There's others to do that sort of work now. Ye're to study your Latin."

Brother Roger's face fell. "Aye, that." He gave a deep sigh and sat up.

"Are you sure you're all right?" I asked, eyeing the distance from the roof to the ground. "That was a nasty fall."

"I'm fine," the novice replied, getting to his feet to prove it. A moment later he collapsed with a whoosh. His face wore a baffled expression. "What's wrong with my knee?"

A shadow fell across us. "What is this disturbance?" I looked up to see the same gray monk who had been outside the gate.

"Father Bede!" the porter exclaimed. "Brother Roger, fell from the roof here."

Father Bede looked sternly from the roof to the novice on the ground. "Had he been in the cloister attending to his studies, this would not have happened."

The porter licked his lips nervously. "I think Brother Urban should have a look at his knee."

"No doubt," said Father Bede. "And no doubt our novice will be wanting a few days in the infirmary, resting his knee while he eats meat like a glutton, neglects his books and sleeps through the holy offices." Roger kept his eyes fixed meekly on the ground. "I will see to it that Father Aidan is informed as to the whereabouts of his wayward novice." The man's black surplice swirled about him as he turned and stalked across the lawn.

The porter stood with his hands on his hips. "The least he could of done is to help us get him to the infirmary!"

"I'll help," I volunteered.

"Thank ye, Master Pilgrim. I'm afraid I can't leave the gate." He got under one shoulder and I under the other, and together we raised Brother Roger. He towered over us as he would tower over most any man. Everything about him was long and thin. His face was pale, no doubt from the pain of his knee, but he was brightening, now that the cloud of Father Bede's presence had passed.

"Fixin' the drains indeed, Brother Roger," the porter chided. Brother Roger's smile looked none too repentant.

"Widow Archer should have no more trouble. The drain is clear. I'll have to see to that gargoyle. His nose is broken off. I could carve a lovely new one with bug eyes like Brother—"

"Others'll see to it, Brother Roger," the porter interrupted.

Roger laughed. "I know—study my Latin."

Roger directed me along the north side of the church and around the east end. He hopped beside me with his hand on my shoulder, his head thrown back to admire the unfinished stonework. "Isn't it marvelous?" he cried when we paused to rest. "Saint Mary's of Glastonbury! 'Twill be the longest church in all England when the Edgar Chapel is finished." His voice rang with pride.

"I was a stonemason once," he admitted. "I worked three years on the Edgar Chapel before the monks agreed to accept me as a novice." He gave me a shy smile. *"Laudate Dominum.* Praise be to God! I don't know much Latin, but I can say *Laudate Dominum!"* He laughed again.

We maneuvered through the infirmary garden, sheltered between the wall of the chancel and the south transept of the church, and into a long pillared hall. Beds lined the north aisle in little alcoves, while the south aisle had been walled off into small rooms.

A monk with a disfiguring strawberry mark on his face tucked a mantle around an elderly brother in a seat by the fire and hurried to us. He clicked his tongue at us. "Now what's happened?"

Roger looked at his feet in obvious embarrassment. "Bit of an accident, Brother Urban. Nothing important, but I twisted my leg, and it doesn't want to hold me up." Roger winced and grasped his knee as I eased him onto a stool. Brother Urban bent over him.

Roger smiled at me. "Many thanks for your—ow—for your help, Master Pilgrim," he said as Brother Urban poked and prodded.

"What has happened to your forehead?" Brother Urban demanded when he stood to find a bandage. He called to his assistant. "Fetch that salve and put some on this boy's head." He knelt to wrap Roger's knee, but continued to address me. "Pilgrim, eh? Take the salve with you. I can spare a bowl of it. Use it morning and evening until the wound heals. Do you hear me? It looks clean enough, but we can never be too sure."

Roger grinned over his head while the assistant dabbed my forehead with an ointment that tickled my nose with the scent of herbs. Brother Urban hadn't waited for an answer to his question. The wound on the back of my wrist throbbed, but if I showed it to him, he would surely ask again how I received it. It would be hard to explain without telling a lie, or worse—the truth. "Thank you," I said instead. "I have come to see my father's cousin, John Thorne."

"John Thorne," mused Brother Urban. "That would be Brother Arthur. I expect you'll find him in the church now. He usually cleans the altarpieces between Prime and Morrow Mass. I could send someone . . . ," he looked around, but the busy assistant was making his way out the door, balancing two chamber pots.

"I can find my way," I insisted, nodding to Roger who grinned as though we were partners in some great adventure.

I retraced our steps around the church to the north porch. It faced the town, and I assumed it was the entrance most often used by the public. I stepped through the great oak doors from the morning sunshine into the cool shadowy dark of the church. To my right were the

Galilee Porch and Lady Chapel the porter had pointed out. To the left, I gazed the length of the nave, past the sweeping arches of the transept and the finely carved quire screen to the tracery and stained glass of the east window. I caught my breath in awe. A huge silver disk, set with a blue stone, hung over the high altar, swaying gently in the currents of air that circulated through the upper regions of the building. It reflected the light from a dozen tall windows and sent shafts glittering into all corners of the church like the Star of Bethlehem itself. The beauty astounded me and left me feeling small and unworthy.

I moved from altar to altar along the deserted north aisle, pausing reverently now and again to admire the beauty. In the north transept I came upon a small man about my father's age. The skin of his tonsure glistened like the cross he polished. He had the short stature and square shoulders of a Norman, but the blueness of his eyes proclaimed that my father was not the only one in the family to intermarry with the Welsh.

I knelt and crossed myself. The chapel set in the east wall of the transept was elegantly proportioned. The image on the altar wore the mitre and carried the archbishop's staff of Saint Thomas of Canterbury. The monk nodded, no doubt assuming I was a pilgrim come to pray, and continued his polishing.

"Master Thorne? Er . . . Brother Arthur?" I inquired.

He shook out his polishing cloth and rested the candlestick against his ample belly. "Yes?" He looked quizzically at me as though he thought perhaps I was someone he should know.

"They told me I would find you here."

The polishing cloth paused while the monk peered more closely at me. "I see." He turned deliberately back to his candlestick, gave it a final caress with his cloth and replaced it carefully on the altar. "If you would like to talk, we'd best go to the little parlor."

He trotted ahead through the arches of the crossing, pausing under the soaring tower to pay respect to the high altar. We emerged from the south door into the shadows of the cloister. Brother Arthur led me to a room on the far side that must have been the warming room in winter, but at this time of year was deserted. There was a carpet on the floor and comfortable chairs around an empty grate.

"May I get you refreshment?" His manner had assumed a stiffness that didn't seem natural to him.

"That isn't necessary," I replied. I fished the ring on the black ribbon from around my neck. "My name is Colin Hay. My father—"

"—is Sir Stephen Hay." He smiled and nodded, barely glancing at the ring. "You have the look of your mother about you." He relaxed. "She made a pilgrimage here many years ago—a woman with a spirit as beautiful as her face. She prayed long for a son who would enter the church." He fixed me with his small blue eyes until I shifted my gaze uncomfortably to the floor.

"She made gifts for the tomb of King Arthur and the altar of Saint Thomas and took home a silver cross as a remembrance of her visit. Why, I believe it was that very cross." He fingered the one that hung on the black ribbon beside my father's amethyst ring and smiled. "Yes, that is the workmanship of our local smith—excellent craftsman. She chose silver and the sapphire stone in memory of the Great Sapphire of Glastonbury. You may have noticed it hanging over the high altar. I often wondered why she had not gone into the church herself. How is your lady mother?"

I studied the pattern of red and black tiles on the floor and opened and closed my mouth a few times. "She is dead."

"I'm sorry." The light in his round face faded. He held the silver cross with its sapphire stone in both hands as though through it he could sense my mother. "I must say prayers for her soul. She would like prayers said from Glastonbury." He seemed lost in fond memories.

Brother Arthur shook himself. "And your father—?" It was almost an afterthought.

The Devil put it in my mind to lie and say my father was well. I longed for this man, who had loved my mother, to think well of me. But it would not do to tell falsehoods in this holy place.

"He is recovering from a wound." The monk's brow wrinkled in concern. "It is a wound I gave him." I held my head high in defiance of my shame. "I blamed him for my mother's death. I have come to purge my soul of sin and give my life to the church as my mother wished." Surely this was the sort of answer a monk would want to hear. I stood with clenched teeth and square shoulders as I had always stood before my father to accept the punishment for my wrongdoings.

"Ahhh." Brother Arthur looked thoughtfully at me. "You know, the abbey is not a place of punishment, nor is penance the same as vocation. A pilgrimage is a fine thing should you wish to purge your soul, but that does not mean you should take vows."

"Please, don't send me away, Brother Arthur." I resisted the urge to kneel and grasp his feet. "Hate is a terrible sin. If I can't get rid of it . . ."

Brother Arthur stood silently, his head slightly inclined, waiting for me to finish. When I didn't, he inquired gently, "Then what? What is it you think will happen if you can't get rid of it?"

"I'll never see my mother in heaven." My voice shook with emotion. I twisted the pouch of money that Walter had given me. "I brought this." I thrust it toward him.

He ignored my offering. Slowly he caressed the ivory beads of the rosary that hung at his waist. "What did your confessor say?" he asked at last.

"He bid me come to Glastonbury." I bit my lower lip and admitted, "It . . . it may have been as much to get me away from my father's anger as his thought that I should take the cowl."

"You did well to come. Your father . . ."

Brother Arthur seemed to be looking back across the years to a time when they both were young.

". . . Your grandfather was a hard man. I pitied Stephen, that he had to outdo every squire in the West Country before his father would approve." I shifted uncomfortably, knowing my grandfather only by the whispered tales of servants and Walter's fearful remembrances.

Brother Arthur went on more briskly. "Your confessor may be right that time away will cool your father's anger. You may find peace and the forgiveness you seek in the quietness of worship and the routine of toil. Goodness knows my candlesticks shine brightest when Father Bede . . . well, when I'm working off a bit of anger." He touched my hand and turned me toward the church. "We will speak with Abbot Whiting after Mass."

At that moment the bells began to toll. "Come."

CHAPTER 5

HEARING MY STORY, THE elderly Abbot Whiting agreed to let me stay in spiritual retreat at Glastonbury for as long as I needed. "You may sleep in the dorter with Brother Roger and Brother Thomas. They are the only novices we have at this time."

"Yes, my Lord Abbot." No doubt the king's recent antagonism toward the monasteries did not encourage young men to choose monastic life.

The abbot pressed his long, thin fingertips together like a spider on a glass. "I will expect you to attend all services, including Matins." I did not look forward to rising at midnight to pray in a cold church. "As long as you are in this house you will submit to those in authority over you and abide by *The Rule of Saint Benedict,* which governs our house and all . . . the Benedictine houses." His voice caught as if he had suddenly realized how few were left.

"Yes, my Lord Abbot."

"You may call me 'Father.'" He didn't know that *father* was not a pleasant word to me.

"Yes, Father Abbot."

"If at any point you find this life distasteful to you, you are free to leave us. You have, of course, taken no vows."

I flushed to think he thought me no more than a fickle child who would change his mind with the waxing and the waning of the moon.

And yet already I wondered if I had chosen well. At the university . . .
But the church was what my mother wished for me. I had failed my
father, but perhaps I could be the son my mother wanted. "Yes, my
L . . . Father."

Contrary to Father Bede's prediction, or perhaps to spite it, at the
hour of the afternoon service Roger limped into the frescoed cloister,
bandaged and leaning on a carved stick. He looked surprised to see
me in a white cassock like his own, but he smiled and nodded and
took his place behind the other novice. He might have said some wel-
coming word if not for the Benedictine rule against idle chatter.

Thomas raised one eyebrow and sniffed at Roger's cane. He was
not much taller than I, although I guessed him to be older. His dark
hair curled carelessly on his forehead. His fair skin was unmarked by
any labor in the sun. I took an instant dislike to him. He had already
looked me over and dismissed me as not worthy of his interest. As
the newest member of the community, I would be the last in line, the
lowest seat at table, the least in everything.

I heard a small gasp of pain when Roger took the step into the quire.
Father Bede scowled at us from across the marble tomb of King Arthur
and began the chant. He was obviously a person of some rank in the
community. I did not want him as an enemy, and yet the small hairs
on the back of my neck rose whenever I felt the search of his eye.

In the afternoon, Father Aidan, the novice master, read to the
novices and to me from *The Rule of Saint Benedict* and explained its
meaning. Then he asked me to read. I read a paragraph about keeping
silence, and he seemed pleased.

"Thomas."

Thomas read easily and carelessly as though the meaning of the
words had no significance for him. His accent reminded me of a
Bristol wool merchant who once lodged with us for a few days while
arranging the purchase of sheep in the neighborhood.

"Roger, your turn," Father Aidan said.

Roger read slowly, tracing the words one by one with his finger.
A schoolboy could have done as well. I was embarrassed for him.
Thomas turned his body aside and looked thoroughly bored, but
Father Aidan praised Roger's progress.

After Vespers, Roger returned to the infirmary to rest his leg. The monks gathered in the cloister for relaxed conversation before the evening meal. Father Bede was anything but relaxed. I had barely entered behind Thomas when he pounced.

"How well do you know Nicholas Thatcher?" he demanded in a voice that stopped all conversation. His brows bristled like blackberry thickets. Thomas raised his inquiring eyebrow at me as though anyone who aroused such ire in Father Bede might be interesting after all.

"Nicholas Thatcher?" The blood drained from my face, and I could only hope the candlelight was not bright enough for anyone to notice.

"You alighted from his cart this morning."

"The Thatchers gave me a ride into town." I clamped my mouth firmly shut to keep from saying more than needed to be said.

"Did he say any word about Bishop Latimer?"

I let my breath out slowly, relieved that I could answer honestly. "No, sir."

"Humph. I'm surprised. That man is a heretic or I'm a fiend." I wasn't certain if he were referring to Bishop Latimer or to Nicholas Thatcher. "Doesn't believe in saints or images or even purgatory."

"I should be careful about accusations you can't prove," said Prior Robert, the only monk present who outranked Father Bede. "Hugh Latimer *is* Bishop of Worcester. Whatever we may think of his ideas, King Henry approves."

"At least for now," Thomas whispered in my ear. When I looked at him in surprise, he shrugged. "Who can tell what the king will approve tomorrow?"

"Hugh Latimer has made more heretics than that German devil Luther," Bede declared, oblivious to the comments of a lowly novice. "He will burn in hell if not before, and it will only be justice."

Some of the monks turned back to their conversations. I suspected that Father Bede's opinions on this subject were well known.

"You are a complacent lot." Father Bede swept the cloister with his glance. "Have you not seen how pilgrimages have fallen off? All this talk of faith instead of the blessed works of the church—"

"Bishop Latimer is not against all works," Brother Arthur protested. "He has preached in favor of the necessary works of tithes and works of mercy like visiting and relieving the poor." Several nodded their agreement. "It is only the voluntary works Latimer attacks. In truth, I see no merit in burning candles or paying for the gilding of images if the poor are abused or the heart is empty of faith."

That seemed reasonable to me, although theological disputes were beyond my understanding.

Father Bede swept on as if he hadn't heard. "Who will give funds for the abbeys if the pilgrims sit at home with their so-called faith?"

That drew the attention of several monks. A burst of air that I took for mirth escaped from Thomas. He leaned casually against a pillar in a manner I would have found more suitable to the velvet coat of a courtier than a novice's white robe.

Father Bede went on. "We are dependent on the incomes of our farms, and if we are not careful King Henry's minister, Cromwell, will take those from us. The very authority of the church is being questioned, and our leadership is too weak to do anything about it. Power! That's what we need! The abbots smile and nod and bow before the whims of ignorant men. Glastonbury should be leading the fight to restore the monasteries to their rightful place."

There was a murmur of unrest among the monks. "What's this?" came Thomas's whispered sneer. "A challenge to the abbot?"

But Bede took no notice. "These men must be stopped or there will be nothing left to us. They are in league with the Devil to destroy us, and Nicholas Thatcher is one of them."

He sat back on the stone bench, his gray face paler than ever. I trembled to be in the path of his fury.

❧

I stifled a yawn as Brother Arthur turned the key in the heavy wooden door at the east end of the cloister. I wasn't used to being up at midnight and again before dawn for prayers. If it weren't for the chill in the air, I would certainly have fallen asleep on my knees. Nor had I expected *The Rule of Saint Benedict* to require rising so early for work.

The ancient iron hinges complained loudly as the door before us swung open revealing a storeroom wedged between the south transept and the chapterhouse. It took a few moments for my eyes to become accustomed to the faint light of early morning, which came from a grating at the far end of a narrow corridor. To the left the corridor was lined with dark oak cupboards. On the right the ceiling dropped and steps led down to a crypt. The entry corridor made a sort of gallery above it.

Brother Arthur struck the flint and lit a candle in a stone sconce. A jumble of gold and silver glittered in its light. I was instantly awake.

I followed Brother Arthur down the steps. He went from sconce to sconce, turning his ample body this way and that as he eased himself among the treasures until the whole room glittered. I marveled at so much wealth. My father would have been drunk with greed.

"The gifts of royal patrons and thank offerings from those whose prayers have been answered after a pilgrimage here to Saint Mary's of Glastonbury," he explained. "Beautiful, are they not, Colin?" He rested his folded hands contentedly on his belly.

In the middle of the low room stood a table piled high with an odd assortment of golden candlesticks and ivory boxes. There were dozens of reliquaries—containers of every shape and size, richly decorated with precious stones. Each held a finger bone, a scrap of cloth, or some other precious relic of a long dead saint. Beneath the table, carved chests with open lids revealed more gilded treasures wrapped in embroidered clothes or thrown about any which way.

Brother Arthur picked up a silver box inlaid with rubies and crystals. "Cromwell's men were not interested in leaving things in order when they inventoried our goods for the king." He sighed. "Then, we have added much as we removed the relics from the church. It is forbidden now, you know, to use relics to raise money." His cheeks drooped, and his arms dropped to his side. "I haven't had the heart . . ."

He straightened suddenly, and his eyes brightened. "But now you are here to help me." He scurried around the table like an enormous black beetle.

"There is so much to show you. This is the gold ring worn by Saint Thomas á Becket when he was martyred at Canterbury. *Dona eis sempiternam requiem.* 'Give to him eternal peace.'" Brother Arthur crossed himself nervously as though a reference to the saint who defied Henry Plantagenet might be construed as treason by Henry Tudor.

We spent the hours before Sext sorting and organizing the reliquaries and finding places for them in the overflowing cupboards. The cupboards were not in the best of order either. Brother Arthur had inventory lists of his own, ancient documents copied by monks now long buried in the churchyard above us.

"Put this in the corner cupboard." Brother Arthur handed me a green silk altar cloth embroidered with gold. As I reached high overhead, I kicked something in the shadows.

"What's this?" I stooped, and my fingers found a loose piece of black velvet. When I pulled it into the light, it dragged something after. The cloth seemed very plain after the rich embroidery of the silks. The nap had worn away in places like patches of fur from a mangy dog. I laid it on the table and felt for whatever had been tangled in it. My fingers touched wood, smooth as silk—a small bowl like a peasant's drinking cup.

I lifted it into the light. It had a yellow sheen and gave off a strange scent like no wood I knew in England. Next to its simplicity, the gilt and jeweled reliquaries seemed no more than whitewashed tombs, full of dead men's bones.

Brother Arthur took it from my hands. "Ahhh." He turned it over carefully. "Look how graceful the lines! How ancient the wood! There is no record of the origin of this bowl. I have already searched all the lists. It is there from the beginning. Perhaps back to Saint Joseph himself."

He caressed the silky surface of the dish. "Olive wood. They say that Joseph of Arimathea . . . 'Twould be just such a cup as this." Tears glittered like cut crystal in the corners of his eyes as he wrapped the drinking bowl reverently in its velvet covering.

"Put it there." He directed me to the top shelf of a cupboard in the corridor on the upper level. It was already filled with gold and silver chalices. The worn velvet covering looked out of place among such riches, and yet when I had shut the doors, the room seemed somehow dimmer and its treasures cheap and tawdry.

CHAPTER 6

AFTER MASS I FOLLOWED Roger and Thomas to the lowest table in the refectory where we shared a platter of fish pies. I didn't mind the silence. Although I would have liked to talk with Roger, I felt reticent in front of Thomas.

One of the brothers stood in the raised pulpit under the window where the light was best to read from *The Lives of the Saints*. "A certain man was accused of stealing, who was, however, innocent."

Thomas gestured to one of the younger monks. His hand fluttered in response, and Thomas made another sign. Father Aidan gave him a firm look, and he returned to eating, but by that time I had realized that many of the monks were carrying on avid conversations without ever breaking the rule of silence.

The monk at the lectern read on. "And they at once seized him, and according to the sentence, put out his eyes, and cut off his ears; then the blood ran into his head, so that he could not hear."

I pushed away the pittance of vegetables I had been eating with a sudden loss of appetite.

After dinner I helped Roger back to the infirmary to rest and took a walk in the abbey grounds to exercise my body. A light rain was falling when I returned through the guest hall courtyard.

Three guests had entered. A strange monk helped an elderly Benedictine from a litter slung between two horses while a young man in a black habit bent his head against the rain and struggled to secure the mounts.

I hurried to help. I took the head of a chestnut gelding just as a groom came running from the stables. The young monk at my side held the other horse and directed the groom to take the litter.

"I thank you," he said in the accents of the north and reached for the gelding.

The guest hall master had arrived to escort the other visitors into the hall. He nodded approvingly in my direction. "Allow me to be of service," I said to the young monk and led the horse toward the stables beyond the hall.

My companion introduced himself as Brother Fergus. His smooth chin looked younger than my own, but he already wore the black of a full-sworn monk. Water dripped from dark hanks of hair around the tonsure shaved on the crown of his head. The stable gave off the warm sweet smell of fresh hay and animals. Rain fell more steadily now, and I was in no hurry to return.

"You've come a long way," I said as we rubbed the horses dry.

"From Lincoln. Our monastery there has been closed by order of the king."

"Have you come to join the brothers here?"

Brother Fergus shook his head. "We have brought Prior Dunstan. He is old and deserves his rest in these troubled times. He longed to see Glastonbury where his patron was abbot. Father Cuthbert and I will return." He spoke with determination. "It is our duty and our calling to serve God in Lincolnshire. If need be—" He broke off.

I studied him over the steaming back of the horse. "What will you do, since your monastery is closed?"

He continued to rub without looking at me. "There is still God's work to be done. The poor are still with us. Prayer is not yet forbidden."

He lowered his voice and turned intense black eyes on me. "Some monasteries have reopened secretly. There is talk of presenting a petition to the king." The horse whinnied and shifted his weight under Brother Fergus's firm fingers. "King Henry's counselors have advised him poorly. He doesn't realize how much the monasteries do for the north. Here in the south, there are inns for travelers and many wealthy people who can care for the poor. In the north there is nothing. If King Henry understood this, he would change his order. I am certain of it."

"But will the king hear your petition?"

"He must." Brother Fergus patted the rump of his horse and left the stall, dusting his hands on the folds of his habit. Rain drummed loudly on the roof, and we sat on a bale of straw to await its passing.

"There are many lords, faithful to the Old Church, who have come to our aid. Robert Aske, Thomas D'arcy—" He stopped abruptly. His wide eyes made him look more like a frightened boy than a monk. "I shouldn't reveal their names."

"By the ring of Saint Thomas, I have already forgotten them," I said.

"To tell the truth," he admitted, "Father Cuthbert fears that some are as interested in defending their independence as in defending the true faith. And many peasants care only for the loss of holidays."

"I heard there was fighting in February."

"Aye, there was fighting. Some there are who think to fight again and to gain by looting. But we will not fight. We will march as pilgrims, a hundred thousand strong, bearing on our bodies the wounds of Christ." He placed his hand over the red and white badge sewn to his habit over his heart. "It will be called the Pilgrimage of Grace. We will carry our petition to the king, and he will repeal the evil laws. He will root out his corrupt advisers, renounce his divorce, acknowledge the Princess Mary as his heir and return us to the holy Church of Rome."

His faith was more than I could comprehend.

"And if the king refuses?"

"There will be no fighting, if that's what you mean. By the wounds of our Lord, nothing is gained from fighting. King Henry won't refuse. He is a good and gracious father to his people, a devout man. God will show him the way."

He looked outside the stable door to where the rain fell like a curtain that cut us off from that other world and its strife. "Father Cuthbert is prepared to lay down his life for the cause if necessary."

He broke a piece of straw into smaller and smaller pieces and dropped them onto the floor of the stable. "The thought frightens me."

I saw his lips form the words more than I heard his whisper above the rain. He shivered and shrank into himself like a half-drowned child.

"My lord abbot and Prior Dunstan were tortured to get them to reveal the hiding place of our riches. It was for naught. We had already given all we had." His face was white as the bread of the Mass, his eyes dark as two bruises.

"I never wanted anything but to be a monk," Brother Fergus whispered, "to live a life of prayer and devotion to God. By the five wounds of Christ, what am I to do?"

"Stay with us," I said. "It's only the small houses that are to be closed. No one will hinder your prayers and devotions here at Glastonbury."

Brother Fergus sniffled loudly and wiped his face on the sleeve of his rain-dampened habit. "My place is in the north with my people." He straightened his shoulders. "When our Pilgrimage of Grace is done, when the king grants our request, then Father Cuthbert and I will return." He turned his eyes on me, and the light of his faith burned in them again. "All this pain will be forgiven, and we will take Prior Dunstan home."

CHAPTER 7

THE NEXT MORNING I returned to helping Brother Arthur in the treasury. The rain was still falling and in the rest time after dinner I made my way to the tomb of King Arthur in the quire before the high altar. I wanted quiet to think of my mother who had prayed for me at this holy place before ever I was born.

The high vaults of the church echoed back the soft footsteps and whispered voices of pilgrims, milling from chapel to chapel. The air smelled of damp wool. In the gloom I nearly stumbled over Brother Fergus, lying with his face to the earth in humiliation before the high altar, his arms out-stretched in prayer. He showed no sign of hearing my startled gasp.

I knelt some distance away and took the rosary beads from my belt. *"Pater noster, qui es in caelis. . . ."*

My father thought courage lay in the thrust of a sword, manliness in draining the wine cup. Yet I had shown myself no better, turning to Walter's sword in my anger and staining my soul with my father's blood.

The *Pater* was followed by ten small beads for ten *Aves*. "Hail Mary, full of grace, the Lord is with thee. . . ."

My mother would have been disappointed in me, too. I abandoned her pious example and gentle teachings to revel in a moment of vengeance.

If only I had the pure faith of Brother Fergus. He believed the best, even of his enemies. He was prepared to do God's will whatever the cost. I fled from my father's just anger and hid behind the skirts of the monks. I was as weak and worthless as my father claimed. I would never be fit to please God or anyone else.

Just when I thought my shame would overwhelm me, I seemed to hear my mother's voice reciting the familiar prayers beside me. So real was the illusion that I glanced over my shoulder to be certain she wasn't there.

But someone was. Matilda Thatcher knelt a few feet behind me. She smiled and went back to her beads. I stumbled and then joined my voice to hers. Together we said the prayers through to the end. I gave Matilda my hand and led her to a stone bench built in the wall.

"Nicholas would not be pleased if he knew I was here," she admitted as she sat. "But I wanted to say a prayer for your mother. We're in town for the fair. Alice insisted, despite the rain." She gave me a bright smile. "Little Wil asks for ye all the time."

"I am well. I found my father's cousin. He looks out for me."

She touched my forehead. "Ye're mending."

"The infirmarian gave me a salve." I used it twice a day on the back of my wrist as well as my forehead, but the wound beneath my sleeve refused to close, although it bled but little.

"I'll tell Wil. He prays for ye every night. He'll like to hear his prayers are answered." I wondered if Alice prayed for me, but Matilda didn't say.

I missed the warm circle of this family, the hungry reading of Scripture, the heartfelt prayers. I had heard many Latin prayers since I arrived, but none had seemed to come straight from the heart as did the plain English prayers of the Thatchers—none except those of Brother Fergus where he lay on the floor before the altar. His thin shoulders had trembled from time to time while Matilda and I made our devotions, but now he lay so still I wondered if he had fallen asleep.

Matilda's motherly eyes rested on him. "Perhaps I should say a prayer for this young monk."

"He's from the North," I explained. "Their monastery has been closed."

She looked at me curiously, but I said no more. I had sworn by the ring of Saint Thomas, an odd choice now as I thought of it. I had never paid much attention to the sainted archbishop before coming to Glastonbury, but the oath seemed to encompass more than the names of the conspirators, which truly I had forgotten.

Brother Fergus got to his feet. The dark curls around his tonsure were still disheveled, but his cheeks had regained their natural color. He looked refreshed as though he had slept the night through in a bed of goose down.

"*Dominus vobiscum,*" he murmured.

"*Et cum spiritu tuo,*" we replied.

Matilda's eyes followed him as he passed through the nave and left by the south door to the cloister. "He's young."

I nodded. She stood to go as well. I stood with her, feeling awkward and for some reason not wanting her to leave.

"Please take my greetings to your father and to your husband. Tell them . . . I am learning many things." She nodded, her eyes cast down. "And greet Wil and . . . and Alice."

"I will. God be with ye, Colin." She touched my hand and glided up the south aisle. Scarcely was she gone when I noticed a flicker of movement in the transept. A figure all black and gray stood looking after her. Father Bede turned malevolent eyes on me.

⁓

A hand reached out and touched my sleeve as we filed in to service. "I will see you in the chapter hall after None," Father Aidan said. His voice was taut with controlled emotion. My stomach tightened in painful anticipation. The chant of the service stuck in my throat. Even Brother Arthur's joyful face lifted to the silvery glitter of the Great Sapphire of Glastonbury above the altar and Roger's booming bass beside me could not draw me into worship.

Thomas raised that irritating eyebrow of his and smirked as I followed Father Aidan to the chapter hall when the service was ended. I tried to look meek for Father Aidan's sake, but it infuriated me for Thomas to see me so.

"Who is she?" the novice master demanded when we were alone. My startled brain thought of nothing to say, but he was too angry to await my answer.

"There is to be no consorting with females within these walls!" he continued. "Absolutely none! This monastery is not a place of debauchery. A tryst in the church is just the kind of scandal Lord Cromwell is looking for—all the excuse he needs to close this house and confiscate its wealth for the crown!"

My mind went numb with horror, and I rubbed icy fingers against my robe.

"All worldly attachments are renounced when we enter here. All!" Father Aidan had been gentle and courteous when he read *The Rule of Saint Benedict* to me, and his patience with Roger's poor Latin was a marvel. Now his narrow face was red and the veins swelled purple from his forehead. "You come under false pretenses and take advantage of the abbot's goodness! He should throw you into the street."

I could stand no more. False pretenses indeed! "We were praying for my mother's soul!" I cried.

He seemed taken aback. "You were praying?" His intense blue eyes examined me closely. "I understood it was a romantic meeting. You touched her."

"I helped her to her feet after our prayers. Surely there's no wrong in that."

"Who is this woman?" His voice was gentler. "Is she a friend of your mother?"

I shook my head. "I met her family on my journey. They came for the fair." I half hoped he would think they came from far and not connect Matilda with Nicholas Thatcher, the suspected heretic.

"I see." The vein no longer throbbed on his temple. His face was regaining the sallow shades of one who spent much time indoors at his books. "And you no doubt told her on your journey of your mother's recent death."

I nodded.

Father Aidan sighed. "Nevertheless, you are not to consort with women of any kind. There are those who would use even the innocent to destroy us." He thought a moment. "If you have a visitor, you must ask my permission to meet that visitor in the parlor. But visitors are discouraged. They will only distract you from your worship. And you are never to meet a young woman without another monk present."

Father Aidan seemed to have returned to his usual calm demeanor. "You must confess this failing and do penance for breaking *The Rule*. I will report you to the abbot. He will decide if the matter should be taken up in chapter with the other monks. Glastonbury has a fine reputation. We must not let it be soiled in these troubled times by a foolish boy who has no sense of decorum."

My cheeks burned with shame. I would also have to confess my ill feeling for Father Bede who had, no doubt, brought this rebuke upon me. If he had recognized Matilda Thatcher, he had not passed on her name to Father Aidan.

"Holy Mother of God, let him not find out who she is," I prayed.

CHAPTER 8

"What have you been up to?" Thomas demanded when Father Aidan dismissed us from the library. I must have blushed like a girl.

"Leave him alone," Roger said. Their whispered voices bounced back and forth through the vaults of the cloister in endless echoes.

"Come now, my dear stonemason. This one is more my kind than yours; he's already in trouble with Father Aidan."

"I'm not," I said, more loudly than I should have. They both looked at me. "I'm not your kind." I wasn't sure yet what kind Thomas was, but I was certain I didn't want to be like him.

A lay servant passed on his way to the refectory carrying a covered dish heavy with the scent of butter and fragrant herbs. Roger looked after him, his lips slightly parted in pleasant anticipation. My mouth began to water.

Father Bede swept around the corner of the cloister walk. "What is this idle chatter?" Thomas, who had opened his mouth to make some reply, shut it quickly, although he rolled his eyes derisively. No doubt Father Bede could not see his expression in the shadows of the cloister walk.

The priest continued. "You will go to separate chapels and say your prayers before your dinner. On second thought, perhaps you will better remember the importance of silence in the abbey if you say these prayers *instead* of your dinner. That will be all. You may go."

Roger shut his mouth abruptly. I inhaled slowly knowing the scent was all the taste I would get. Thomas scowled and set off for the crypt of Saint Joseph. I followed Roger into the church where he turned toward his beloved Edgar Chapel. I crossed the nave and knelt in the Chapel of Saint Thomas, trying to figure out what it was I was supposed to be sorry for. I was relieved that Father Bede had interrupted the conversation.

❦

Father Cuthbert and Brother Fergus left early the next morning, or Brother Fergus might have risen to my defense. After all, he was present when I met with Matilda although I doubt he was conscious of anything beyond his own troubled prayers. I paced nervously in the cloister as I waited outside the chapter hall for, being only in retreat, I was not yet a member of the community. Perhaps it would have been better to ride north with the pilgrims and face with them an uncertain fate.

"I will not go home a failure," I muttered with clinched fists. "I will not hear my father say I am not man enough even for a monk." And if I did go home, might I yet be hanged for attempting a murder? For that matter, I did not know that my father had survived any infection from his wound. My own wounded wrist ached beneath its binding. I clasped my hands together in an effort to stop their trembling.

The monks were long about their business. Word had come that the shrine of Saint Thomas had been pillaged at Canterbury. The king had proclaimed that the archbishop, martyred by an earlier King Henry for opposing his authority, was no longer a saint. Not one precious stone or leaf of gold was left. Even the bones had been scattered to the winds. There was much to discuss about the import for our house at Glastonbury.

Father Aidan gestured from the arched doorway. "You may enter. Do not be afraid, Colin. I will speak on your behalf."

My head trembled only a little as I tried to nod my thanks. I passed before him into the chapter hall. A patch of sunlight from leaded windows high above our heads fell on the floor like broken shards of glass. The members of the community sat on stone benches around the walls. All were equal except the abbot's seat at one end, topped by a carved stone canopy.

Several faces looked sternly upon me, and I had no doubt that Father Bede had spread the word of my infraction. Brother Arthur sat to the right of the door under a carved gargoyle with a face as fat and cheerful as his own. I avoided his eyes, dreading to see his disappointment. I could feel Thomas's eyes on my back and imagine the derisive smile on his thin lips. "Already in trouble," he was no doubt thinking.

The Abbot nodded to me. "I believe our young brother has something to say to us."

I forced my legs forward over the scattered light on the floor to kneel and kiss the abbot's ring. If I rushed a bit, it was only because I was so anxious to put this moment behind me.

"I have sinned, Father, and brought dishonor on the community. I spoke privately with a woman of my acquaintance in the church yesterday. I repent of my error and humbly ask to be permitted to stay." There, it was done. I was tempted to add, "We were not alone. Brother Fergus was there." I clinched my teeth together to keep from explaining that she was only a friend and the encounter was not planned. Father Aidan had told me that trying to justify my action would appear as pride. My heart fluttered in my chest, and I wiped my sweaty palms on my habit.

"Meeting privately with a woman is a serious offense," Father Abbot said slowly, "however unplanned it may have been." I looked up, grateful that he had said what I could not.

"It is a grievous sin indeed," said Father Bede, seated to his left. "Women, with their filthy, lecherous bodies, are the tools of Satan for the downfall of men. Consorting with them before the very altar of God is an affront to all that is holy and cannot be tolerated—"

Abbot Whiting raised his hand for silence. "I have heard, Father Bede. It is true that avoiding the temptation of women is one of the reasons for taking up the cloistered life. Does anyone else have advice to offer in this situation?"

Father Aidan spoke behind me. "Colin is quite new here and not yet accustomed to our ways."

"Did you not read him *The Rule*?" Father Bede demanded.

Abbot Whiting straightened in his seat as if surprised by the vehemence of his tone.

"I did," Father Aidan said quietly. "And I believe that he understands better now what is involved in this life."

I swallowed hard and stared at the embroidered cushion under the abbot's feet. The floor was hard and cold beneath my knees.

"My Lord Abbot," Prior Robert began calmly. "We must consider the possible implications of this—incident." Several voices murmured agreement. "Under current regulations, anyone who objects to what we do may journey to London at the abbey's expense to lodge his complaint with the proper authorities." He shook his head thoughtfully. "Any discontented tradesman or scandalized peasant may seize the opportunity to take a holiday in the capital."

Father Bede pounced upon this support. "Prior Robert is right! It is important that we deal seriously with this offense and leave no opportunity for such a complaint."

"Please don't send me home," I blurted. "I won't ever do it again. I swear to you. I never meant—"

The abbot again held up his hand for silence. "We understand that you are repentant, Colin. If you were not, I would already have sent you away. It is a question of appropriate discipline in light of . . . shall we say . . . the antagonism to monastic houses currently prevalent in some quarters."

I wasn't sure if he meant the things that people like Wilfrith Thatcher were saying about the uselessness of monks, or the threat that Thomas Cromwell could move against all monasteries and not merely those whose members were few.

"And of course," the abbot continued, "you are free to go if you do not wish to submit yourself to the discipline of this house."

"No! Please. I want to stay. I will do whatever you ask."

"If the young man had come to me in private confession," Father Bede said in a cool voice, and I silently swore never to confess to him, "I would have assigned him as penance forty days of bread and water followed by a pilgrimage of prayer at the Stations of the Cross on the Tor."

Father Aidan and Brother Arthur were not the only ones to gasp. "That is very harsh," said Father Aidan. "Forty days! Such a difficult penance has not been given at Glastonbury for a hundred years."

Father Bede raised himself to his full height. "Thanks be to God, such a blatant disregard of *The Rule* has not occurred in a hundred years! Not in Glastonbury, the oldest and greatest house in England and the jewel of Saint Benedict."

"He is a pilgrim in retreat," said a voice from the back of the hall. "Would not a pilgrimage of prayer be sufficient?"

"He's a pilgrim who *claims* he wants to be a monk," Father Bede corrected him. He looked personally insulted. "My Lord Abbot, a pilgrimage of prayer is no more than any good Christian should do to show his devotion. I do not think that ten days of bread and water are sufficient to break the pride of this young rebel. It is my opinion that he should not be here at all. He has already been known to consort with heretics." His eyes narrowed, and he looked at me as though I were something that had crawled from the drains of the lavatory. I straightened my shoulders and refused to lower my eyes.

He pointed a bony finger in my direction. "This one has an independent spirit. Humility is not to be found in him."

Anger rose up in me. I would prove myself to this man who despised me as much as my father.

"I'll do it." The words bubbled out of me like effervescent water from a mineral spring. "I will fast forty days on bread and water and then climb the Tor—on my knees, if need be." Father Bede drew back at my outburst. "I do not wish to bring this house into disrepute," I said more calmly. "I will do whatever is necessary."

Abbot Whiting pressed his fingertips together and looked slowly around the hall. His expression was grim, and I realized how little he liked to give Father Bede his way, but I had left him no choice.

"It is done then." He placed his hands deliberately in his lap. "Colin's penance will be forty days of bread and water, followed by climbing the Tor to pray at each of the fourteen Stations of the Cross." He looked thoughtfully at me.

I rose and backed out of the room forcing my eyes to stay on the floor with more humility than I felt.

CHAPTER 9

"I AM PROUD OF YOU," Brother Arthur said as he unlocked the heavy oak door of the treasury. The creak of its hinges drowned the growling of my near-empty stomach. I had been too upset to eat more than a small portion of my bread and water.

I stared incredulously at him. "How can you be proud of me? I have been here but three days and already broken *The Rule* and brought the monastery into disgrace."

He smiled serenely. "You didn't mean to break *The Rule*, and you confessed your shortcomings and accepted discipline. Perhaps not as humbly as you might, but . . ." He patted my arm as my mother would have done. "Methinks Father Bede has a proud spirit of his own."

Brother Arthur was not the only one to comment on my acceptance of discipline.

"Clever of you to look so humble and repentant," Thomas mused when he found me alone in the dorter before Compline. I was lying on my back on my pallet studying the shadows cast by the rafters and wondering if I could really go forty days smelling pea soup, fish pies and roasted vegetables and eating only bread and water. I had been glad for the Benedictine silence during the day and deliberately avoided the conversations allowed in the cloister at this hour. Thomas apparently didn't notice my lack of response.

"You've got the abbot on your side now. I never managed that even if my father is a generous patron of the abbey." His face showed momentary regret before he brightened and went on. "If you want to meet women, Colin, you must be more subtle."

"I swear on the tomb of King Arthur, I never intended—"

He laughed outright. "The tomb of King Arthur? You *are* an infant. You don't really think the bones of Arthur are buried in this church, do you?"

The lamp flickered, but he must have seen my gaping mouth.

"The monks planted those bones—old bones of a very large man, killed in battle, no doubt—but they were found at a convenient moment after the Great Fire, when the abbey was desperate for money." He leaned back against the wall. "All the best scholars say there never was such a king. It's all a bit of fancy, full of inventions to suit simple females. We know better now. At least, some of us do."

I sat up. I wanted to leap on him and shut his throat with my hands so that no more of these words could escape. It was bad enough to say that the king my mother had adored never existed, but to suggest that monks and holy men of God had practiced deception? It was more than I could bear. And yet, much as I disliked Thomas, I knew that he was far more learned and sophisticated than I.

"Father Aidan won't give you a straight answer, but you can ask Prior Robert. He doesn't say anything aloud because it would not be in the best interest of the abbey, but he doesn't believe any of it. Don't ask Father Bede. He believes every word from Merlin's magic to the Holy Grail. Merlin's magic is witchcraft and devilment, of course, but the Holy Grail is another matter." He paused and his face lost its mocking look for the moment. "There is power, and then there is power."

He gave a short laugh. "And I'm thinking there's more of it at court than in the church. Father Bede may have missed the point altogether."

The bells rang for Compline, and he said no more.

"We have been asked to assist in the library," Father Aidan explained as he led Roger, Thomas and me to the north walk of the cloister. "The king has given orders that every mention of Thomas of Canterbury be removed from all books. In a library as large as that of Glastonbury, it is a formidable job. Father Bede needs our help."

If I had not had such a dread of displeasing Father Bede, I would have looked forward to the opportunity to peruse the abbey's books and manuscripts.

The librarian was bent over a heavy tome on a slanted reading table. He squinted in the pale autumn light. The thick volumes piled on his desk drew me like a lodestone. I mentally translated the title *Estoire del Saint Graal* on a crumbling leather cover: *The Story of the Holy Grail.* How my mother's eyes would have danced to have me read her such a tale. *De Antiquitate Glastonie Ecclesie,* read another in slightly better condition—*Concerning the Ancient Church at Glastonbury.* I leaned forward. Surely such a book would tell of the finding of Arthur's bones. If I could read it for myself, I would know if Thomas spoke truth or only from the deceptions of his own heart.

The gray head of the monk rose beyond the desk like a monster from the sea. "You—will—not—touch—any—book—on—this—table." Each word was clipped and separate from the others, and his eyes showed white all the way around their gray centers.

I jerked my hand back from the volume I had touched without meaning to. "Yes, Father." The words nearly choked me. I could feel Thomas shaking with silent laughter beside me.

Father Aidan's voice was calm and soothing. "There, there, Father Bede. The boy meant no harm. He is awed by the riches of our library."

"See that he leaves them alone except under the strictest of supervision."

"Yes, Father."

"What are you smiling at?" His gray eyes glared at Thomas from under his bristling brows.

Thomas's face was an instant mask of piety. He bowed reverently. "Nothing, Father." But there was still mischief in his eyes.

Father Bede looked us up and down as if to determine if our aid would be worth anything. Roger shuffled his large feet. He clearly felt as nervous about this assignment as I did.

At last Father Bede stood and led us to the tables beyond him. "You may begin with these books I have laid out." There was a book of sermons on the table he had assigned to me. A Latin grammar was laid out for Roger. He pointed Thomas to a moral treatise. They didn't look nearly as interesting as the books on Bede's desk.

"Saint Thomas—I mean, Thomas of Canterbury—may have been used as an example in these." It was the first time I had seen the man flustered. "And I don't think the content will do you any harm," he continued. "Use the ink I have provided. *Not* what is in the cupboard. A single line will do. Do not—waste—the ink."

He returned to his own desk where I could feel his eyes boring into my back. I did indeed find a reference to the former saint in the very first sermon in the book assigned me. I dipped my pen and drew a single line through the name as Father Bede had instructed. It seemed odd to cross out a man's name and pretend he had never been. The line I had drawn was very pale. I started to dip my pen again. "A single line," Father Bede had said, and yet the name was still clearly visible.

Thomas was stirring the ink in his pot and inspecting it with a puzzled expression on his face.

"This ink is very thin," Roger whispered.

"Silence," came a stern voice behind me. "It is not necessary for tongues to wag in order for fingers to work."

Roger nodded to me. It was on the tip of my tongue to challenge the old man about the quality of the ink. He gave me a stern look as though he knew exactly what was in my mind and bent back to his work.

So that's his plan, I thought with grudging admiration. It was a kind of deception like passing off the bones of an ancient warrior as those of King Arthur. No one could accuse us of disobeying the king's order, and yet nothing would be lost from the Glastonbury library. Father Bede may have been as stubborn and demanding as my father, but he was not stupid.

~

"Come with me to the infirmary, Colin," Roger said when at last Father Bede released us. "Brother Urban has been asking after you." We walked slowly, and he leaned heavily on his cane. He insisted on doing everything with the community, even painfully climbing the stairs to the dorter at night.

"Ah, here he is, our acrobat who climbs abbey roofs and leaps on unsuspecting pilgrims!" called one of the elderly monks by the fire.

"I did no such thing!" cried Roger in response. "And here is the pilgrim himself to testify to the truth." He thrust me into their laughing midst.

"All for the love of the Widow Archer," teased an old man whose teeth were gone. "She's a mite old for you, lad. Best keep your mind on your vows!" The others grinned knowingly.

"Ah, Colin!" Brother Urban approached us. "How is that forehead? Let me look at it." I bent my head for him to examine. "That's healing nicely, but since you're here, let's put more ointment on it. I expect what I gave you is nearly gone." It was. I stood quietly, feeling shy and awkward, while he moved toward a locked cupboard in the corner.

"I seem to have left the salve in Father Dunstan's room," Brother Urban said. "I'm sure he won't mind. Roger, sit down and put that leg up. I'll be back to rewrap it in a moment. Colin, come with me."

Brother Urban led me to one of the little rooms in the south aisle. I lingered in the doorway.

"Come in. Come in where I can see you," a firm voice invited. It was a stronger voice than I expected from the frail form propped on the bed cushions. His hair was white as snow, although his face was not as old as I had first supposed. The skin was slack as though he suffered great pain, but his smile was warm and his eyes lively and curious.

"This is Colin," Brother Urban said.

"Ah, yes. Brother Fergus spoke of you."

I blushed. This must be the prior of the northern abbey. I knelt to kiss his hand. His skin was cool to the touch, stretched and puckered with scars not yet faded to white. It smelled of the strong herbs in

Brother Urban's ointment. I remembered what Brother Fergus had said about torture, and my breath caught in my throat.

Brother Urban found the ointment and dabbed some on my forehead. I was preparing to go when Father Dunstan held me back. "I need a young friend to pass the time now that Brother Fergus and Father Cuthbert are gone," he said. "It gets lonely for an old man who can't get about."

I doubted he would have chosen me if he had known I was under discipline, but Brother Urban set a stool for me near the bed, and I sat down.

"So you are Colin," the old man said when the infirmarian had gone. "A fine saint's name."

My mother had often told me the tale of Saint Collen as a child— how he conquered the pagan, Bras, and converted a whole people to Christ; how he scattered holy water and banished the faery kingdom of Gwyn ap Nudd from the very tor that rose over us here at Glastonbury. At night on my bed I used to imagine myself fighting the powers of darkness as my namesake did. I would not flinch before the pagans or stoop to the Devil's charms. I would face the demons of the underworld without fear and scatter them before me.

What a fool I was! When Satan offered me vengeance, I took up a sword against my father and shamed my mother's memory. And rather than face the penalty of my wrongdoing, I fled to Glastonbury like the coward that I was.

"I'm no saint," I said, staring at my hands in my lap.

"No," the old man said slowly. "And if you thought you were, it would be proof enough you were not."

I looked at his clear blue eyes. "You mean . . . it would show I wasn't humble enough for a saint."

"Are you?"

"No. I'm proud and insolent. Just ask Fa—" I broke off and lowered my head, ashamed of my bitterness. When I looked up, he was gazing steadily at me. He seemed to see into my soul as Father Bede had done that first day on the street, but instead of condemnation, there was compassion in his eyes.

"Ah, Colin," he said. "A saint starts out no more holy than you. I'll let you in on a secret—a saint is but a sinner who's been forgiven and made over by the grace of God."

Forgiven. That was the hard part. I didn't think Saint Collen had ever tried to kill his father.

CHAPTER 10

I GREW LEAN AND STRONG ON my simple diet of bread and water. On Sundays Abbot Whiting permitted me a small dish of crisp leaves grown in our garden, and roots scraped clean even if they had not been cooked. At first I felt like an ox grazing among the raw herbs, and only hunger forced me to consume them, but I grew to enjoy the sharp bite of dark green watercress and the crunch of yellow carrots.

In the rest time after dinner I often asked leave to walk in the grounds. I was drawn to the fishpond on the far side of the cider orchard where the Tor could be seen rising beyond the nearer, lower Chalice Hill. In a few weeks I would climb that hill. I would show them all that I was strong enough, devout enough. When I was done, the load of guilt for what I had done to my father would be gone.

It was October. The leaves on the apple trees had turned yellow and every light breeze plucked a few more from the branches to drift to the orchard floor. I rounded the east end of the church, and neared the north porch. Three horses trotted briskly into the yard. An old woman, who by her plain dark dress and wimple must have been one of the widows from the almshouse, cried out and jumped from their path. The horsemen never glanced her way. They alighted near me and tossed their reins to the porter who had come running after them.

"Where is Abbot Whiting?" the first man demanded. He was a

broad-shouldered man dressed in a brown velvet coat trimmed in fox fur and gold braid. The sleeves of his embroidered doublet were slashed to show the soft white of his shirt. "Robert Layton on king's business. Speak up now."

"He is resting," I stammered. "After dinner the monks always—"

"Did I not say this is king's business? Take me to him immediately."

"Yes, sir."

I led the men through the old cemetery, past the guest hall to the abbot's private garden and lodging. At the door I paused.

"Hurry up, lad. This is important."

I knocked timidly. A porter opened the door.

"King's messengers," I explained.

The large man pushed past me, and the others followed. "Where is the abbot?" Layton demanded in a voice guaranteed to wake anyone who might be resting. He drew a sealed roll from his pouch and stood tapping it on his hand.

"I will call him." The porter bobbed his head submissively several times and hurried off.

I stood just inside the door. My hands were cold and clammy. Whatever this business was, I feared it would not be good news for the abbey. The men strolled around the hall inspecting the chests and hangings and speaking to one another in low voices as though they were considering purchase. One lifted his head and looked at me.

"Fetch us something to drink. We are thirsty after our journey."

"Yes, sir." I darted across the garden to the abbot's kitchen and brought back a pitcher of watered wine and three pewter cups. When I returned, the men were not in the hall, but I heard their voices from a small office on the left. The heavy oak door was slightly ajar and Brother Basil, the abbot's secretary, stood just inside.

"I brought wine for the visitors," I whispered.

Brother Basil opened the door, and I slipped into the small reception room. Abbot Whiting sat in an elaborately carved chair, studying the unrolled document. The men stood before him, legs wide apart and their feet turned out in what I guessed to be a courtly fashion. They held their arms wide and curved in an attitude that struck me as menacing until I realized that their large, puffy sleeves prevented their arms hanging naturally at their sides. Layton pushed back his velvet coat and rested his hands on his hips, exposing a broad, muscular chest.

The abbot's face was as gray as Father Bede's, and his shoulders slumped with the weight of all his seventy-nine years.

"But . . . but how can we?" His hand came up to his mouth as though to keep it from saying more and betraying to these strangers the unrest he felt.

I set the cups on a little table and concentrated on pouring the wine. When I looked up, the abbot was still pale, but he straightened his shoulders and spoke with the firm confidence of an accomplished host.

"You will stay with us this evening. I will have beds prepared for you in the guest hall, and I would be honored if you would dine at my table. In the morning . . . I will bring this business to the chapter."

I held out a cup to Layton, but he ignored me, his full attention on the abbot.

"What is there to discuss? The king has asked you for a hundred men to go against the insurrection in the north—these so-called pilgrims." His lip curled in a sneer. "Do you propose to deny him what he has asked? Would you defy your king?"

I nearly dropped the cup. *The north?* I thought. Brother Fergus had wanted no part in an insurrection. He had been sure the king would hear their peaceful petition. "There will be no violence," he had promised.

"No, of course, I would not defy the king." Some of the abbot's confidence seemed to have fled. "We are all his loyal subjects. But a hundred men? The harvest is not yet fully in. Our manors are stretched to their limits. Not a man can be spared."

"You have many manors." The man reached for the cup I had been holding. "From Cornwall to Berkshire. Ask each one for a few men. Is that too great a thing?" He lifted his cup in a toast to our monarch before he drank.

The abbot looked at him steadily. His mouth moved a few times as though to speak, but he turned his eyes once more on the paper in his hand. I served the two attendants.

"We will do what we can," Abbot Whiting said. "Colin, please show these gentlemen to the guest hall and see that they are well cared for."

"Yes, Father."

"When they are settled, return here. I will require your services this afternoon."

I looked up, startled.

"Father Aidan tells me you write a clear hand."

"Yes, Father."

I led the men back through the garden and delivered them to Brother Gildas, master of the guest hall. I was tempted to linger to hear what other news the courtiers might have to tell, but the abbot had asked me to return, and I was not sorry to escape their proud ways.

When I returned, I found Father Bede and Prior Robert with the abbot and Brother Basil in an inner room. I hung back in the arched doorway. They seemed to be composing a document.

"'The manor of'—fill in the name—'is requested to send'—leave a space here. Prior Robert and I will discuss the numbers each manor should send." Abbot Whiting drummed his long fingers nervously on the desk. "It should really be discussed in chapter, but—" He shook his head. "This will be difficult. 'Requested to send'—here you will write the number—'fighting men to Glastonbury Abbey by' . . ." and the abbot paused, as if to consider how long he might delay the inevitable—"'by the first day of November in the year of our Lord fifteen hundred and thirty eight to assist our king in putting down the enemies who have rebelled against his revered authority and undermined the security of the realm. Each man should provide his own weapons' and so on and so forth. You know how it should go."

"Yes, Father." Brother Basil nodded and took the paper.

They looked up. Father Bede's bushy gray brows met in a scowl when he saw me. "What are you doing here?" he demanded. "As one under discipline, I should think you would use your rest period to pray for your insolent soul."

Father Abbot put a restraining hand on Father Bede's arm. "I have asked Colin to help with the copying." He nodded to his two fellow officers. "I will meet you in the parlor." Father Bede's eyes shot fiery darts at me as he and Prior Robert passed.

I stood in the doorway, knowing I would rather eat bread and water for a year than write the letters that would muster men to fight Brother Fergus and Father Cuthbert. Was there not some trick we could use like watering the ink to avoid doing this terrible thing? From Abbot Whiting's face I was certain he liked it no better than I.

"Father, have we no choice?" My voice cracked like a youth just coming into manhood.

Brother Basil drew in his breath sharply and frowned at me.

But the abbot replied quietly, "Colin, my son, sometimes the choice is made by those in authority over us. It is not our place to question, but to obey."

He looked at me, and I knew he spoke of my obedience to him as much as his own to the king. The struggle that painfully twisted my gut must have showed on my face.

"Dissension is a terrible sin, Colin. It leads to war and suffering. We must not give it a chance to divide this land as it has in the past. England must stand united. At a time like this we must set aside our own convictions and support our king."

I dropped my eyes. "Yes, Father." I had much to learn.

⸎

I spent the afternoon and evening copying letters. Glastonbury owned as much of Somerset as did the bishops of Wells and Winchester put together, and many manors in other counties of the Southwest besides. Twice in my haste I blotted the page I was working on. The first time I started over, but when I erred again Brother Basil insisted I continue.

"This is not a gospel you are copying, Colin," he reminded me. "No one will care about an extra bit of ink on the page." It irked me to send an imperfect letter, and I vowed to be more careful.

Brother Basil and I were excused from both Vespers and Compline. A servant brought us supper and although he set a pittance of fish and vegetables at Brother Basil's elbow, he pushed it aside and took only bread and water with me as we continued our work.

As for me, the bit of bread I tasted turned to lead in my stomach, and I took no more. My hand ached, and my eyes burned from straining in the failing light. The wound on my wrist was finally closing over, but now it ached. Each time my stomach made its loud complaint, I sent up a prayer for those I was betraying.

"We will finish in the morning," Brother Basil said at last. "Come directly after Prime."

"Yes, Brother."

The sound of feasting came from the guest hall as I passed. The king's messengers were enjoying their stay.

The great church was quiet. The monks had long since gone to their rest. I entered the Lady Chapel, passed through the Galilee porch, and climbed the steps to the great doors of the nave.

A forest of arches and columns stretched before me into the gloom—the longest church in all of England, Roger had said. At the far end, above the high altar, the Great Sapphire of Glastonbury glittered in the candlelight like the star of Bethlehem pointing the way to the Christ Child. I crept between the pillars of the north aisle, and the Great Sapphire slipped in and out of my vision, drawing me ever forward.

At the crossing, I fled. I was too ashamed of my part in this business to come nearer the holy place. Instead I darted into the north transept. There I found another penitent, stretched on the tile floor of the Chapel of Saint Thomas. It was Abbot Whiting. The archbishop's miter and staff had been removed and the image proclaimed to be Saint Thomas the Apostle, but I had no doubt which Thomas was in his mind.

In the morning when the messengers departed, Thomas the reluctant novice went with them.

⟡

"These are from the strongboxes in the church, gifts for the upkeep of the chapels."

Brother Arthur emptied a bag of coins onto the table in the back corner of the crypt and began to separate them into piles of pennies, half pennies and the occasional coin of greater value. The piles were pitifully small. "We must enter the totals into these ledgers."

It was the thirty-eighth day of my fast. I pulled up a stool and sat beside him. There was a calming rhythm to sorting and counting, and a sense of satisfaction in forming systematic piles and neat rows of numbers. Brother Arthur verified my total of the offerings for Saint Joseph.

"Amazing," he said. "My count never comes out right the first time." He smiled and pulled down the ledger from a high shelf.

"Enter the amount here," he directed. I dipped my pen and wrote the number where he showed me. A footstep sounded in the gallery, and a child appeared on the steps.

"Ye have a visitor, Colin," the page said. "Brother Basil says ye're to meet him in the guest hall. He's tall—and wears a black armband." The boy's eyes were wide. He knew as well as I that a black armband meant there had been a death.

Brother Arthur closed his eyes a moment, and I thought his lips whispered a brief prayer. "Go, my son, and God be with you."

I stood slowly and smoothed the wool of my cassock. My mind had gone suddenly numb, and I couldn't think whose death would mean anything to me now my mother was gone. Unless . . .

I looked quickly at Brother Arthur, who was no doubt thinking the same. I had heard no news from home in all these weeks. Had my father lingered long from the wound I gave him and only now left this world for the next? The scar on my sword arm felt hot. I pressed it while I tried to calm the beating of my heart. I might yet be hanged for murder.

The boy darted from the room, and I followed more slowly.

The guest hall was nearly empty when I entered. In a corner near the hearth sat a man. His back was to me. His clothes were too colorful and too fashionably cut for the sheriff of our parish in Wales. He was tuning a harp.

"Llwyd?" I asked, not believing my eyes.

He laid down the harp and turned to me. "Colin? You look—like a monk."

I nodded vaguely. I couldn't keep my eyes on his face. They kept straying to the black cloth tied around his sleeve.

"Your father is well and sends his greetings," Llwyd said.

Then it could not be my father for whom he wore the black arm-band. I began to relax. "You mean he didn't disown me?"

Llwyd chuckled. "To the contrary, your father is quite proud of you. He tells the story to anyone who will listen, and you become a better swordsman with every telling. Mind, he doesn't mention that you are in Glastonbury. He always leaves the story hanging where you run off and implies you are gallivanting about the countryside sowing wild oats." My mouth was hanging open, and I shut it with a snap.

Llwyd put a hand on my shoulder. "He wants you to come home. He has no skill in running an estate. Your mother, bless her soul . . . ," he glanced toward heaven and crossed himself. "Your mother always managed the servants. They would do anything for her. Your father . . ." He cleared his throat loudly. "Well, you know your father."

I nodded.

"I think those ledgers of yours have been gathering dust, and more corn found its way into a barrel than into the barns this autumn."

"What about Walter? Walter understands what's needed."

His face grew suddenly grave. "Walter is dead."

All feeling seemed to run out of me like spilled water from an overturned vessel. I remembered Walter's trembling at our mother's bedside, his horror of any sign of mortality. "How did this happen?" I asked.

"He fell from his horse."

"Walter's an excellent horseman." My brother could leap stonewalls and small rivers on his stallion. He had always been invincible.

"Aye, but he had been drinking, he and your father. They were coming home late. Walter might not have been hurt, but . . . he fell into the stream."

"The stream?" The stream by the manor was but a few inches deep, except after torrents of rain. "Didn't Father pull him out?"

"Your father . . . was a bit confused."

"Confused? Too drunk to pull his son and heir from the stream?" A sea of anger broke over me like waves crashing on the rocks. "Walter died because Stephen Hay could not think to pull him from the water!" I set aside for the moment that my brother was too drunk to pick himself out of the stream.

"Colin." Llwyd laid a hand on my shoulder.

I pulled away. "Leave me."

"Your father is a changed man. Broken. He has sworn no liquor will ever pass his lips again."

I laughed like a simpleton.

"We all doubted, but these three weeks he has taken not a drop. He is daily at Mass. Daily he makes confession, and daily he prays for the souls of your mother and your brother and the baby sister who died."

Tears flowed silently down my cheeks.

"He wants you to come home."

I shook my head. "Llwyd, nothing has changed. For a few days or weeks he grieves his loss, but his piety will not last. I'm not the man my father pretends I am. Nor will I be. He may be proud of me from a distance, but he would soon find fault with who I really am."

Llwyd squeezed my shoulder. "I'm not so sure. I think he's realized you are more than your mother's lapdog."

I cringed.

"Think about it. He's all alone. The time of the monasteries is ending—"

"Not at Glastonbury," I insisted. "Only the small monasteries are being closed."

"You know that is not true."

I did know. Some larger houses already had closed "voluntarily," turning their assets over to the crown. We were pressured to do the same. How much longer could Abbot Whiting hold out?

"You're not even a novice, Colin. You have made no commitment to this life. And, you are the heir."

The heir. I had always longed to be loved as my father loved Walter.

"I never asked to be heir. I never begrudged Walter his place. I wanted only my own—to be seen for who I am."

Llwyd never moved, but something in his eyes reminded me of Mother's pain. I steeled my heart against it.

"I'm not going home," I said. "I am needed here. I, Colin Hay, have skills the monks value, skills my father laughed at. I will not be reforged in my father's image. I cannot become what he wants me to be."

I stood and looked at my childhood friend.

"Stephen Hay has no heir," I said with steady voice.

CHAPTER 11

THE SUN WAS NOT YET UP on the fortieth day of my fast when a small group of pilgrims gathered in the orchard to climb the Tor. The weather was balmy for November, but a sharp wind still buffeted our robes. Abbot Whiting arrived to give us his blessing.

"I will accompany you as far as Chalice Well," he said.

He led us out the back gate and around the base of Chalice Hill to where two streams flowed from a little valley at the foot of the Tor. One slid over stones as red as blood while the other coated all it touched with white. The little procession turned up a well-worn path. The air was cold and damp.

"The white stream flows from under the Tor," Brother Arthur explained. "Sometimes its waters rush out, and sometimes they are no more than a trickle. They say the hill is hollow, filled with caves, but no one knows the way in."

He spoke quietly in my ear, but his voice sounded far away. I was tired from the vigil I had kept all night in the Chapel of Saint Thomas, whichever Thomas it was. I was more tired from grieving for my brother and the loss of the person I could never be.

The abbot paused beneath the circle of naked apple trees that surrounded the little shelter covering the red spring, and Roger pulled back the wooden lid.

"It is said," the abbot began, "that when holy Joseph of Arimathea came to Glastonbury, he brought with him the cup of Our Lord, in which he had collected the very blood of the crucified Christ from the cross."

The wound on my arm throbbed—the wound my father had given me for my sin. It had finally closed, but today it was red and hot and the skin puffed up as though infection was about to burst forth. I had let no one see. I couldn't let them know the pain inside. The pain was my penance as much as climbing the Tor.

Behind Abbot Whiting, Father Dunstan, the prior of Brother Fergus' abbey in the north, leaned on the arm of a page. Father Dunstan had known pain. He had endured and conquered. So would I.

The abbot continued. "Saint Joseph rested by this very well, and when he dipped the Holy Grail into the waters of the spring, they turned red as you now see them in memory of Our Lord's death."

He nodded to Father Aidan, who reached down a carved drinking bowl from a niche in the shelter.

"The true cup has been lost," Father Aidan explained. "Some say it was buried with the saint, others that it appears to those who are worthy as in the days of King Arthur. But wherever the true Grail is, let us drink in remembrance."

He dipped the cup where the water flowed from the well shaft and left its red mark on the stones. He passed it reverently to the abbot. Father Dunstan leaned forward a little, lips parted like a child eager for his turn. Abbot Whiting drank and held out the cup to me.

"Colin, this is your pilgrimage," he said. "Drink from the waters of Chalice Well."

Father Bede made a sound deep in his throat. It occurred to me that, as the next-ranking member of the community, he had expected to drink next. The sound made me look his way. Beyond Father Bede, in the shadow of the trees, stood a stag. For a moment it seemed to be a man on horseback with the head of a stag. But the shadows were deep here between the two hills when the sun had not yet risen above the water-logged peat beds of Avalon. And when I looked again, it was only a stag with his kingly antlers held high, surveying us as if to ask what threat we posed to his domain.

I took the cup from the abbot and lifted it to my lips. The water was cold and tasted of iron. When I had finished, the stag was gone. I breathed deeply and returned the cup to Father Aidan. He filled it again and passed it to the others.

"The stream flows ever the same," murmured Brother Arthur when he had drunk. "Like the love of Christ. It does not come and go as the White Spring on the other side of the valley, but is the same yesterday, today and forever."

"Amen," Roger said.

Father Dunstan closed his eyes, tilted his head back and drank deeply. When he opened his eyes, the Tor was before him.

"How I wish I were young and could climb," he said. "To climb such a hill would be almost like climbing Mount Calvary itself." He sighed deeply and passed the cup to the next monk. "I always longed to make a pilgrimage to the Holy Land."

Abbot Whiting gazed toward the green slope dotted with grazing sheep. "If it were not for so much business—the running of the estates, settling of the tenants disputes—I, too, should like to climb."

Father Dunstan laid a thoughtful hand on the abbot's arm. "You will climb the Tor one day, I think."

Abbot Whiting laughed lightly. "Not today. Perhaps next year when this business with Chancellor Cromwell has been settled." But Father Dunstan didn't laugh, and his face grew troubled.

We knelt, and Abbot Whiting made the sign of the cross over each of us in turn before he led the way out of the valley.

The sun was just rising over the moor. Soon it would disappear into thick clouds overhead, but for the moment pools of water glittered among the grasses like bits of silver or jewels adorning the cover of a gospel. Waterfowl called to one another.

Roger blinked in the brightness and turned aside. So did I. I glanced over my shoulder. There in the bare trees where the valley curved around the base of the Tor and the waters of the White Spring trickled down, I saw him again. This time it was clearly a black horse and not a stag. On his back was a man, wearing a cloak of some deep color swallowed in shadow. And on the man's shoulders sat the head of a stag with a five-point brace of antlers. I shuddered at the sight of evil.

Roger gave a sharp intake of breath beside me.

The stag-man stood motionless. He stared after the little party exiting the valley, oblivious to his presence. Only Roger and I watched him. And he watched us. At last he inclined his thorny crown toward us, like a king acknowledging our presence, and turned and disappeared into the trees toward the White Spring.

Roger turned to me, his eyes wide. "Did you see?"

I hesitated.

"For a moment, I thought . . ." But he didn't finish.

"You thought what?" I asked.

He shook his head. "It was a stag, wasn't it?" He shivered, and I thought that he had seen what I had seen and sensed what I had sensed, but we were both too frightened to speak of it.

⁓

When we emerged from the little valley, the sun was just disappearing into the cloudbank. It shot its last rays into our faces, and the glitter on the waters ceased. Father Dunstan hesitated where the paths divided. The abbot was already some way along the track to the abbey.

Father Dunstan turned his face toward the steeply rising Tor. "Like a pilgrimage to Jerusalem!" he said. He made the sign of the cross over me one last time. "God bless you, my son." Then he, too, turned toward the abbey.

The seven of us who were to climb, made our way to the level field where the fair had been. A scattering of yews more ancient than the abbey itself stretched ahead. They must have once shaded a great avenue, but now there were wide gaps and only a few twisted trees to mark the path. A cold rain began to fall.

At the entrance to the avenue stood the first station. I tried to focus my mind on the picture carved in the little pillar there—Christ condemned before Pontius Pilate. I now knew something of what it was to stand in the judgment hall, exposed to all. But Christ was innocent; I was guilty.

We finished our prayers more or less together, and Father Bede and some of the others strode ahead up the hill. The grass was slippery, and little rivulets ran down through the mud. I started toward the second station behind Father Aidan and Brother Arthur.

I fell before we reached the third station. My foot slipped on the wet grass, and I came down heavily on my knees. My hands sank into the yellow mud, burying the beads of my rosary. I felt the wound on my arm split open and warm fluid soak the bandage beneath my sleeve.

"Dear Colin," Brother Arthur murmured. "You'll be wet and cold, and we've hardly started."

From under my hood I could see Roger's sandaled foot step near, and his hand touched my shoulder.

"Up, my boy," Brother Arthur said aloud. "You can manage."

I stood so quickly to prove him right that I nearly over balanced. My head felt light, as though my soul watched from someplace outside my body.

I steadied myself and looked down. The front of my white cassock was streaked with mud. I tried to rub it clean, but my dirty hand only made it worse. Rain washed the beads of my rosary. I looked up. The lower hill hid the summit and nothing could be seen of my goal. Father Bede, I had no doubt, was there to see that I fulfilled every jot and tittle of my penance, but he and his group had grown impatient and moved ahead.

It was only after the fifth station that we passed over the brow of the hill, and Saint Michael's Church came into view. The heavy rain had ceased and only swirls of fine mist obscured the tower.

I began to climb again. I slipped once more. The front of my robe was heavy with accumulated mud.

The seventh station.

The eighth station.

The ninth. This is where Christ fell for the third time. No, not here. That was far away in Palestine where the sun burns hot and the winds blow dry from the desert. The cold rain had long since soaked through the wool of my cassock.

The tenth station: Christ stripped of his garments. The wind swept across the moors and threatened to strip me of mine. A cloud had settled so low on the Tor that the tower showed as no more than a shadow in its whiteness. The entire valley was blotted out. Nothing existed except this expanse of wet, green hillside, the pillar before me for prayer and the ghostly tower that was my goal. Tiny specks of ice rattled against the pillar and shrouded the ground in white.

"Colin, we must go on." Father Aidan raised me to my feet. I stumbled forward.

I fell again. The way here was steep and the wet grass gave no traction. My hands in the mud were red and chapped. A network of red lines covered the back of my right hand where the infection had spread. I clung to the grass and pulled myself forward. I would do this even if it were on my hands and knees. Water dripped off my hood and ran around me. Inch by inch I pulled myself forward.

At the eleventh station I stretched myself facedown on the grass as I had on the floor of the church that first night after killing my Father. My breath rasped in my throat. My lungs ached each time I drew air into them.

But no, I hadn't killed my Father, had I? Walter said I only wounded him. I wanted to kill him. Guilty in my heart. I imagined nails piercing my hands as they had those of Christ. I deserved those nails. I deserved to hang. Why did he do it?

I dragged myself across the grass. My knees no longer held me up. I was only vaguely aware of the others standing around me—voices rising and falling in prayers that pulsed through my veins. Roger, Brother Arthur, Father Aidan. Even Father Bede, his voice chanting ceaselessly, lending me its strength. They clustered in a sort of windbreak, close about me in the wet grass. But still the wind came through. It seeped between their feet and through the fibers of my cassock. I could hear it howl over their chant around the top of the tower and feel it whirling madly in my head, tossing about stormy thoughts of sin and death and suffering.

The twelfth station stood on a level place in front of the small chapel. A stone cross rose from a pedestal, and on it, an image of our crucified Lord. Blood trickled down his cheeks from the crown of thorns on his head. It ran from the cruel nails in his hands and feet, and flowed from the wound in his side. I closed my eyes and moaned. That wound in his side, so like the wound I gave my father.

I opened my eyes. I lay in a puddle of blood that flowed from that side. It surrounded me and soaked the white wool of my robe with stains that could never be washed away. The side of my face lay in the blood, and its stench filled my nostrils.

I raised my head to the cross, but it was not the eyes of Christ I saw staring down at me. They were my father's eyes, full of derision.

He put his face close to mine and laughed. "What kind of man is this? Not man enough to be a monk. They'll send you home in disgrace. Ye're not worth so much as a stillborn girl."

He laughed again, and antlers sprouted from his head until it became the head of the stag-man in the wood beside the White Spring.

I closed my eyes and moaned again. When I opened them, it was not a cross I saw, but a gibbet. On it hung the boy who had stolen my father's ponies. His face was blue and swollen. The birds of the air had pecked at his eyes. Then it was not the boy's face. It was Brother Fergus. His pilgrim badge was sewn to his robe. His bare feet hung a few inches off the ground and rain dripped from his dark hair and ran down his dead face.

But no, the hair was not dark. It was thin and white and the face was Abbot Whiting. Though he was not yet dead, strong arms reached to take him down. There was no mercy in their faces, but only a death more horrible even than hanging.

"God have mercy on me, a sinner," I sobbed.

PART 2

THE CUP

CHAPTER 12

I AWOKE IN THE INFIRMARY.

"God be praised," said Brother Arthur. "I thought you would join your mother and the saints of heaven."

"You've been ill three days and three nights," Roger said.

"How did I get here?" I asked. "Did I finish the stations?" I shivered.

"Aye, you finished—all fourteen, though Roger here had to carry you down on his back." Brother Arthur chuckled. "It pays to have the strength of a stone mason in the abbey." He smoothed the woolen blanket and tucked it in around me.

Roger leaned close and whispered, "Next time you break the abbey rules, do it in summer!"

I managed a half smile. At least, I think I did. I tried.

"Why didn't you tell us about your arm?" Brother Arthur asked.

I looked at where it lay outside the cover. It was freshly bandaged, and although the hand was still puffy, the red lines were nearly gone.

"Brother Urban poulticed it," Roger said. "All sorts of herbs. He put in onions like they use for plague, and even bread mold." He turned up his nose in disgust as though he had never heard of such a thing.

Brother Arthur waited, but I had nothing to say in answer to his question. "You're tired," he said at last. "We'll leave you to rest and return after Vespers."

Brother Urban came with a cup of broth, which he fed to me like an infant. It tasted of chicken, and I savored every mouthful, but I fell asleep before the cup was empty.

When I woke, the November afternoon was growing dark. A thin form loomed near my head, the face hidden in the shadows of a monk's hood. The fading light caught the beads that clicked in his hands as he recited whispered prayers. He made a low sound in his throat.

"Father Bede?" I murmured. He startled and gripped the beads as though embarrassed to be caught praying for such as me.

"Merely confirming your improvement. Someone must report to the abbot." But I was sure Brother Urban would report all that was needed to the abbot, if Roger and Brother Arthur did not.

The infirmarian bustled in. "Ah, Father Bede. You have been here a long time. How is our patient?"

Father Bede growled. "I was just going." He left abruptly.

Brother Urban watched him go, then turned back to me with the broth he had brought. "You should have told me about that arm. We could have saved a lot of trouble." He stuck a spoon of broth in my mouth.

I swallowed it and two more spoonfuls. "I was ashamed," I said at last.

"Hidden wounds fester," Brother Urban said, "the same as in the heart." He fed me another spoonful of his warm, savory soup. "You'll be well ere long. You slept as sound as a newborn child today, not like before, tossing and turning with fevered dreams."

The dreams came back in fits and visions. Sometimes it was Brother Fergus who hung on the gibbet; sometimes Father Cuthbert, his companion. But the face that came most clearly, dark and horrible, writhing in agony before the weathered stones of St. Michael's tower, was that of Abbot Whiting.

I closed my eyes to shut out the memory and saw instead my father's face. "Not man enough for a monk!" he spat. His teeth were black with the rot that comes from eating sugar. Horns sprouted from the thick tangle of his hair, and he threw back his head in raucous laughter as at the Michaelmas feast so long ago. The horns grew into a full brace of antlers, and the hair on his face spread until it had become the stag-headed god, Gwyn ap Nudd. I shivered.

"There, there." Brother Urban set the cup on a small oak table. "I should not have reminded you of the dreams." He fussed with the blanket and a small bolster at my head. "Tsk, tsk. You moaned and cried and begged Abbot Whiting for mercy."

Or was it Abbot Whiting for whom I begged mercy? I shook my head when he offered the cup again. My stomach felt like it would give up the broth I had taken. "No more."

"But you must get strong. Abbot Whiting is very concerned for you."

"Later. Let me rest now."

The bell for Vespers began to toll. It was a soothing sound that made me think of candles and incense and my mother's low voice chanting prayers in our chapel at home. I had finished the fourteen Stations of the Cross, and yet I could not remember the final two. I felt no more forgiven than when I crossed the Severn. How could God forgive what I could not forgive myself?

I drifted to sleep and slept right through Roger and Brother Arthur's visit, not waking until morning.

The next day I felt stronger. Abbot Whiting came with Brother Basil. "You have shown a deep devotion to God," he said. "None in chapter would stand in the way of your taking vows as a novice, if that is still your desire."

None? Not even Father Bede?

"That is my desire," I said aloud. I would be one of them. I would be worthy.

That morning there was a little rice in the broth along with bits of chicken. Father Dunstan brought it and sat with me while I ate it, talking of his dream of the Holy Land. I chewed slowly.

"Is there news from the north?" I asked when his talk lapsed.

Father Dunstan gazed at the small window as though he could see as far as Yorkshire. "They say the pilgrims stopped at Doncaster. They await the Duke of Norfolk. He has promised to talk with them on the king's behalf." He did not sound as confident as Brother Fergus had been that their appeal would be well received. "I think the men of the manors will not need to fight."

"That's good, isn't it?" I asked, for his voice sounded resigned to great sorrow.

He stared at the scars on his palms for a long time before he answered quietly. "Fighting and war are always failure."

I took another spoon of rice and broth and let its warmth slide down my throat. My visions were only fevered nightmares, and no reflection of what was really happening. After all, the abbot was well and strong. He had been twice to visit me. The pilgrims were stopped and waiting. All would be resolved peacefully.

CHAPTER 13

WHEN I HAD RECOVERED sufficiently to leave the infirmary, I took my vows as a novice. The treasury was in good order, and I now spent mornings in the abbot's office, assisting Brother Basil. One morning after the Christmas feast, Father Bede left the abbot's inner office.

"Colin, come with me. Brother Arthur will no doubt need your help," he said.

I looked up from the small writing table at which Brother Basil had placed me. The secretary nodded, and I followed Father Bede's clipped stride across the old graveyard.

"I trust you are behaving yourself in the abbot's presence," he said as he strode purposefully across the garden, through the cloister toward the treasure room.

"Yes, Father." I felt old resentments rising.

"I would not want Father Abbot to be disappointed in my recommendation."

I was so shocked that I stopped still and stared.

Father Bede stopped, too, and looked over his shoulder. "Come along, boy." I hurried after.

The treasury was locked. Father Bede hesitated, and I found myself enjoying his discomfort.

"He may be in the church cleaning the altarpieces," I said at last.

We found Brother Arthur in the Edgar Chapel. Father Bede looked around as though seeing the chapel for the first time. "The work is not yet finished here," he said. Only Father Bede could focus on the unfinished quire stalls and bits of incomplete stonework and ignore the elegant fan vault that rose from the side bays and the completed tracery window over the remains of King Edgar. "Where are the workmen?" Father Bede asked.

Brother Arthur inclined his head politely. "I believe they have been busy elsewhere. There is always work to keeping an abbey of this size in repair."

"I see." Father Bede examined a space where the paneling was only partially installed. He turned and looked directly at Brother Arthur. "One hardly notices the workmen and what they are doing." His gray eyes returned to the space behind the paneling.

He cleared his throat. "Father Abbot sent me to find you. I am to choose a suitable gift for Lord Chancellor Cromwell."

Brother Arthur put down his polishing cloth impatiently. "Another? Cromwell has already received a manor, the income of the abbot's proxy and more pieces of silver and gilt than I care to recall."

Father Bede stood primly with his hands in his sleeves.

Brother Arthur sighed and turned toward the cloister. "Then I shall need Colin's help to reach to the higher shelves."

In the treasury Father Bede sent me searching through every chest and cupboard. He dismissed the simpler items and only examined the most modern and elaborate of the chalices. He compared the weight of silver crosses and candlesticks and demanded that I pull out the most jewel-encrusted reliquaries.

"What we give the chancellor must be something of great value and unique to Glastonbury," Father Bede said. "Something that will impress the Lord Chancellor with our power and the value of having a strong abbey behind the king."

"Why not the Great Sapphire?" Bitterness curdled Brother Arthur's voice, and I busied myself with sifting through a chest of silver plate, embarrassed by his pain. To Cromwell and the king, all this was merely wealth. To Father Bede, I suspected, it was prestige and the heritage of a church that rivaled Saint Peter's in Rome for antiquity. To Brother Arthur, it was beauty and ancient holiness offered to God.

Brother Arthur went on. "There is nothing of greater value or uniqueness to Glastonbury than the Great Sapphire—unless you found the Holy Grail."

Father Bede started and dropped the candlestick he held. Its weight must have been seven pounds of pure silver. It crashed against a jeweled casket he had also been considering and scratched the gold inlay of the cover.

Brother Arthur clicked his tongue and examined the damage. He passed it to me. "Rub it well with polish, Colin. You can get that scratch out."

I took the casket and began to rub with my cloth although I didn't know why. The chancellor would not notice the scratch. He would only tease out the gold of the inlay, pry the precious stones from their settings and melt down the metal for coins. That was what had happened to our previous gifts.

"What is up there—in that black cloth?" Father Bede demanded. The doors to the chalice cupboard stood open. He pointed to the wrappings of the olivewood drinking bowl.

I hesitated.

"Fetch it down," Father Bede demanded.

"I really don't think—" Brother Arthur began. His face had turned a sickly shade of puce.

Father Bede cut him off. "I want to see what it is."

I looked at Brother Arthur. He set his jaw and nodded slowly for me to obey. My legs felt as heavy as roof beams as I climbed the stool. Perhaps Father Bede would change his mind.

"Have you considered this cross?" Brother Arthur picked it up.

Father Bede ignored him. "Can you move no faster?" he prodded me.

My fingers tingled when I touched the wrappings. I pulled them to me. Back on the floor, I unwrapped the cup. I marveled at the calm I felt, the assurance that what God willed would be accomplished.

Father Bede made an impatient sound and dismissed me with a wave of his hand. "Only wood. It's of no value."

Brother Arthur let out a long slow breath, and his shoulders relaxed. I smiled at him and wrapped the cup again in its velvet cloth and returned it to the top shelf.

"This reliquary will do," Father Bede said. "And that tray." It was solid silver weighing more than the candlestick, and its handles were set with rubies and sapphires. A scene of the Tor from our orchard was etched in its surface.

Father Bede surveyed the riches in the room. He picked up a golden chalice. "This is the cup of Saint Patrick, is it not?"

Brother Arthur turned pale again, and he reached a trembling hand.

"I shan't take it," Father Bede said quickly. "Something like this should never leave the abbey." He gave the sacristan a direct look. "When Cromwell's men return, they will choose for themselves what they will take. It would be well if some of the most . . . holy items . . . were out of their sight." He caressed a pair of candlesticks richly encrusted with jewels and set them deliberately next to the chalice.

Brother Arthur stood as still as a gilded altar image. I didn't dare to breathe.

Father Bede continued. "The stonemason would know how to do it. I believe he is quite skilled." I wondered what Roger would think of being hauled into this.

He picked up the reliquary and the tray. "I will carry these to the abbot for his approval. Colin, you may stay and help Brother Arthur to put these things away, but do not be late for Mass."

When he was gone, I exploded. "Is he telling you to hide some of the abbey's treasure? You can't! They would know from the lists. You would never get away with it. And where could you hide it?"

"In the Edgar Chapel," Brother Arthur said slowly, staring at the doorway where Father Bede had disappeared. "The construction is not yet complete. Father Bede is right. Brother Roger would know how to do it."

"But you mustn't, Brother Arthur! It's too dangerous. What if you were caught?"

"How would we be caught, Colin? The lists you speak of are old and not always accurate. Many gifts have already gone to the Chancellor."

He turned a determined eye on me. "The treasure is ours, Colin. Until we give it, it belongs to no one else. If we choose to store it in the walls of a chapel instead of in a storeroom under the chapter house, there is no sin in that."

"I don't think the Lord Chancellor Cromwell would see it that way."

"Cromwell will not be chancellor forever. This too will pass." He moved slowly around the room picking up first one beloved item then another. He opened the doors of the chalice cupboard. "We could not hide much. Only the most precious; only the most holy." His eyes caressed the velvet covering of the olivewood bowl. "Reach it down again, Colin."

I obeyed more quickly than I had obeyed Father Bede.

"It is silver and gold and jewels that Cromwell wants," Brother Arthur said when I had laid the drinking bowl in his hands, "not a piece of wood as old as our faith." He caressed the smooth grain of the cup and touched his finger to the rim and then to his lips to kiss. "They would cast it aside and trample it in the dirt. Even Father Bede disdained it and he has been seeking the Holy Grail all his life, or I miss my guess." He closed his eyes and drew the fragrance of the ancient wood into his lungs. He opened his eyes and looked straight at me.

"You saw how we found it, tossed in a corner. Next time it may be damaged." He turned to survey the clutter of cups and chalices in the cupboard. He raised his soft chin and the muscles of his face tightened in determination. "I will not give what is holy to dogs or throw pearls before swine."

He thrust the olivewood cup into my hands. "Take this to Father Dunstan. He will know its worth even if Father Bede does not. When Cromwell's men come, they will not miss it, nor are they likely to search the infirmary."

I took the cup in its wrappings from his hand. Before I could go, he spoke again. "If you see Brother Roger, tell him I would like to speak with him."

I did not see Roger. I had no intention of drawing him into Father Bede's plot. The door to Father Dunstan's cell was closed when I reached the infirmary.

"Colin, what are you doing here?" Brother Urban inquired. "You aren't ill again, are you?" He reached a hand toward my forehead.

"I am well. I came to see Father Dunstan."

He smiled and raised his eyebrows, as he nodded toward the elderly monk's closed door. "The abbey is troubled today, I see."

The door opened, and Abbot Whiting stepped through. He caressed the ring on his left hand. With a start, I recognized it as the ring of Saint Thomas, or rather Thomas of Canterbury, that Brother Arthur had shown me on my first day in the abbey. Brother Urban swept a deep bow, and I sank to my knees. Abbot Whiting nodded and made a sign of blessing, but his mind seemed to be still with the former prior in the little cell behind him.

When he had gone, I stuck my head around the door. "Father Dunstan?"

"Colin! How kind of you to come."

"I brought you something." I pulled the drinking bowl from my robe and carefully unwrapped it. "Brother Arthur asked me to bring it to you. He said you would know its worth."

He took the wooden cup from my hands and held it as gently as if it were a newborn babe. He lifted it to his nostrils and drew in the scent as Brother Arthur had done. "Ah, Colin, I can smell the very air of Palestine! Can't you hear the wind in the cedars and the waves on the shores of Galilee?"

I heard nothing but the rattle of plates in the hall, but I had no doubt that he could hear the voices of archangels if he listened for them.

He turned the bowl over in his hands. "It is very ancient." He looked intently at my face, as though he could there read the answers to his questions. "This must be one of the most precious treasures of your monastery."

I swallowed. "Brother Arthur wants you to keep it safe. He is afraid. . . . If Lord Chancellor Cromwell's men come again, they will not know its worth. It may be damaged."

"And Brother Arthur knows its worth. He knows what this is?" His blue eyes pierced through me.

Brother Arthur had implied things he hadn't said, and I would not be guilty of spreading rumors. "It's olivewood. He believes it is from the Holy Land. The records don't say."

A smile of gentle amusement crinkled Father Dunstan's eyes before he closed them and kissed the rim of the cup. He took a deep breath and let it out very slowly.

"Tell Brother Arthur that I recognize the worth of his treasure. I will keep it safe. I am honored by his trust."

CHAPTER 14

"BUT *HOW* CAN YOU FORGIVE?"

Roger leaned toward Father Dunstan, who was going straight to the problem that worried us both.

We went often to visit the elderly northern monk in the infirmary hall. He seemed stronger. He spent his days ministering to the old and sick, helping Brother Urban feed the ones who could not manage for themselves and speaking words of encouragement to those in pain. Roger and I enjoyed his tales of saints and of the Holy Land. But some days, like today, we talked of deep and worrisome things, like Brother Fergus and Father Cuthbert and their dreams of freedom to worship.

Their pilgrimage to ask an earthly king for grace had been for naught. The Duke of Norfolk made promises and then betrayed them. Once the tens of thousands had dispersed, their leaders were arrested for treason, Father Cuthbert and Brother Fergus among them.

"Yes, Father Dunstan," I demanded. "How can you forgive such injustice?" Some days I cursed those pilgrims for fools, and other times I wept for their innocence.

The old man sat on his stool near the tiny altar in his cell where the olivewood drinking bowl now rested like some relic that helped him to focus on the passion of Our Lord. He studied his own scarred hands.

"It is Christ in me who forgives. I do not have it in me, but he does."

Roger and I stared at him. Father Dunstan fixed me with his gaze as though some bitterness in my tone had exposed the pain in my soul. The wound on my arm had healed, but not the one in my heart.

"Colin, 'tis a curious thing: Only those who are forgiven are able truly to forgive. And only those who forgive are free to receive forgiveness."

He returned to slowly tracing the scars on his palms. His voice was gentle and soothing as a lullaby and brought unwelcome tears to my eyes. "If we harbor bitterness, we will seek revenge, and our cause will be overcome with evil." He looked again at me and I set my jaw. "This is the way of Christ, Colin, the way to which He has called us."

<hr />

Father Dunstan talked of moving to the dorter some day soon. But in the cold and damp of lingering winter, he took a chill. The fever was not high, but his body was old.

"I do not think he will last the night," Brother Urban whispered on the third day.

I set down the cup of broth I had been trying in vain to spoon into Father Dunstan's mouth.

Brother Urban picked it up to carry away. "I shall send for someone to hear his last confession."

"I'll go," Roger said. His voice was low and heavy.

It was Abbot Whiting who came. I knelt and kissed his ring when he entered the little cell. "Father," I began, but my voice caught in my throat.

He laid a hand on my head in blessing. "This is no time for sorrow, Colin. It is a time of rejoicing when one of God's holy servants enters His presence at last. Wait outside while I hear his confession, but don't go far. I have need of you. Father Bede is bringing the elements."

I glanced back as I left the tiny room. For all his talk of rejoicing, Father Abbot looked as sorrowful as I. I think Father Bede expected the abbot to ask him to assist, but instead it was me he wanted. Roger,

Brother Urban and a few of the other monks who had valued the old prior, crowded into the tiny cell with us.

"I have brought the chalice of Saint Dunstan," Father Bede said importantly. "I thought it would be appropriate for one named after the saint."

The abbot shook his head. "Father Dunstan has requested that we use this olivewood cup." He lifted the drinking bowl in his hands.

"But is it consecrated?" Father Bede demanded.

"It is. Father Dunstan has been using it in his personal Mass for some time now. Colin, we will begin."

I had often assisted our parish priest at Mass. I knew where to hold the prayer book and when to hand the abbot the holy water. I knelt and crossed myself at all the appropriate times.

Father Dunstan lay pale against the cushions. The thin white hair around his tonsure spread on the bed linen like fragile silks of a spider's web. Father Abbot said the prayers over the cup. The olivewood drinking bowl reflected the glow of the candles that lit the tiny altar where it rested.

Father Dunstan must have rubbed it with some of Brother Arthur's polish, I thought. But the glow seemed to grow until it outshone the candles on either side. I could not tear my eyes from its beauty, and yet the abbot continued his prayers in a heavy voice. He lifted the cup, and it was as if a blaze of light filled the room. The whitewashed walls gleamed like noonday sun on snow. The gold thread in the abbot's cope blazed like flames.

The light reached into my very soul and exposed every secret thought and desire. I fell to my knees, tears streaming down my cheeks.

Dómine, non sum dignus. Lord, I am not worthy.

The abbot turned and offered the cup to the man in the bed. I caught the scent of cinnamon and cloves and fragrant wine far richer than any our cellars held. Far off voices chanted faintly.

Holy! Holy! Holy!

I knew not the tongue. But I knew without doubt the meaning of the words.

Father Dunstan's face glowed with the same unearthly light as the cup. His skin was firm and pink, and a ring of golden curls encircled his head. I was looking into the face of a young man a few years older than myself. Perhaps I should have been surprised, but I wasn't. I knew him to be the Father Dunstan of the days of the Yorkish King Edward, when the priest had first made his vows to our Lord. His eyes danced with joy, and he reached eager hands to grasp the offered cup.

"Drink ye all of it," Abbot Whiting recited.

Father Dunstan gulped the wine, tears like liquid crystal running down his cheeks. It was as though he could not get enough of what that cup contained, yet could not believe his good fortune to have tasted even a drop of it.

He laughed, the irrepressible joy of an infant spilling over in de-light at communion with his God. I laughed with him, the sound coming out almost as a sob. How could anyone in that room refrain from laughing and crying and shouting for joy at the goodness of God, yet Abbot Whiting continued the prayers without pause.

He lowered the cup and the light waned. The distant voices faded, and I smelled again the herbs of the potions Brother Urban used against the fever. The walls glowed no more than newly washed wool and then dimmed to their usual shadows. The cup faded to a polished gleam, and then, with only the light of two candles in the room, even that was gone. Nothing remained but the yellow grain of olivewood, very old and very worn.

I sprinkled the abbot's hands with holy water, and my own hands shook with emotion. I held the prayer book in a daze. This world of shadows seemed but a passing dream after the blazing reality of the cup.

The prayers ended. "Rest now," Father Abbot said to Father Dunstan.

I looked at Father Dunstan. He lay back upon the cushions. His snowy hair still glimmered with traces of the light that didn't come from the candles, and his eyes were bright with excitement.

"It's the fever," Brother Urban said. He laid a hand on the old man's forehead, then removed it with a puzzled look. "But he doesn't feel warm."

Indeed, Father Dunstan's cheeks were not quite so pink as I had seen them a few minutes before. Nevertheless, they showed healthy color.

"The cup. May I hold the cup?" Father Dunstan stretched out a hand whiter than the linen coverlet.

"Of course." Abbot Whiting nodded to me.

I reached for the cup on the altar. It stung my fingertips with the spark that comes when you touch metal on a dry winter's day. I drew in my breath sharply and pulled back.

"What's wrong?" Father Bede hissed behind me.

Abbot Whiting turned to me. "Bring him the cup, Colin."

The Rule of Saint Benedict places obedience to one's abbot on a level with obedience to God. Although I feared to touch it again, I nestled the cup in my palms and lifted it gently. It felt warm as a womb and soft as a mother's breast. My hands tingled with such life that I could feel the blood circulating in my veins. The tingling crept up my arms to my shoulders, and if it had reached my head I would either have fainted or shouted for joy. But Father Bede grabbed it from my hands before I could relinquish it to Father Dunstan.

"You're slow to obey."

It was as though my arms had been wrenched from my body. I gasped in pain. Abbot Whiting looked uncertainly at me.

Father Bede turned the cup over in his hands, brushing the surface with his fingertips. He looked from the cup to me and back again. Did he feel some shadow of the tingling I had felt?

I put my hands into the sleeves of my cassock to hide their trembling and fixed my eyes on Father Dunstan. He smiled a knowing smile and nodded as though we shared some secret.

"Curious thing, isn't it?" Father Bede said. "It must date from well before the fire. I would have said I knew all Glastonbury's treasures, but this—I must consult the lists."

"Father Bede, Father Dunstan asked for the cup." Abbot Whiting had not moved from where he stood.

"Yes, yes, of course." Father Bede studied the bowl as he crossed the room. Even then he hesitated before handing it to the man in the bed.

For the merest instant I saw once more the Father Dunstan who had been. Or perhaps it was Father Dunstan as he would be in the kingdom of heaven, full of strength and vigor. Then there was again an old man, clasping an olivewood bowl to his breast, like the Prophet Simeon must have clasped the infant Christ in the temple.

"We must let him rest," Father Abbot said. Brother Urban put out the candles and motioned us toward the door. I was the last to leave, and when I looked back I wasn't certain if it was the young man or the old who lay in the bed.

CHAPTER 15

FATHER ABBOT SENT FOR ME after Prime. "You will be happy to know that Father Dunstan is doing quite well this morning," he said. "There's no sign of fever, nor of the weakness he has experienced in the last few days. Brother Urban says his recovery is a miracle."

"*Laudate Dominum,*" I breathed. "Lord be praised."

The abbot sat back in his carved chair, his fingertips pressed together in the gesture that was common to him. The ring of Thomas of Canterbury glistened on his hand as Abbot Whiting looked steadily at me.

"Colin, what did you see last night?"

I could feel the blood drain from my face. "What did I see?" My voice came out as a tight squeak.

"I was concerned with Father Dunstan and with the words of the prayers. But the others say you trembled and shed tears and blinked as though in a bright light. They believe you saw a vision. And now with Father Dunstan's wondrous return from death's shadow, I wonder if more happened by his bed than I saw."

I clasped my cold hands tightly to stop their shaking and fixed my eyes on the cushion at his feet. If my Lord Abbot had seen nothing unusual, how could I tell him? Did I think myself more holy than the head of our house?

He waited patiently for me to speak.

"I saw . . . I saw a light. It came from the cup. It filled the room, and I supposed that all could see it." The curious interest in his eyes told me others had not. "And I saw Father Dunstan. He was not an old man, but young and strong and eager to drink from the cup."

Father Abbot nodded slowly. "Have you seen such things before, Colin?"

My lips went numb and my hands were lumps of ice.

"I know when you were ill, you suffered in dreams." His voice was kind, but the muscles of my stomach gripped my middle. "Do you have reason to believe these dreams came from God?"

"No, Father Abbot," I said quickly. "They were mostly about my father—and sometimes Father Cuthbert and Brother Fergus with the pilgrims."

His fingers stopped their gentle movement and his palms pressed together in an attitude of prayer. After a few moments he broke the silence.

"Colin, I think it best that you not speak of these things, except, of course, with Father Dunstan. No doubt he, too, saw this light. In chapter I will ask the others not to question you. But if you see anything else, I hope you will come to me. I know that your relationship with your father was not close, but God is your Father now, and on earth I stand in His place."

I rubbed the thick scar that had formed on the back of my wrist where my father's sword had wounded me. "Yes, Father."

He looked at me as though he suspected I held something back. I blinked several times, and pushed away the memory of his face in my vision of the Tor.

❧

"You saw Him, didn't you?" Father Dunstan demanded when I visited his cell that afternoon. Brother Urban had given me a curious look when I passed through the infirmary hall, and I saw the lay brothers whispering together, with glances in my direction. But no one broke the abbot's order not to question me.

"I saw you," I began.

"Not me! Not me! The Lord Christ! He came to me and offered His blood from His own cup. I saw the marks—the wounds He took for my sake. Oh, poor scarred hands, the marks of His love." He clasped his own hands to his breast as though feeling the pain. "Abbot Whiting saw nothing, nor did Brother Urban. I think perhaps you, Colin, saw the glory."

"I saw the cup, glowing with light, and I saw your joy."

"Oh, Colin, the joy of knowing my Savior waits for me, that He gave Himself for me and has prepared a place to receive me forever into His presence. I feel new—like I could live forever. And yet I long to leave this body and live with Him." He shook his head with a look of impatience.

He sighed and looked thoughtful. "'Tis for the abbot God leaves me yet a while. He carries a heavy load. I can do little to bear him up, save in my prayers. He must choose which king he serves."

He studied the wooden cup in his lap.

"Colin." I tore my eyes from the cup and looked at his face. "When I am gone, take this to the abbot."

"But Father," I protested. "You aren't going to die. You have recovered from the fever. You're quite well. Brother Urban says it's a miracle."

"I know what they are saying, Colin." He shook his head and caressed the smooth side of the cup. "Miracles—how little we know their purpose."

❧

I dreamed again that night.

I saw the cross in front of Saint Michael's Church atop the Tor, but the cross was empty. There was no image of Christ stretched upon it. Nor was there any gibbet. The mists of Somerset swirled around me. They were not cold and biting as they had been when I climbed the Tor, but balmy and fragrant with apple blossoms. From the mist a man stepped toward me. His garments glowed with the same light as the cup. His face was kind, and he smiled gently. He reached a hand to raise me from the trampled mud before the empty cross.

He spoke to me, not in Latin, but in my native English, "Man thy sins are forgiven thee."

I'd heard those words before. I could still see the Tor's mist-shrouded summit, but superimposed upon it were the smoky rafters of a small, rude peasant's room. Alice's golden head bent over the book on the table, and she read firmly by the flickering lamplight, "I say to thee, 'arise, take up thy bed and go home to thy house.'"

For the first time I understood the man's complete helplessness. Nothing could he do to save his body or his soul. There was nothing I could do to save mine.

Not on the Tor.

Not in the abbey.

Alice's voice faded. There was only the man standing in the mists of the Tor with his hand stretched out to me.

I took it.

⟨∾⟩

Father Bede found me next morning after chapter. He drew me into the undercroft of the dorter as the others filed to their work.

"Brother Colin." It was the respectful tone he normally reserved for the abbot or prior. "I had one or two questions about your experience when our dear Father Dunstan was so ill."

I stiffened. "Father Abbot told me not to speak of it," I replied.

"Of course not!" He drew back and creased his brow. "This is not something to be flaunted for personal glory. We to whom God grants special insights must keep a humble spirit before Him."

He emphasized the word *we* and laid a friendly hand on my shoulder. It weighed like a yoke of iron. "You have done well to be humbly silent on the subject. The abbot was most wise to discipline your haughty spirit with that fast."

I drew back, but he continued. "When Father Abbot asked you not to talk about this, he was referring to the monastery in general and the idle talk that, unfortunately, occurs in the cloister or in the infirmary hall. He was not referring to the leaders of the house. After all, I am third in rank after Prior Robert. Father Abbot shares freely with both of us all the business of the house."

"Then he has told you?"

Father Bede cleared his throat. "Father Abbot has been busy of late. That is why I thought it better not to trouble him, but to interview you directly."

I nodded to the priest. "I will be happy to answer your questions, Father Bede." His smile was gracious, but his gray eyes reminded me of a hawk that had spotted a hare hiding in the grass. "I will speak with you about it as soon as Father Abbot gives me leave."

I turned toward the offices.

～

After that, I frequently saw Father Bede lurking in the infirmary. *Lurking* was the word that came to mind, for he had no business there. He plagued Father Dunstan with requests to see and handle the cup.

"We give up all personal possessions when we enter these walls," I heard him say on one occasion. "The cup belongs to the abbey for the boon of all. For the abbey its power should be used." How he would have used it, I didn't know, but the abbot did not support his request, and the cup stayed in Father Dunstan's care.

Rumors flew about the vaults of the cloister. How had the cup escaped the notice of Cromwell's men? Was it invisible when enemies approached? Someone noted that not one had died in the infirmary since the cup had come there, though a number of old men had taken shelter with us from the smaller monasteries that had been closed.

Once, when Father Dunstan was sitting in the infirmary garden, he sent me to his bedside for the cup, which now seldom left his sight. Entering the cell I surprised Father Bede, his hand inches from the cup on the altar.

"Father Bede?" I said in pointed challenge. My voice startled us both as it echoed about the small room. My hands felt cold and clammy. I didn't know if I was more angry or frightened at being the one to confront him.

He jerked his head in my direction, his face contorted in a quick spasm before he brought it under control. He slid his hands into his sleeves.

"I am looking for Father Dunstan," he said at last. The words were ordinary, but under them ran a current of barely restrained passion.

"He is in the garden," I said. "I'd have thought you passed him when you arrived."

His mouth opened and closed before he said, "I must have been preoccupied." He closed his mouth and brushed past me without another word.

I picked up the cup and returned to the garden. Father Bede disappeared at the other end of the walkway. If he had spoken to Father Dunstan, it was no more than a word.

CHAPTER 16

THE WINTER RAINS HAD BEEN constant, but now the weather eased. Father Abbot was anxious to leave for his country retreat at Sharpham Manor, a couple miles outside Glastonbury. He had sent word to London that he would not attend the spring session of Parliament. Although he had no specific physical complaint, he was past eighty, and I was sure a retreat would do him good. He left shortly after Mass and took me with him, since Brother Basil was needed to assist Prior Robert at the monastery.

Abbot Whiting led the way on a gentle mare. I followed among the entourage of servants. A merchant's cart rattled up Spital Street past the hospital for the poor that gave it its name. The cheerful noise of business on the High Street was a clamor after the quiet of the cloister. It had been months since I had been out in the world.

A fine mist hung over the River Brue at the ford where our party crossed. Its banks were alive with swaying yellow daffodils, the heralds of spring. It was easy to imagine the hand of the Lady of the Lake rising to reclaim the sword Excalibur when King Arthur died, for all Thomas's assurances that the tales were not true.

The road looped south to avoid the soft ground of Hulk Moor. Although a man might pass on foot if he knew the way, there were few places where the water-saturated ground would bear the weight of horses.

The abbot seemed to sit taller in his saddle, and his horse almost danced in eagerness as we approached Sharpham. We turned north into a drove and thence into a lane lined with elms that met overhead, enclosing us in a tunnel spread with the delicate green of infant leaves. A herd of deer grazed near the tall stone house at the top of the lane. They raised their heads to observe our passing and returned calmly to crop the dew-drenched grasses.

On that first afternoon at Sharpham, Father Abbot called me to the room where he and the steward were working. "Colin, take a look at these." A large ledger was spread before him on the table.

"Here are the expenditures, my Lord Abbot," the steward explained. "You can see that the income is not enough to cover the management of the household here, much less sustain the abbot's table in Glastonbury. Perhaps a little less . . ."

The abbot motioned to me. "You have seen to your father's accounts, haven't you? These make my head ache. Perhaps if you and my steward look them over together, you might come up with some solution. Or at least be able to explain to me why we are bleeding money like a slaughtered calf."

"Yes, Father Abbot." I glanced at the steward, who gave me a hard look.

The accounts were not kept in quite the same form as my father's, but they were neatly done and up to date. The steward seemed pleasantly surprised when I caught on so quickly. The reason for the drain of money was obvious. We spent more than we took in. More local ale and cider and fewer bottles of fine imported wines from France would help, as would removing roast swan's tongue from the Christmas menu. The horses kept in the Sharpham barns for the use of the abbot's noble guests were a significant drain, but I doubted he would agree to sell them. In the end we conspired to recommend a few minor economies.

"About the horses," the steward began.

Abbot Whiting waved a hand. "It is important for one in my position to provide generously for his guests. I must not be seen to be weak or powerless, especially now."

In the end he was pleased with my work. "Train him," he instructed the steward. "The recent laws keep cloistered monks in their cloisters. That makes it difficult for us to administer our estates. But Colin is not yet a monk. He is free to go where I send him. He is good with numbers, isn't he?"

The steward nodded his agreement, and I flushed at the affirmation.

Three days after we returned to Glastonbury the abbot sent me to another manor. I traveled on my own, carrying letters from the abbot. I wore a set of clothes Father Aidan had found for me. They were rather old fashioned, but I had grown nearly a span since coming to the abbey, and my own no longer served.

"It will raise fewer questions," he said as he folded my white novice habit.

The steward had been warned that I was coming and had the books in order, although the ink for the last several months was all the same, and the handwriting declined so that I suspected the entries had been done hurriedly at one sitting. I found some errors, corrected them and assured the steward that the abbey was still in control of the estate. I missed the abbey. There was no one with whom to say the Hours and only a handful who gathered at the parish church for Mass.

I had known a strange peace since the vision of the cup in Father Dunstan's room. I still hesitated to call it the Holy Grail, although that was one theory whispered among the monks. The term had the feel of a dead relic, no more real than the bones of King Arthur beneath the marble tomb in the chancel, which were not real at all if Thomas was to be believed. This vision was very alive. Father Dunstan had beheld the living Christ. I had not seen my Lord in the infirmary cell that wondrous night, but I had no doubt that it was He who had reached out to me on the misty top of the Tor in my dream.

Odd. I had grazed my forehead on the floor of the church in penance for my sin against my father. I had let the wound on my arm fester. I had fasted forty days, kept vigil at the altar of Saint Thomas, climbed the Tor, praying at the Stations of the Cross, and spent three days near death in the infirmary. Yet through it all I had felt not a whit more worthy of anyone's acceptance, much less the love of God, than on the day I fled my father's house. But when the Man from the mist, the One who told the paralytic his sins were forgiven, said the same to me . . . then I felt free. Not perfect. I would never be as holy as Brother Fergus, dedicated to serving the poor, willing to die for the chance to do God's will.

I stared at the ledger on the table before me and shivered at the thought of the young monk I had known for only a day. At this moment he was locked in a prison cell in London awaiting . . . what? Could their Pilgrimage of Grace end anywhere but the block or scaffold?

I added a column of figures and confirmed the steward's math.

I was still a long way from forgiving my father for all he had done, but I sensed that something inside me had begun to change. I no longer felt at home with bitterness. The heretics preached salvation by faith alone. Faith was all I had when I reached to grasp the hand of the Man in the mist. Even that was stunted and desperate.

Could it be enough?

CHAPTER 17

I DREW A PALE LINE THROUGH the name of Thomas of Canterbury. Laying down the pen, I rubbed my cramped hand. The thick scar above my wrist itched. I turned to gaze out the leaded glass window at the cloister garden, run riot with summer roses.

Father Bede pounced like a cat waiting at the mouse hole. "No dawdling. You spend enough time away from the abbey. You must make up for it with diligence when you are here."

I bent again to my work. Though his words remained harsh and demanding, I suspected that he might see some hope for me. He had recommended me to Brother Basil after all, and for all his complaining he wasn't willing to release me from the hours I spent in the library.

"I don't know what the abbot is thinking," Father Bede murmured under his breath, "letting a novice cavort about the countryside."

There was no one in sight for him to criticize but me, and the high standards he held for the abbey demanded that he criticize someone. Thomas was gone. Roger had recently taken his final vows; now he helped the schoolmaster teach the younger boys. I suspected his own long struggle to learn Latin made him a patient teacher. I missed his company. We had become as close as I had always wished I could be with Walter.

Walter. I stared at the hand that held my pen and saw instead an image of his boyish fist guiding my chubby fingers to form my first letters. I felt my brother's arms across my shoulders, drawing back the bow with me, directing my shot so it hit the target, albeit the edge, and praising my success as though it were my own. My eyes blurred and my nose began to run. I sniffed and wiped it on my sleeve.

"Silence," Father Bede demanded.

A schoolboy in the livery of a page entered the cloister and handed the librarian a folded and sealed paper, then stood with his head respectfully bowed.

I bent over the volume of saints' lives, but my eyes watched while Father Bede broke the seal and opened the paper. He smiled faintly.

"So, the abbot has need of my advice," he murmured. He closed the book in front of him and rose from his stool. "No doubt it concerns the letters that arrived this morning from London," he said a little more loudly. He looked around, and I quickly lowered my eyes.

"Colin."

"Yes, Father."

"Carry on. I am trusting you to behave in my absence as you would if I were present."

"Yes, Father." There was a time when he would not have trusted me so far.

He crossed the cloister garden followed by the page and went out by the door closest to the abbot's apartments.

I let out a great sigh, stretched my back and massaged my hand, things I would not have dared to do if Father Bede were present. The opening and closing of the cloister door sent a breath of sweet air around its corners. A hinge creaked. The door of a book cupboard swung slowly open. It creaked again with an irritating sound. I rose to shut it.

But it wouldn't shut. The latch was set in the locked position, but it hadn't caught. I couldn't open the latch and shut the cupboard without the key. And the key was the one around Father Bede's neck.

My heart began to pound. This was the forbidden cupboard. My eyes fell on the treasures inside, books of many sizes, stacked on one another, volumes on alchemy and witchcraft and the wisdom of the Druids. Some that I assumed to be the oldest were wrapped in protective cloths. Perhaps the history of the abbey was there—the book that would tell of the finding of King Arthur's bones.

I glanced around the library. A book lay open on the desk near the east aisle. The monk who had been studying it could return at any moment. But he was not there now.

I reached out my hand to the cupboard, and drew it quickly back. No. I would not look.

Carefully I closed the door of the cupboard as far as it would go. As long as there was no breeze it would stay there as it had when Father Bede was in the room. I turned my back on the cupboard and started for my desk.

The book Father Bede had been studying still lay on his table. He always assigned himself the most interesting titles, often ones from the forbidden cupboard, far too old to contain the name of the former saint. The light in the north aisle of the cloister was not bright in the afternoon. Nevertheless the gold letters embosomed on the leather cover caught my eye. *De Antiquitate Glastonie Ecclesie. The History of the Church at Glastonbury.* This was the book I sought.

"It must be the hand of God that led me to it," I marveled.

I lowered myself onto Father Bede's chair and opened the cover. The name of the author, William of Malmesbury, was written in antique script on the first page. I leaned forward. Thomas had said that the bones had been found shortly after the Great Fire. That was on Saint Urban's Day in May of 1184, Father Aidan had told me. This book was very old. No doubt the fire would come near the end. A faint breath of air cooled my hot face as I turned to the back of the volume.

But the account ended fifty or sixty years before the Great Fire—a lifetime before the monks who had found the bones that now lay in the tomb at the front of the church. Disappointment ran out of me like wine from a burst barrel. I would never know if the monks were deceivers or not.

"What—have—you—done?"

Father Bede stood over me. His gray eyes had turned to molten pewter, and his pale face was livid with color.

The door of the locked cupboard had swung open with his coming.

"I didn't—" I began.

"I trusted you and you have abused that trust!"

"But—"

"Are you not sitting in the place of your betters, reading a book you were not authorized to touch?"

His gray brows pushed together in an angry scowl. "Did you not break open the lock to this cupboard to gain access to what is forbidden?"

"No, Father. I swear!"

"How then is it open?"

"The latch! It didn't catch when you locked it."

He twisted the neck of my cassock in his powerful fist as though I were no more than a naughty pup.

"The door was swinging open," I went on. "I only meant to shut it."

"Are you accusing me of carelessness?" He drew himself to his full height. "I who have served this library for forty years?"

"No, Father. I only said . . ."

He dragged me to my feet and pushed me toward the abbot's offices. "If I had not come back for certain papers, who knows what mischief you would have done?"

"I did nothing!" I insisted. "It was you who left the cupboard open!"

"You insolent child of the Devil, do you dare to speak that way to me?"

I knew I had sinned. I should not have spoken to him so. "I'm sorry," I said. I didn't feel it, but I dreaded the humiliation of being dragged before the abbot.

"I will see to it that you are very sorry."

Brother Basil looked up when we entered. His mouth fell open in bafflement.

"This boy broke into the cupboard of most valuable books, read things not intended for novices and had the insolence to speak disrespectfully and accuse me of failure in my duty," Father Bede said when he saw the abbot. "I demand that he be locked in the punishment cell." His hand still twisted my garments awkwardly.

Abbot Whiting cleared his throat and looked pointedly at the librarian. Father Bede released me, and I adjusted the folds of my cassock. My hands were damp with sweat, and my left thumb scrubbed at the scar on my wrist.

"Colin, did you break into this cupboard?

"No, Father. The door was swinging open. I meant only to shut it."

"He lies!" Father Bede roared.

Abbot Whiting kept his eyes on me. "Did you read books you were not authorized to see?"

"I . . ." I had. I lowered my eyes. "Yes, Father."

"And did you speak disrespectfully to Father Bede?"

I knew I should try to look humble, but I raised my head defiantly. "I did."

"His pride and insolence must be brought in line," Father Bede demanded. "He should be flogged."

Abbot Whiting looked at the compulsive movement of my thumb against my wrist. "I think a night in the punishment cell will suffice," he said quietly. There was compassion as well as disappointment in his voice. "Brother Basil."

"Yes, Father."

"You may see Brother Colin to the cell."

Brother Basil took my arm gently and led me away. Father Bede's voice rose behind us in angry explanations of the importance of discipline. Whatever regard I might have begun to have in his eyes, I had certainly lost.

The punishment cell was in the cellars beneath the refectory. It was dark and musty smelling. There was no window but a grating in the door to the poorly lit corridor. Brother Basil lifted the key from a nail in the wall. "I'm sorry, Colin."

I shook my head. I had only myself to blame. He locked the door. His footsteps echoed up the corridor, and then there was silence.

I sat on the stone bench built into the wall and stared at my hands. The skin around my scar was red where I had rubbed it. Why did Father Bede always bring out the worst in me? Like my father.

Tears coursed down my cheeks. Once they began to fall, they would not stop. I wept for my mother and my brother and my infant sister. But most of all I wept for the father I longed to please and never could.

CHAPTER 18

ON THE TWELFTH OF JULY, Father Dunstan died quietly in his sleep. Brother Urban found him with hands clasping the cup. His lips were curved in a gentle smile of peace and joy. Father Bede appeared in the infirmary to claim the cup before the lay brothers had finished washing the body. Fortunately, Brother Urban knew Father Dunstan's intention as well as I did, and by then it was already in the hands of the abbot.

The next day word reached us that the leaders of the Pilgrimage of Grace had been executed, including Father Cuthbert and Brother Fergus. I wept for them and spent the night alone in prayer in the Chapel of Saint Thomas.

❧

Abbot Whiting himself celebrated the Requiem Mass. Whether it was his own desire or pressure from Father Bede, he used the olive-wood drinking bowl rather than any costly chalice. I do know that there was much whispering in the cloister, and most of the abbey servants and a good many from the town were present for the service.

"'Tis the Holy Grail," they whispered.

I chanted with the others as I filed into my place. Roger assisted the abbot today. The cup on the altar seemed small beneath its delicate embroidered veil. Could this indeed be the cup of Our Lord, the chalice of His last supper brought to England by Saint Joseph, the cup that once held the very blood taken from the cross of Our Lord's passion? The Holy Grail—vision at King Arthur's court, pursued by all his knights and achieved only by the holy Sir Galahad in the castle of the Fisher King? That faery castle was said to rest somewhere in the swamps of Somerset, perhaps on this very Isle of Avalon, now called Glastonbury. In my mother's tapestry the Holy Grail had glittered with gold. This was only polished wood, but that night in Father Dunstan's cell I would have sworn it glowed more brilliantly than any precious metal.

My palms were wet and cold despite the heat of the summer's day, and my woolen cassock stuck to the sweat of my body. If the light shone forth again, what would it reveal? I remembered great joy that night, but I also remembered how exposed I had felt. What would the light show of the bitterness I yet harbored against my father, my resentment toward Father Bede?

I glanced through the carved quire screen to the townspeople crowded in the nave. These people had come to see a miracle. One whispered to his neighbor and pointed to me, alone in my white novice gown now that Roger wore black. I knew they were marveling that a lowly novice had seen the miracle. What did they expect of me? I was not so holy as Brother Fergus or even as Roger, my patient stonemason friend.

Hoc est enim corpus meum—This is My body.

Abbot Whiting spoke the words of consecration. The little bell rang as he bowed in worship of the crucified Body of Our Lord.

"My Lord and my God," I responded in Latin with the monks and the crowd on the other side of the screen. They leaned forward to glimpse the raised Host, the bread that had become the very flesh of Christ. There was perfect silence in the nave as the abbot uncovered the olivewood drinking bowl and took it in both his hands.

I blinked. For a moment I seemed to glimpse the Man who had reached to me through the mists on the Tor. He smiled as though we shared some secret.

Hic est enim calix sánguinis mei—This is the chalice of My blood, of the new and eternal covenant.

The vision faded. Abbot Whiting raised the ancient wooden cup over his head, and no one needed the ringing of the little bell to tell them this was the moment for which they had come.

Brother Arthur's face glowed. Roger's eyes were moist as he fixed them on the raised cup. Father Bede leaned forward, his body as tense as the highest string of Llwyd's harp. Even the monks who usually said Mass privately in one of the side chapels at this hour were in their places with all their attention on the high altar. Sunlight streamed through the arched windows of the church, and the Great Sapphire hanging overhead tossed its silvery shards into every corner of the quire, but the cup shone no brighter than any piece of ancient wood, dull and ordinary next to the gold and silver adorning the altar.

There was a sigh as of disappointment from the nave when the abbot lowered the cup, and a rustling of garments as people turned to see any sign in their neighbors of having witnessed a miracle. Several monks stared in my direction, and I could feel the intensity of Father Bede's gaze.

There had been no fiery glow from the cup. Part of me was disappointed and the other part relieved. But when it came my turn to drink from it, the wine was sweeter than any I had ever tasted and had about it the scent of cinnamon and cloves.

CHAPTER 19

THREE DAYS LATER I DONNED secular clothes and rode out to check the accounts of yet another abbey farm. My horse followed a mill-stream until it emptied into the River Brue. Its meandering course had long ago been tamed and forced to run between straight banks, draining the broad, flat peat bogs on either side.

The day was bright on the ripening fields. Ahead, the water had been allowed to stand. Reflecting sky and moor, it glimmered gray as steel for miles—Meare Pool, the source of most of the fish that reached the abbey tables. A stone building stood in a meadow, just beyond where the track left the river. The smell of drying fish was stronger than the bundles of new thatch in the cart that stood in the meadow.

A familiar figure rounded the building, stepped toward the cart, and paused to look at the approaching rider. "Colin? That be ye?"

A broad smile spread over Wilfrith Thatcher's weathered face. "Dinne think ye'd still be in Glassonb'ry. How be on, lad?" He reached a hand and patted my horse eagerly as though he were genu-inely glad to see me. "I see ye're no longer takin' rides in the carts of yeomen." I had no answer for that, but it didn't matter because he hardly paused. "Nicholas."

Nicholas's yellow head popped over the ridgepole of the half-thatched fish house. "Hello, Colin." He deftly caught the bundle of thatch Wilfrith tossed up to him.

"My greetings to you, Master Nicholas," I called. "As usual, you are hard at work."

"The man don't know the meanin' of rest save on the Sabbath," Wilfrith sighed, but with a proud gleam in his eye. "I picked good to get him for Tildy, though she had a mite to say on the matter. Now if I can jest do as well by Alice." He gave me a wink, and the heat rose in my cheeks.

Wilfrith laughed and slapped his thigh. "Knew ye'd never be a monk, lad. How's your hand at turnin' a plow?"

I stammered and shifted the reins in my hand. My horse stretched his neck for a bite of the tender grass that grew at the side of the road, and I occupied myself with making her behave.

"Send me up some more thatch," Nicholas called, as much to distract his impish father-in-law as for need of material, I thought.

"Dinne be wastin' good thatch," Wilfrith said. "'Tis only a fish house—not the new barns at Sharpham, ye know." Nicholas grinned and winked at me.

"Those barns'll take a pretty cartload of thatch, I tell ye."

"Sharpham Manor?" I asked.

"Aye. Ye know it?"

"Beautiful place—the abbot's favorite retreat. He goes there often as he can."

Nicholas gave me an odd look. "Where ye say ye been keepin' yourself?" His tone was casual, but his manner suddenly wary. "Not at the abbey, by your dress."

I looked down at the padded doublet I wore. "Why yes, the abbey," I said. "I'm assistant to Brother Basil, the abbot's secretary. I oversee accounts of the abbey manors. I'll be at Meare for a few days." I nodded toward the large stone house at the top of the meadow. That was where Brother Basil had told me I would find the steward. "I hope to have time to come and see you."

"I see." Wilfrith rubbed the stubble of his chin thoughtfully. I'd spoken loudly enough for both men to hear and both were quiet for a moment. "Abbey accounts, eh?" Wilfrith muttered and turned away to lift another bundle of thatch. He looked back at me, bobbing his head as though searching for something to say. The moment stretched into awkwardness. I had disappointed them. I opened my mouth to say something and make it right, but there was nothing to say.

"Well, I'll be going then," I said, fearing something precious had been lost. Nicholas nodded but seemed suddenly preoccupied with lashing the next bit of roof.

"Good day to ye, Colin," Wilfrith said quietly, and I wondered if he too grieved the loss.

I felt their eyes on my back as I rode up the lane, and it was all I could do not to turn around and ask their forgiveness for . . . I knew not what.

The manor was a cold and silent place, but James Toogood the lay steward welcomed me warmly. He had undoubtedly felt the pressure of maintaining the abbey lands without the monk who used to oversee the property. The demands of work made it difficult for him to make the journey into Glastonbury to consult with the abbot.

He led me into a small upstairs room that looked out on a lush meadow sloping gently to the river and pool. The Mendip Hills, far off on the horizon, rose like an edge on the flat platter that was the Vale of Avalon.

The steward had been expecting me. Ledgers were neatly laid out on a table by the window where they would catch the best light.

"I trust ye'll find all in order." Master Toogood nervously clutched his hands. "I do me best by the abbey. I'm a godly man. I might have entered the church meself if me wife hadn't got herself with a young'un."

I wondered how she had managed such a thing without his help, but I only patted the massive account folio. "I'm sure the abbot appreciates your efforts. If you will show me where the brothers left off, I will begin there."

The books were in good order. Most entries tallied the quantities of fish sent to the abbey or the collection of rents from the tenants. The name *Thatcher* was on the list. Part of their rent was exchanged each year for labor in thatching the manor buildings. The dovecote had been recently redone, and the amount agreed upon for the fish house was recorded.

I took only a short break for midday meal, and my eyes were

beginning to feel strained when Master Toogood brought a clay lamp.

"Will ye be continuing, or will ye be wanting some dinner?"

I straightened and eased my aching back. "Some dinner would be nice, thank you." I gave a great sigh. "I don't find many problems here. I should finish on the morrow."

"Very good."

I found it difficult to make conversation at dinner. I was tired and had lost the knack of exchanging pleasantries through the discipline of silence at abbey meals. My host bounced endlessly from subject to subject, complaining of hoof rot in cows and mites on the sheep. One tenant he suspected of poaching fish from the abbot's pool and another of some other offense.

"We even have a nest of heretics in our midst," he said.

I choked on the bite of meat I was chewing.

"Some of our best tenants, too," he went on.

I coughed violently and reached for my glass of watered wine. "Are ye all right?" Master Toogood asked and pounded my back until the piece of meat was dislodged. By then he'd forgotten what he'd been saying as my fit began.

"The cider apples look good this year," he said when I had my breath again.

I had lost my appetite. Even the chance to eat roast lamb instead of the abbey's usual fish did not tempt me.

"I think I'll take a walk in the village," I said when dinner was finished.

"Of course! No doubt ye'd like to stretch your legs after sitting all the day. I'd be happy to accompany you, but—"

"No, no. I'll be fine." I could see he was not anxious to go out, and I was desperate to escape his endless chatter.

Besides I hoped to visit these "heretics."

"The village is small. There's no fear of getting lost. It was an island before we began draining the bogs round about."

"So I've been told."

I escaped at last into the lingering evening. The clouds of the day had broken and a faint golden glow still showed in the west. I passed the church and the little whitewashed inn. A light shone in the window and the voices of laughing men carried into the night. A narrow lane led to a small village green, which I guessed held the weekly market. The green, like the street, was empty.

The Thatchers' cottage was the last in the row, and I thought I could see it where the higher ground began to slope back toward the bogs and a thick growth of thatching grass thrust above the carpet of fog. A shadowy figure could be seen pausing at the door and then disappearing inside. Perhaps it was Alice. I stepped quickly, eager to see my friends.

The latch of the door had not quite caught. The faint light of a lamp shone through a small gap, and I could hear Nicholas speaking earnestly.

"Hello," I called, knocking lightly. "Anyone home?" The voice grew silent and there was a faint rustling sound. "Nicholas? Matilda?" The door swung open although I hadn't meant to push it. More than a dozen pairs of eyes turned toward me from around the room. I heard a sharp intake of breath from the woman nearest the door, but otherwise the silence was complete.

"Colin!" A child squealed and leaped from the floor at Nicholas's feet. Wil had grown by half a head since I'd last seen him. He had stretched into a sturdy boy. "Ye're back!" He reached for my hand and pulled me into the room. "Look, Father! Colin's here."

No one yet moved. They might have been the carved images of saints on the quire screen of the abbey church of Saint Mary, but their clothes were dusty from the day's labors and smelled of sweat. I met Nicholas's eye. A book lay open in front of him. I swallowed and tried not to look too closely.

"Hello, Colin." His voice was steady, but it didn't hold the welcome Wil had expected, and he looked questioningly at me.

Wilfrith rose from his seat. "Colin! Jest a few friends and neighbors come to bide the evenin'." He extended his hand to me and nodded at his guests. There was a general rustling. A few exchanged whispers.

"Jest friends and neighbors," agreed a man with a wandering eye who nodded to the man next to him.

A tall, broad-chested fellow stood. "We best be goin' now. Come along, Elwina." A sturdy young woman with a missing front tooth rose slowly. She glanced nervously from Nicholas to me as she followed her husband. Two others slipped quietly out behind them.

"I didn't mean to interrupt," I began lamely.

"'Tidn't no matter. We've all had a long day, and folks needs their sleep." Wilfrith shook my hand and nodded at his guests who took their leave in ones and twos and slipped into the night.

I stood in the middle of the small room, Wil clutching my hand and looking bewildered. When the others were gone, I noticed Matilda sitting on a bench in the corner, her arms protectively around Alice. Alice didn't look much like she needed protection. Her chin was held high, and her eyes blazed. I turned my gaze back to Nicholas, who stood above the open book.

"Sit, Colin." Wilfrith patted a stool beside him. "Matilda, fetch our guest some refreshment." Matilda rose awkwardly from the bench and lifted a wooden cup down from its shelf. She was heavy with child.

"How did ye find James Toogood?" Wilfrith asked.

"He is well—and he keeps accounts in good order."

"Father! Did ye know Colin was here and ye said nothin' about it?" Alice leapt to her feet, hands on her hips.

Wilfrith rubbed the stubble on his chin. "Nicholas and me run into Colin on the Glassonb'ry road today." I watched Matilda pour cider from the jug in the corner. "He be workin' with Abbot Whiting's secretary."

A small gasp escaped Matilda. She replaced the cider jug among the rushes on the dirt floor a bit more abruptly than I expect she had intended.

"He come on abbey business," Wilfrith went on meaningfully.

Alice took the cup from her sister's paralyzed hands. She looked straight at me as she thrust it in my direction. I had forgotten how blue her eyes were. She too had grown in the last few months. Where Wil's body had stretched long and thin, hers had filled out in pleasing shapes that made my heart beat faster.

My fingers brushed hers as I took the cup. "Thank you, Alice." I swallowed several times before I remembered to lift the cup to my

mouth. "Thank you," I said again when I had swallowed some cider.
I had to tear my eyes away from her before I forgot completely what
I intended to say to Nicholas. "There's an English Bible in the parish
church now, you know," I blurted. "There must be one here in Meare
as well. You can read it any time. That's the law."

"Humph," Wilfrith grunted.

Nicholas looked at me steadily from under his thatch of yellow
curls. "Readin' in church's not the same as readin' at hearth, free to
talk of the meanin' without someone hoverin' at your shoulder, tellin'
ye what to believe."

Nicholas would never let someone else do his thinking. I could see
that. "But what about the others? They're not in their own homes."

Nicholas was silent. Alice was not. "Jest because a neighbor drops
in after supper, dinne mean we forget our custom of readin' from the
Word of God. We dinne stop when ye were here, did we?"

I didn't remind her how frightened they had been or that the
English Bible had not appeared on the second night. "A neighbor?" I
tried to laugh lightly. "Half the village was here!" I looked from one
to another, but no one seemed to appreciate my humor.

"Humph," Wilfrith grunted again. "And the other half be at the
inn, drinkin' their lives away."

Nicholas laid a hand gently on his father-in-law's arm. "Colin, our
neighbors also want to hear God's Word—without the priest explain-
in' away its meanin'. They're simple folk who don't yet know how
to read for themselves, though Wil'am and John are learnin'. John's
quick, near as quick as Alice."

I set my half-empty cup on the boards by the worn Bible and leaned
forward. "It's dangerous, Nicholas. Unlearned people can get all sorts
of strange ideas about what the Bible means."

"Is that what they taught ye at the abbey?" he asked quietly. "To let
other men do your thinkin', acceptin' what they say without lookin'
to know if it be true or not?"

My fear for them made me angry. "But man, you don't have a
license to preach!" Matilda winced at my outburst. Alice's blue eyes
were hard as steel daggers. I took several deep breaths and struggled
to push the anger down.

"You've never studied," I explained more calmly. "Do you think your priest doesn't suspect? The steward knows."

"Oh, Nicholas!" Matilda clasped her arms to her belly.

I closed my eyes and tried to think, but Alice's blue eyes seemed to bore through my closed lids.

"The abbot's a good man, but he's got to answer to others too. What if he found out? You could be thrown off the land or worse. You're preaching as well as reading, or I miss my guess."

"We aren't heretics, Colin, only ordinary folk seekin' to know God's Word and live by it. We read a bit and pray at the end of the day, just as you in the monastery do in your service of Compline—nothin' more."

I looked from Alice's proud face to Matilda's swollen belly. "Nicholas, for their sakes . . ."

"If Nicholas dinne read it, I would," Alice snapped.

"Alice!" The name came as a hiss from her father.

I blinked back the moisture that collected in my eyes. I cared for these people! How could they risk everything? My mind flashed back to the day the abbot had set me to writing the letters to the manors calling men at arms to fight the Pilgrimage of Grace in the north. What was it he had said?

"Sometimes the choice of right or wrong is made by those in authority over us. Our place is to obey." Even as I said it, I wondered if the abbot still believed it. There was no uncertainty about what Alice believed.

"Ha! Them what sets the laws? They fits them to their fancy."

Nicholas shook his head at me. "No one tells us what to believe. We search the Word of God." He laid a hand on the open book before him.

With a long sigh, I turned toward the door, shaking my head. "I've heard more than one speak of you as heretics." I looked at Nicholas. "It's a terrible risk you take. Don't blame me when they come pounding on your door."

I shut it firmly behind me.

CHAPTER 20

I RETURNED TO THE ABBEY after dinner the next day. The service of
None had just finished when I delivered Master Toogood's letters to
the abbot. There were two, both heavily sealed with wax as though he
trusted me no more than his other messengers.

"Thank you, Colin. You found all satisfactory?" He broke the seal
on the first letter and began to scan its contents.

"The cows and sheep are producing well," I reported. "The fish
house has a new roof. Master Toogood would like to do some repairs
on the weir. I believe he has explained that in the letters."

"Yes, yes. It's here." The abbot laid down the letter and looked at
me. "Thank you, Colin. I believe Brother Basil has some work for
you." He picked up the second sealed letter. I bowed deeply and left
the room.

"Colin." The abbot was already perusing the second letter. "Have
the page send Prior Robert and Father Bede to me, please."

The young page scampered out the door when I gave him the instructions, and I settled at the worktable in the reception room with
Brother Basil's documents.

Father Bede scowled at me when he and Prior Robert arrived in
the office. I sighed. After what he saw as my latest misdeed, he would
never consider me good enough for his beloved Glastonbury.

They were a long time alone with the abbot. Father Bede's voice rose in anger, but I could not catch his words through the thick, stone walls and heavy, oak door. Surely if James Toogood had some complaint against me, Father Abbot would have called me in. I held my pen too long, worrying instead of writing, and a large drop of ink fell on the page.

"Oh, no! I've spoiled it."

"If you blot it and scrape it, it will be fine." Brother Basil did not seem overly concerned.

I used a bit of blotting paper and scraped the page carefully with the knife at my belt. I rubbed my neck to massage the muscles that had increasingly tightened as the officers of the abbey remained sequestered.

"Colin, are you feeling quite all right?" Brother Basil looked at me oddly.

I swallowed the acid taste in my mouth. "Perhaps I'm not accustomed to the rich food at Meare."

"You should be bled more regularly," the monk advised. "I myself am bled monthly. The flesh we're given in the infirmary is as strengthening as the release of evil vapors in the bleeding. You may go and see Brother Urban if you wish."

"No. I don't need bleeding." But as Vespers drew near and the three did not emerge from the abbot's office, my disquiet grew. They were probably discussing appropriate discipline for me. Father Bede would be arguing for another fast if not another night in the punishment cell. I finished the document and took it to Brother Basil.

"Thank you, Colin. This needs two copies." He handed me another paper, and I returned to my seat. "Colin," he said before I had sat down. He studied the document I had just handed him. "You have missed two lines."

"I have?"

"Yes. This entire section." Brother Basil sighed and shook his head. "It must be done again. Go and ask Brother Urban for a brew of herbs to settle your stomach. You look terrible."

He pulled out a fresh sheet of paper and began to copy the document himself as the door to the inner office opened. Father Bede and Prior Robert backed out, bowing to the abbot as they took their leave.

Father Bede's face was scarlet. Prior Robert shook his head sorrowfully and followed him from the office. But neither one looked at me.

"Brother Basil," Abbot Whiting called.

"Coming, Father." Brother Basil glided into the abbot's office carrying paper and pen. "Go on, Colin. You're no use here."

I was puzzled as I made my way to the infirmary. If I were the one they had been discussing, I was certain Father Bede would have given me one of his piercing looks. He would want to be sure I knew the rod was about to fall on my back. But if not me, who? What had those letters from the steward contained? Hoof rot and mites could not have made Father Bede so angry. Perhaps poaching from Meare Pool or—

My mouth went suddenly dry. Heretics! This family had already angered Father Bede, so more about them might be enough to make him forget even my inadequacies.

I hurried toward the infirmary. I definitely needed something to settle my stomach now. How could I have been so concerned about myself? I never thought—but I had warned Nicholas. "What if the abbot finds out?" I'd told him. The abbot might very well know. Frankly, I was less concerned about what the abbot knew and could do than about Father Bede. And I had carried the letter.

I must find a way to warn them.

❧

"So shall all heretics perish from the earth!" Father Bede's sermon rang out past the quire screen to the handful of pilgrims in the nave. They trembled with delicious fear at the fate of the wicked, secure in the assurance that their pilgrimage kept them out of harm's way, whatever sins littered their past or would enslave their futures.

I too trembled—for Nicholas and the Thatcher family. I could tell the abbot that I had forgotten something at Meare. That would give an excuse to return. What? I could think of nothing convincing. Brother Basil kept me busy copying urgent documents, and I was sure he would not have let me go, no matter what I had left behind.

A message had been carried to James Toogood, but I didn't know what it said. I might have sent word to Nicholas by the same messenger if I had known before he left, but I didn't. Besides, I could not be certain that the man would even give my note directly to the Thatchers. If the steward were to see it. . . . No, there was no one I could trust with this.

Neither Nicholas nor anyone else had been brought to the abbey jail. I knew the abbot would not allow any of his people to be dragged before his rival, the bishop at Wells. Surely no serious action had been taken.

And yet Father Bede's ranting homily did not bode well.

On the third day, I unexpectedly found a way to warn them. The urgent documents were finished, and I was sent to Westhay to inspect the records. It was a small farm, and I didn't think the work would take more than a day. The place lay beyond Meare. If I rode hard, I would have plenty of time to give my warning in person, if time indeed remained for the Thatchers.

The waters of the pool were ruffled by a strong wind, which had dispelled the morning mist. Wild fowl, startled by my horse's pounding hooves, rose and settled again in the rushes near the south bank.

I passed several people as I rode up the slope away from the water. The inn by the parish church seemed to be doing a brisk business. It was market day, and the grass of the village green was littered with peddlers and customers. I urged my horse through the crowd, eager to reach the last house in the village and give my warning.

"Knives! Sharpen your knives here!" The whir of a spinning whetstone came from the booth beside me.

"Fine laces and ribbons! Buy a fancy piece for yer lady, sir?" An eager boy, all large teeth and tangled hair, lifted his overflowing tray to thrust his wares against my thigh.

"No! Give way!" My horse snorted a complaint when I twisted the reins impatiently to pass the young hawker.

"Ye can have these." A fruit merchant extended hands laden with apples toward some boys. "Too many worms." Clutching several apples each, the boys darted beneath my horse's head and through the crowd to the far end of the green. Much as I wanted to get on to the Thatchers' cottage, the flow of people forced me with them. The crowd was thicker here, and my stomach lurched at what I saw over their heads.

Stocks had been constructed. They had not been there a few days before. The wood was pale and new. In them a man was held by his head, hands and feet. His yellow hair was matted with rotten vegetables already thrown, and his face was streaked with blood from a cut beneath his eye. My stomach wretched at the disgusting mess, and my horse danced in place as I hesitated.

"Take this, heretic!" shouted one of the boys, who loosed a wormy apple with the force of David's sling. The man looked up, and for a moment I saw the face before the apple hit his nose and started a fresh flow of blood. It was Nicholas.

The crowd laughed. "'Tis what ye deserve!" someone yelled with an inebriated slur. "Makin' yourself out better than us. Think ye're good as a priest, eh?" The boy threw another apple. It brushed Nicholas's cheek and splattered on the wooden frame by his head.

My heart thumped against my ribs, and the pulse in my neck threatened to close off the air passage. This had come of the letter I'd carried.

I looked around but saw no one I recognized from the evening at the Thatchers. Where were his friends? Why didn't they stand by him? Yet, what could they do?

Slowly I turned away and urged my horse to a trot as soon as I was free of the crowd. I could hardly see as I passed the rest of the village, from tears and the irritating smoke blowing from the last house. The cottage was intact. After all, it belonged to the abbey and was only let to the Thatchers. My throat was constricted and my knees wobbled as I dismounted. A heap of burned wood lay in the yard. An arc of cartwheel pierced with broken spokes poked from the ashes. A scorched piece of ticking from a straw mattress fluttered in the breeze that scattered ash into the road and scalded my throat. I coughed. The door stood ajar.

"Hello? Is anyone here?" I approached the darkness of the doorway, waving my hand in a vain attempt to dispel the stench of burning.

The cottage was nearly empty. After the bright light of day, it was difficult to see. The rushes of the floor were scraped aside by the dragging of heavy objects. Even the boards and trestles of the table were gone, no doubt to fuel the fire outside. The large chest from the corner was pulled into the center of the room. A few items of torn clothing were tossed about. Most had no doubt been claimed as spoil or thrown onto the fire in the yard.

A stirring drew my attention to the corner.

"Alice? Is that you?" Matilda's voice was weak. The straw tick she lay on was ripped open and the smell of smoke clung to it as though it had been thrown on the fire and retrieved before it burned completely. There was no sign of the great bed she and Nicholas had slept in. The corner was dark. Her form was small and thin.

"It's Colin."

"Colin?" Her voice caught as if she wondered what new evil was come upon them.

"Matilda, I . . ." I stepped forward and stopped. There were no words to say the grief I felt.

A shadow blocked the light from the doorway, and I turned.

"I'm back, Tildy. See! I told ye I'd not be long." Alice stood with a pail in each hand. She had come from the bright light, and no doubt I was hidden in shadow.

"Who be there?"

I stepped into the light.

"Colin! Come to see how your work fared?" She dropped the pails and threw herself on my chest, beating with clinched fists. Water spilled across the dirt floor and splashed my boots.

"Alice, no!"

I gripped her wrists to protect my face, but she wouldn't stop struggling and sobbing.

"See what ye've done?"

All my efforts to stop her could not do what a low moan from the tick on the floor did. She broke off her cries, tore from my grasp, and rushed to Matilda's side.

"I'm sorry, Tildy. I spilled the water. I shouldn't have gone and left ye. He didn't hurt ye, did he? I won't let him!" She shot me a fierce look.

My arms hung helpless at my sides. "I'll get more water."

"I'll not take your water!" Her icy blue eyes cut like twin blades, but Matilda murmured something she had to lean close to hear. She bowed her head, and I wondered if she were crying.

When she spoke, it was so low I had to strain to hear. "Where the pool empties into the Brue. There be a clean flow of water there." Her voice was low, and she didn't look up.

I retrieved the pails from the muddy floor. When I returned, Alice moistened a scrap of cloth in one of the pails without looking at me and used it to wipe the soot from Matilda's face. I looked around for some sign of an infant, but there was none.

I idly picked up one of the torn garments and laid it in the trunk. I fished a baby's dress from among the rushes that carpeted the floor. It had been sewn with tiny stitches my mother would have been proud of. I rubbed the dirty boot marks on it, but they didn't come off.

"Shall I push the chest back into the corner?" I asked.

Alice shook her head. "'Tis all the table we got now. Jest shut the lid."

I closed the lid and shoved the chest so it stood square in the room as the trestle table once had. The dinner hour had come and gone. Hunger pangs rumbled in my stomach, but the girl made no move to prepare anything. I could see no sign of anything to prepare.

"Where's Wilfrith?" I asked fearfully.

"He took Wil to a cousin in Godney. Dinne want him seein' what they be doin' to his father."

"I'm sorry."

She turned on me, but much of the fire had gone, and she didn't speak right away. "They come durin' prayers," she whispered. "Two nights after ye was here. They come with sticks and clubs and torches. They broke Wil'am's arm—him what has the wanderin' eye. They beat Nicholas senseless and dragged him away. Tildy tried to protect him so they started in on her."

Alice was crying now. I could hear the sniffles between her words. "They beat her 'til she started to scream that the babe was comin'. The midwife dasn't come. Only me and Elwina to help." I strained to hear her words.

"The child was no bigger than the doll Tildy made me of rags

when I was a babe meself. He was beautiful as Wil, but . . . too small."
She gave me a desperate look as though even now I might do something to save the child. "He gasped for air. He might of lived but for
the smoke of the fire they made to burn our things."

She shook her head in despair. "They burned it all—to be sure
'twas hot enough to destroy the book. All the while the priest was
shoutin' that this was what come of denying God and Holy Church."
She spat the words, as if cleansing her mind of any remaining affec-
tion for priest or altar.

"How will you live?" I asked.

"Why should ye care—you or James Toogood?" Fire reignited in
her eyes.

"I didn't betray you, Alice. I fear I carried back the letter Toogood
wrote about you, but I swear I didn't know what was in it."

"Ye might have guessed. Ye told they'd come knockin'! Who but
yourself told Toogood?"

"He already knew. Toogood told me at dinner about heretics in the
village. I was afraid he meant you."

"So ye should of known what was in the letter."

There was nothing I could say.

"What will you eat?"

"Elwina'll bring us sommat—when her family has eaten, and her
husband is gone out. He wants no part of us now."

"And Nicholas?"

"They'll let him go. Tha's what Martin Baker said, like as not tonight after the market is done. They won't throw us off the land. Too
good of workers, me father and Nicholas. The abbot don't want to
lose them. He jest has in mind to teach us a lesson." She looked back
at Matilda, who had fallen asleep.

Running footsteps sounded in the yard. Wilfrith's form blocked
the light. "Alice? Matilda? Is everthin' a'right? Who's horse be in the
yard?"

"'Tis Colin, Father."

"Colin?" His voice turned dark with rage. "Git ye out of this house,
and may I never see the face of ye again in this world! 'Tis sure I'll not
be seein' ye in the next, where ye be goin'!

I stood as one turned to stone. How could I defend myself? Alice was right. My thoughtlessness about the letter had betrayed them.

Wilfrith came at me. He was not a large man, but his anger gave him strength. "Git out of this house, ye servant of the Devil, afore I break the commandment and tear ye to pieces fine as dust!"

I glanced again at Alice and Matilda in the corner. They would not still their father's anger. They shared it.

"Alice," I begged, "tell Nicholas I took no part in this—not of my own will." Struggling to control my emotions, I stepped around the angry man and through the door into the sunshine.

He followed me, as though to dump into the street the very memory of my presence. I swung my leg across the horse and looked one last moment at his angling frame in the doorway.

"I'm sorry," I said again. The muscles of my neck seemed to reach around my skull to crush it.

"Git!"

CHAPTER 21

THE DOORMAN'S VOICE CHASED determined footsteps down the corridor. "I'm sure the abbot will see you in a moment if you let me inform him." The page sat higher in his chair and fixed his eyes on the doorway, as did I.

"I will inform him myself." A tall broad courtier swept into the room. It took only a moment for me to recognize Richard Layton, the messenger of Chancellor Cromwell. Three companions followed him.

Layton marched into the inner office. "Good afternoon, Abbot. We require lodging and hospitality. You will assign your workmen to build cases for us. Our orders are to relieve the abbey of its superfluous plate. My men are surveying the altars and the treasury. We wouldn't want anything to be—misplaced in the confusion." The final words came out with a sneer.

My breath came in short gasps as though the muscles of my frozen chest refused to expand. I caught one of the courtiers watching me from the corner of his eye, and tried to compose myself. His smug expression looked vaguely familiar, but the shock had locked my mind.

"I'm sure you are most willing to give us your assistance," Layton went on before the abbot had recovered enough to speak. "There's no point in excess silver and gold going to waste at a time when your king has need of it. Now if you will excuse me, we have had a long journey and would like to rest." He exited the inner office with clipped strides, his heavy boots sounding on the polished boards.

Brother Basil followed on silent slippers. "Colin, please show these gentlemen to the guest hall."

I knew I should reply, but no words came out. I ordered my body to its feet, but my brain seemed to float somewhere outside it. I led them across the abbot's garden to the hall where he lodged his guests.

"I didn't expect to see you still here," said the courtier, who had stepped beside me.

"Thomas?" Once my fellow novice, his hair had grown longer, and his satins and velvets were a world away from the modesty of novice white.

"I told you that the power is at court, not the church." He laughed. "The church was my father's piety, not mine. I've convinced him to see reality."

"But we need spoons," Brother Gildas was saying as we entered the guest hall. He spread his arms protectively over a pile of silver on the table. "We entertain guests of high estate. They expect silver spoons." His voice was high and tight. One of the courtiers sniggered. Thomas wore an amused smile, and I wanted to use a stool to dislodge it from his face.

Instead I addressed the monk in charge of the hall. "Brother Gildas, I have brought guests requiring hospitality."

"Leave the spoons." Layton strode forward. "It's excess church plate we are after, not the household silver. Be about your job." He shooed his unruly men out the door. As they left, he brought a spoon close to his face, scratched it with a fingernail and examined its quality before returning it to the sideboard.

I left as soon as I might and fled toward the cloister. The abbey swarmed with soldiers. They blocked gates and searched any who tried to leave. Monks cowered in the library like helpless sheep waiting a turn to be sheared.

A soldier swung the handle of his dagger against the lock of a book cupboard and broke it open. Father Bede looked up from his desk as though noticing the intrusion for the first time. His hand closed on the key that hung around his neck.

The soldier dragged out one of our most beautiful gospels and began ripping off its silver clasps. "What purpose does this serve? Ye can close it with iron as well as silver." He tossed the silver into a bag and let the book fall. Hand lettered and illuminated pages tore and folded as they caught the table's edge and crumpled on the floor. He reached for another.

Father Bede rose to his feet, his face as white as death. "Wretched, pestilent fellows!" he cried, stepping forward. One of the monks gripped his arm. Father Bede shook him off. "Sons of the Serpent! Instruments of Beelzebub!" Father Aidan and I helped restrain him. The book he had been studying lay forgotten on the table. "Children of Antichrist!" he screamed. Even we three had to strain to hold him back.

The soldier laughed, a loud and bitter sound the cloister walls had never heard. "What know ye, old man? I serve King Henry. If he be the Devil, he be a handsome one—with me wages in his hand."

Father Bede lunged toward him, but we held him fast.

"Lock him up!" the sergeant ordered, and two soldiers stepped forward. I looked at Father Aidan. We must have all relaxed our hold in our uncertainty of what to do, for Father Bede succeeded in breaking from our grasp only to be seized by the soldiers.

"Take him to the holding cell," the sergeant demanded. "Every abbey has one, though I be sure you lecherous hypocrites never use it."

"I'll show you where it is." Thomas stood in the doorway. Bitterness showed in his eyes, and I suspected he had seen the inside of that cell more than once at Father Bede's insistence. I shivered at my own memories and took a step toward them.

"Do you want to go with him?" Thomas asked in a voice so low it commanded silence. I locked my eyes on Thomas's. My heart quickened in my chest. I wondered at how near I was to saying yes. But what would that serve? I shook my head slightly and melted back into the crowd of monks, but I never took my eyes from the back of Thomas as he led the soldiers holding Father Bede through the south door.

"You will know the power of Glastonbury and of the Holy Grail!" Father Bede screamed. "You will fall like the dragon and the whore of Babylon and burn forever in the lake of fire!" His voice echoed through the abbey corridors until it was lost in layers of stone and earth.

I looked after them. I could almost smell the must and feel the dark damp of that cell. I remembered my tears and nightmares. Father Bede . . . my father . . .

We stood silent as pillars of salt. Brother Arthur's normally ruddy face showed pale by the light from the cloister garden. The soldiers began to laugh and mock Father Bede's curses.

"You will know the power!" one cried, pointing a trembling finger at his fellows. They guffawed and slapped each other. When I looked back, Brother Arthur lay slumped against the doorframe of the treasury.

Roger's flaming head bent over him. "He's fainted! We must take him to the infirmary."

"No one leaves the cloister!" the sergeant ordered. All humor was forgotten. "Put him in the refectory."

I helped Roger carry Brother Arthur into our dining hall off the south cloister walk. A trickle of blood flowed from his temple where he must have struck his head when he fell.

"Is it safe?" he murmured when he saw Roger. "Is the cup of Saint Patrick safe?"

"Hush!" Roger whispered fiercely. He looked around to be sure no one could hear. "Hush, Brother. It will be all right."

"And the cup," Brother Arthur went on as we laid him on one of the long benches. "The olivewood cup is with the abbot. It will be safe, won't it?"

"That cup is wood, Brother Arthur. It'll be safe," I reminded him. "It's silver they want."

"But if they knew . . . if they knew what it was . . ."

"If they knew, they wouldn't believe. You rest. There's nothing you can do about what's happening."

I motioned to Roger with my head. Out of earshot of Brother Arthur, I gripped his wrist. "The cup of Saint Patrick—you've hidden it, haven't you?"

Roger's innocent face was incapable of lying. He shuffled his large feet and couldn't meet my eye. "They won't find it," he said at last. He squared his shoulders with a confidence I didn't feel.

I glanced from him to Brother Arthur on the bench. The older man seemed to be aging before my eyes. "Let's pray they don't." I crossed myself.

The others were herded into the refectory to keep them out of the way of the soldiers. I was not allowed to return to the abbot, who, I was told, would be staying in his quarters with Brother Basil. At the hour of Sext, Prior Robert organized us to say the Office. Roger led the right side of our improvised quire in place of the imprisoned Father Bede. Somehow in the crisis, young as he was, he inspired us with his peace and confidence in our Savior. The familiar psalms steadied our minds and most of us stayed on our knees in prayer throughout the hour of dinner and our usual rest time.

At None we recited the same service we would have prayed in the Church of Saint Mary. If I prayed loudly enough, I could drown the voices of the soldiers and the sounds of the first crates arriving from the workshops and the treasures being packed. We stayed on our knees fasting until after the service of Compline.

The sounds from the cloister had ceased, and when the prayers were done, our guards herded us like sheep to the dorter—each to his own cell to sleep. No one rang the bell for Matins, but we all woke, our bodies accustomed to rise at that hour. We found the doors locked, so each man knelt at the entrance to his cell and prayed the prayers.

We were confined to the dorter for two days, allowed only to make trips to the reredorter morning and evening to relieve ourselves. We were brought bread and water twice daily. Guards told us the cooks and lay workers had all been sent home except a handful to prepare food for our "guests." By the sounds from the refectory in the evening, it was evident that they were making free use of our wine cellar.

On the morning of the third day we were released. The soldiers were gone. Several monks, including Brother Arthur, were moved immediately to the infirmary. Brother Urban had won his fight to keep the infirmary cooks, but the shock of the siege was too much for the elderly inmates. Two had died.

After settling Brother Arthur in a soft bed, Roger went straight toward the Edgar Chapel. I went with him. The church seemed bare. King Henry's servants had left us one cross and one pair of candlesticks for each altar. They were the least jeweled and contained the smallest weights of gold or silver of those we had possessed only days before. A few altar cloths remained, but none with any significant amount of gold thread.

"Look!" I gripped Roger's arm and held him back. There was nothing over the high altar save a broken cord that had once held the Great Sapphire of Glastonbury.

"It's gone!" Roger broke from my grasp and ran down the south aisle of the quire to the Edgar Chapel. He burst through the entrance and turned to the left. When I arrived panting after him, he was staring at the paneling.

He turned to me, his face pale as newly fallen snow. "It's all right. It's all right," he said again slowly.

I stared at the paneled wall. He was right. They wouldn't find it. No one would look behind the paneling of the chapel. Some abbey churches had been torn down, but they wouldn't destroy Glastonbury. It was too old, too sacred, too rooted in the history of England. The chalice was safe. Roger was safe. Brother Arthur was safe. I turned and followed Roger back to the cloister.

Father Aidan was picking through the litter of books on the floor of the north aisle. "The Gospel According to Saint John." He held a bundle of loose pages in his hands. His voice had the dazed sound of one who could not grasp what he was seeing. "The cover is gone. . . ." I remembered it was all of silver, richly decorated with precious jewels. "They even took the title page." He looked at us as though he could not fathom why, although I had no doubt it was for the gold leaf of the elaborately embellished capital letters.

I tried the treasury door. It was not locked. It swung open to reveal a near-empty room. Chests and cupboard doors stood open. A piece of silk lay trampled on the floor, but every item with gold thread that might be picked out had been removed. The cupboards were empty, but for a few of the simplest chalices and patens for the saying of Mass. At least they had left us those.

Roger knelt behind me and crossed himself. *"Domine misere mei.* Lord, have mercy."

I bent to examine one of the bits that littered the floor. I drew back my hand in horror—bones and teeth and locks of ancient hair—the contents of reliquaries that had been carried off for their silver, gold and jewels.

"What sacrilege!" I gasped.

"Father Bede was not far wrong," Roger whispered.

"Father Bede!" I gasped and stared at Roger. "He's locked in the punishment cell!" I turned and ran from the room with Roger close behind me. I bolted out the west door of the cloister and around the corner to the little door that gave access to the cellars.

"Father Bede, are you all right?" I called as I fumbled in the darkness for the key on the wall. The stench of human waste came from the cell. What if the key wasn't there? What if they had taken it with them?

"Here it is." Roger plucked it from the wall and thrust it into my hand.

"Father Bede?" I twisted the key in the lock as Father Aidan entered the corridor with a lamp.

"Is he all right?" the novice master asked.

The door swung open. "Father Bede, they're gone. You can come out now."

Father Aidan stepped forward with the lamp, wincing at the smell. The light showed the librarian, sitting hunched on the bench that was built into one wall. He looked up slowly. His eyes were deeply sunk in his sickly face.

"I looked, and there before me was a pale horse!" he muttered in Latin. "Its rider was named Death, and Hades was following close behind him." His voice grew louder as he looked at us and rose to his feet. He was nearly shouting as he stepped toward us. "They were given power over a fourth of the earth to kill by sword, famine and plague, and by the wild beasts of the earth!"

I fell back as did Roger. Father Bede stood in the corridor reciting the Revelation of Saint John like a prophet. His hair was disheveled. Both his tonsure and his beard showed three days of growth. He hadn't washed in that time, and I doubted he had been fed. But it was his eyes that held me—eyes that blazed like coals from the pit.

"Father Bede." Father Aidan laid a hand on the librarian's arm. "We have all had a difficult time. Let us go to the infirmary and rest."

CHAPTER 22

THE STEWARDS SHOWED A surly attitude that summer of 1539, for they knew that the days of Glastonbury Abbey's oversight were numbered. They would not long answer to Abbot Whiting. Their management was heavy-handed, their accounts sloppy. Complaints against the abbey from tenants became frequent. If I did not hurry my horse along the road to Glastonbury on that warm day, it was because I dreaded to make my report and add to the worries weighing the abbot's shoulders.

The Tor rose on my right, crowned with the tower of Saint Michael's. Roger had talked of climbing again. I was certain Brother Arthur would join us, and perhaps the abbot. He had said he would climb this year, although the business with Chancellor Cromwell was far from resolved. Would such a climb help Father Bede who suffered from fits of madness since the departure of Cromwell's men?

Suddenly I had a longing to drink again from the Chalice Well, as we had that day last November. I left my horse at the tithe barn and turned up the thickly wooded valley between the base of the Tor and Chalice Hill. I followed the stream until it separated into two strands, flowing almost side by side, one that coated the rocks red as blood and the other that crusted every fallen leaf or twig with white. They had flowed so for hundreds of years, and the minerals deposited by the white stream had built up into tiny grottos and pools.

I paused where the red stream flowed down from the left, and looked up the valley where I had seen the stag-man. I had tried to convince myself that I had seen only a vision, like my other dreams that day. Roger had seen it as well, though; of that I was convinced. Despite the warmth of the afternoon, I shivered.

I made my way up the lower slopes of Chalice Hill through the garden to the spring. I lifted the oak well cover, which was etched with an ancient pattern of interlinking circles, and took down the cup from its niche in the shelter.

The water was as cold and pure as I remembered. It ran down my throat and spread its strength to my limbs. I studied the cup in my hand. It was made of ash and carved with scenes of the last supper, the crucifixion, and Saint Joseph. I turned it slowly, letting the pictures tell me their stories.

The olivewood cup in the monastery was much simpler. It now sat on the small altar in Abbot Whiting's room, and he used it, as had Father Dunstan, in his private Mass. I saw it from time to time in his office, but never saw its glory as that night in Father Dunstan's cell.

I sipped again from the cup in my hand, and said a silent prayer for the abbot, the abbey and myself. Then I said another for Brother Fergus, the Thatcher family and others like them over England who hungered for God and were willing to suffer and die for what they believed.

When I got to my feet and replaced the cup in its niche, I saw a stag watching me from a thicket deeper in the valley. The sun was still high and the afternoon bright. I had no doubt that it was a stag. But it turned its huge brace of antlers and gazed at me with the same kingly dignity I had seen in the stag-man that day. We stood some moments, staring at one another, until at last the great beast turned and walked slowly into the trees toward the White Spring.

I didn't realize I had been holding my breath until I let it out.

The wood was not so thick with undergrowth at this time of year, and for a moment I was drawn to wander deeper, to follow the path of the stag. But instead I retraced my steps along the red brook where it flowed down through the garden, back into the little valley to meet the White.

When I reached the valley I paused and looked back up the hill. There was no sign of the stag, and yet I felt the presence of evil. It was a bitter taste in my mouth that threatened to overpower the taste of iron from the water of Chalice Well.

Or did I taste my fear? I thought to return to my horse at the tithe barn.

But no. I would prove to myself that I was not afraid, that I was a man. I turned up the valley. The White Spring appeared not to have one source as did the Red Spring but to seep from many places on the steep sides of the Tor, leaving its lacy formations among the leafy green of the hillside. The path was damp, the ground soft beneath my feet. A short way above Chalice Well the way curved sharply around a projection of the hill. I caught my breath.

The scene might have come from one of Brigit's tales in my childhood. The hill rose as sharply as walls on three sides. All was white flowstone, dotted with exquisite ferns and delicate flowers of the sort that delight in shade and wither in the sun. The elegant tracery of our Lady Chapel paled beside the glory of what God had here designed.

I took a step forward before I realized I had found the stag. He stood majestically, a full seventeen hands high, his crown of antlers broader than the height of a man.

I was not alone in his presence. Father Bede stood before him, his head bowed, his arms stretched beseechingly. It was the stance of a priest in adoration before the high altar.

As I watched, the king stag turned his head and gazed at me, and when he did, he was transformed before my eyes. It was no mere animal who stood in the valley but a man with the head of a stag, sitting atop a black horse.

I gasped. Father Bede turned. He startled and for a moment a look I almost took for fear crossed his face. Then it turned to anger.

"You! What are you doing here? The abbot sent you on business. He did not give you leave to go traipsing around the countryside for your own pleasure. If your business is done, you should be back at the abbey, praying for the salvation of your soul."

Anger and hate like I had never seen shot from his eyes. I took a small step backward before I resolved to stand my ground. The stag appeared once more to be only a stag. Yet he did not flee despite the priest's shouting, but looked away, as if the madness of men was none of his concern. Father Bede advanced toward me with menace. "You know nothing of prayer and repentance. You live off the abbey, then go off into the world, abusing the generosity of the abbot and bringing disrepute and the king's wrath with your mischief. You are a scoundrel bad as any heretic!"

If Father Bede looked for me to wither in fear and obeisance, I was no longer the young pilgrim seeking refuge. These were not the Abbey walls. At the word *heretic* I could think only of Nicholas in the stocks. Whatever this man had suffered at the hands of the soldiers, he caused suffering aplenty with his smug piety. My resentment erupted.

"You know nothing of God or of the people you hurt. There you sit, cloistered in the abbey, seeking your own salvation and private knowledge while you rain judgment on any who seek to know the God you claim to—"

Father Bede drew his cassock around him and raised his head with dignity. "You forget yourself, Colin. Give a thought to whom you speak."

"I . . ." The strong ties of Benedictine rule tugged at me. I had indeed forgotten myself. I had nearly told him that the "heretics" of Meare were my friends. But all he seemed to notice was my failure to show respect. "I'm sorry, Father," I murmured. I was not sorry, and such a lie would have to be confessed before I next took Mass. I would no doubt pass another night in that horrible cell beneath the refectory.

"You will say seven *Aves* and ten *Paters* in the Saint Joseph Chapel after Compline, and perhaps God will see fit to forgive your impertinence. Mind you, I will be there myself to hear your prayers. Now go."

I was relieved that he evidently did not intend to denounce me to the abbot. When I reached the abbey, the abbot was preparing to depart for Sharpham. He took me with him, and in the confusion of our hurried departure, I didn't tell him what I had seen at the White Spring.

CHAPTER 23

Benedictus sit Deus Pater.

ABBOT WHITING'S SHOULDERS hung limp, and his voice carried an intense tiredness in its dull tenor, as though he hardly heard the words of the Mass he had recited every day of the fifty years since his consecration as a priest. Even the quiet country air of Sharpham Manor was not enough to lift his spirit.

> Blessed be God, the Father, and the Only begotten Son of God, and also the Holy Spirit: because He hath shown His mercy towards us.

The servants of the household knelt reverently behind us. I rang the little bell at the appointed times and offered the vessels of holy water and wine. The abbot mixed them in the olivewood drinking bowl that served him always as a chalice these days.

The abbot bowed low over the host and repeated the words Christ used the night in which He was betrayed.

> *Hoc est enim corpus meum*—for this is My Body.

Betrayed. It was Christ's friend who betrayed Him to the authorities to be beaten, mocked and hung on a cross. Judas Iscariot, who had been His companion for three years, sent Him to death with a kiss.

Three gibbets on a hill. Three crosses had stood on Calvary. That was the common form of execution in those days, however inhumane. Now it was the hangman's rope.

Abbot Whiting knelt and adored the host. I came to myself and remembered to ring the little bell. He rose and held the bread high over his head for the cluster of faithful to venerate. I rang the bell three times. Its tinkling was the only sound in the chapel.

The image remained before me. Three gibbets on a hill. My skin was cold, but I felt the sweat forming on my forehead. My breath came in short, shallow gasps. The tower of Saint Michael's church rose behind three gibbets. I felt faint.

Abbot Whiting knelt once more and adored the Body of Christ. My numb fingers rang the bell one more time.

Simili modo postquam coenátum est.

Abbot Whiting slipped the cloth off the olivewood cup.

> In like manner, after He had supped, taking also into His holy and venerable hands this goodly chalice, again giving thanks to Thee, He blessed it.

The ancient wood of the cup had been well cared for since Brother Arthur had pulled it from the treasury and sent it by my hand to Father Dunstan. It had a golden sheen.

The abbot made the sign of the cross. His words flowed on a river of intense longing.

> . . . And gave it to His disciples, saying, "Take, all of ye, and drink of this: for this is the chalice of my blood, of the new and eternal covenant: the mystery of faith: which shall be shed for you and for many unto the remission of sins."

I stared at the altar, not daring to breathe.
The cup glowed.

As oft as ye shall do these things, ye shall do them in remembrance of Me.

I rang the little bell as the abbot genuflected and adored the Precious Blood of Christ. Tears ran down his cheeks, and I knew that he too saw the gleaming light. Rising, he thrust the cup high over his head. With such a gesture King Arthur must have raised Excalibur to triumph over the pagan hordes invading the Britain of his day. With such a gesture William claimed the field at Hastings.

A light exploded from the cup, brighter than sunshine on the heights of Mount Snowdon, hotter than liquid silver in the furnace. It spilled over the crucifix, the altar, and Abbot Whiting, filling the room with such glory that I forgot to ring the little bell. It rang on its own as I fell to my knees, trembling in adoration before the miracle of God's presence. And yet there was no sign from the gathered household that they saw the glory.

Slowly, very slowly, the abbot lowered the cup and set it back in its place on the altar. I drew into my lungs the scent of eastern spices, and in the silence heard the far off chanting of heavenly voices:

Holy! Holy! Holy!

Abbot Whiting picked up the cloth and covered the cup, but a piece of linen could not put out the light. Although it no longer filled the room, it shone through the veil with a power that would not be quenched. He knelt and adored, and I barely remembered to ring the bell one more time.

The tears did not cease to flow as he recited the prayers after consecration. His face knew a joy I had never seen in him as he reached the final doxology, making the sign of the cross with the bread over the chalice.

Per omnia saecula saeculorum—world without end.

"Amen." Never had I meant the word so completely. "So be it."

Somehow we got through the final prayers of the Mass. I remembered to ring the bells and make the correct responses. He caught my eye when I poured water and wine over his fingers to purify them. Although the light of the cup was fading, a light had been lit inside Father Abbot.

Et verbum caro factum est.

He read the last gospel from the prologue of Saint John.

And the Word was made flesh and dwelt among us, and we saw His glory, the glory as of the Only begotten of the Father, full of grace and truth.

"Deo grátias," I proclaimed the end of the Mass. "Thanks be to God."

There was a shuffling at the door to the chapel. I turned to see the doorkeeper.

"If it please Lord Abbot." He was the only member of the household whose duties had not permitted his presence at the daily Mass. "There be a boy at the door. He says it's important, but I dinne let him interrupt the blessed Mass." The man crossed himself hurriedly.

Father Abbot looked as jolted by the return to ordinary realities as I. "Colin, see what he wants. I'll be in my room if you need me."

I followed the doorkeeper. A boy leaped from the step where he sat. He was streaked with sweat and mud and looked like he had fallen in the bog more than once. It was Wil Thatcher.

"Colin! I come as fast as I could across the moors. Ye've got to warn the abbot! Soldiers be comin'."

I drew in my breath sharply.

Wil went on. "Me father saw them on the London Road headed for the abbey. Lots of them, ridin' fast."

I raced back into the house, lifted my cassock to my knees and took the stairs three at a time. "Father Abbot! Soldiers are coming!"

He stood at the front window of his office, contemplating the olivewood cup. His shoulders were square, his manner serene. Through the open window I could see beyond the elm-lined lane to the sheep drove from the town of Street. Already a troop of men-at-arms galloped toward us. A fog descended on my mind like the mists that creep from the bogs at evening to hide the traveler's path.

Abbot Whiting looked at me and extended the cup. "Take care of this. It should not be lost."

"But, Father!"

"Take it home to Wales with you. Keep it safe. England will have need of it in time to come." He turned back to the window and calmly watched the approach of the soldiers.

I held the cup in my fingertips. The fog on my brain seemed a little lighter.

"I'm glad you never took your final vows, Colin. You will be a good landlord to your tenants. You are learning to temper justice with grace." He was sending me home—to my father. "It is grace England needs, not wars," he continued. "A true pilgrimage of grace."

He twisted the ring of Saint Thomas of Canterbury on his finger, he who would always be a saint in our minds, whatever Henry Tudor said.

The first of the riders, carrying the royal banner, reached the lane and turned in. My heart fluttered like a captive bird, and I slipped the cup into the breast of my cassock.

"We do not deserve forgiveness and yet God forgives." He took my hand and ran his finger along the scar above my wrist. "Father Dunstan taught me a conundrum. I'm not sure I understand it yet. Only those who are forgiven are truly able to forgive. Yet only those who forgive are free to receive forgiveness."

I pulled my hand away.

The clanging clatter of armored riders dismounting rose to the window from the yard. The abbot watched them through the glass until a banging began on the front door. He crossed himself. Then he gave me one more, long look and strode past me, out the doorway and down the stairs to meet the soldiers. For the briefest moment I caught the scent of cinnamon and cloves.

PART 3

THE GATES OF ANNWN

CHAPTER 24

THE ABBOT INVITED THEM TO enjoy the hospitality of Sharpham Manor, but Layton refused, angry at the inconvenience of not having found the abbot waiting at the abbey. He insisted on taking him back to Glastonbury, bound and under guard. Soldiers were left to search Sharpham for evidence to be used in the trial.

My teeth clenched. "For anything that might support your lies!" I muttered.

"Colin, please assist these men as you would me," the abbot instructed before two soldiers hoisted him roughly onto the back of a horse.

"Yes, Colin. Assist them as you would me," Thomas mimicked. It was all I could do not to strike his grinning face.

"Thomas!" Layton said.

"Yes, sir!" The former novice sprang to attention like one of my father's hunting dogs. I felt a secret satisfaction to see him grovel.

Layton tilted his head to inspect the imposing façade of the abbot's retreat to its highest gable. "This house and all the property of Glastonbury Abbey now belong to the crown. Search the abbot's study." He nodded to me. "The servant will help you. Bring me anything suspicious that you find."

"Yes, sir. I will, sir. I know you will be pleased."

"See to it." Layton turned, and the troop of soldiers galloped down

165

the lane. Only a few were left to guard Sharpham. I craned my neck to find Abbot Whiting, serene and dignified in the midst of the departing troop.

Thomas jerked his head for me to follow him into the house. "You heard him. Show me his papers."

"Most are in Glastonbury. This is a place of retreat."

A sly grin spread across his face. "Making it ideal for hiding something he doesn't want seen." He gripped my arm and steered me through the door.

I could feel conscious control creeping through my body, preventing me from grabbing his throat. Attacking his attackers would not help the abbot.

Thomas dropped my arm. "Where are his papers?" I led the way to the first floor study, feeling like Judas Iscariot although I could think of nothing incriminating that could be found there.

Thomas sprawled in the abbot's chair behind the worktable in his office. "So? Bring me the papers. You're supposed to help me, remember?"

I went to the cupboard, willing myself to hold the same control the abbot had shown. I brought a stack of documents and set them on the table. I didn't trust myself to speak.

"What's this?" he demanded.

"The records of the estate."

"What do I want with those?" He roughly pushed them aside.

"You asked for his papers."

"Give me his personal papers, the ones that show his treason against the king."

"You were one of us and well know he has committed no treason against the king."

"Of course, he has. If the king says he's a traitor, he's a traitor. The king does not lie." He thrust an angry finger into my face, but I did not flinch. "Show me the evidence!"

"Look for yourself. There is no evidence."

"There is and I'll find it, and you will wish you had helped me."

All that morning I brought him whatever he asked. He found nothing. The accounts were neat and in order. I had checked them myself. There was little personal correspondence, and what there was made no mention of politics.

Thomas swept the table with his arm, dumping records and documents onto the floor. "Show me the evidence!" he screamed.

I said nothing.

"I need dinner." He stood up from the table. "Do you eat anything besides fish in this house? I want meat and fowl." He strode from the room, and I could hear him calling the cooks to serve him.

I knelt on the floor and gathered together the fallen papers. Although my stomach was empty, I had no desire to eat. Mechanically, I rearranged the documents and stacked them neatly in the cupboard, although I couldn't imagine who would ever look at them again.

After his dinner, Thomas went to the abbot's room. He took a long rest, no doubt enjoying the comfort of Sharpham. It was midafternoon, well past the hour of None, when he came bounding down the staircase, calling for the groom to saddle his horse.

"I found it!" he told me triumphantly when I came out of the study where I was almost finished repairing the damage of his earlier investigation. He shook a book in my face. "He possesses a treatise on the king's divorce—a popish document that proves his disloyalty to the king! We have him now!" He strode through the front door. I listened to the pounding of his horse's hooves on the lane until they faded in the distance. A breeze rustled the leaves of the ivy around the front door. Insects hummed in the meadow. Somewhere in the house a door shut. I turned and went back into the study, sick at heart.

⟶⟵

I slept that night in the new barn. The house no longer belonged to the abbey, and I was not allowed a bed there, although I was permitted to collect my cloak. I wrapped the olivewood cup carefully in a spare tunic and used it to pillow my head. I was reluctant to close my eyes in sleep for fear of dreams and visions of gibbets on the Tor. But when sleep came, my dreams were of gentle breezes on the Brecon Hills and a day when my father took Walter and me hawking. I fell and skinned my knee but didn't cry, and for once my father was proud of me.

When morning came, a gentle rain was falling. I went to the kitchen door, and the cook gave me bread and a cup of cider before I began my walk back to Glastonbury. The horse I had ridden was now locked in the stable, the property of King Henry.

I took the path that twisted and turned over Hulk Moor, seeking the higher ground. I did not run headlong as Wil had the day before and so avoided missing the way and plunging into the bog. The long swamp grasses bent mournfully, and rain dripped steadily from them.

I carried the cup in the pouch at my belt. Many a workman carried his cup so, and it would not attract attention there. Although I wrapped my cloak around me and wondered when I would next see a fire, I wasn't cold. A curious warmth seemed to come from the pouch as from the roasted tubers my mother had me carry in winter as a child.

My body might be warm, but my brain was numb. I put one foot in front of another until I had crossed the River Brue and reached the town, and the clouds that clustered thick around the Tor dropped behind the houses and shops.

A crowd of people milled outside the abbey. Dogs added their barks and howls to the confusion. A table had been placed in the street by the gate. Thomas sat at the table, trying to control a raucus queue.

"Here, here," he snarled. "Be patient. I'll take your statements. Anyone who can testify to the abbot's treason will have the opportunity." He sat behind the table with paper and ink. Everyone talked at once, and I could make out no individual complaints, but I recognized some who had objected to the enclosure of a field the previous spring. They were ignorant men who couldn't read like Nicholas or Alice. They thought only of their own bellies and went like sheep where their leaders told them.

I pushed through the crowd to the gate. Seeing my white novice habit, the guard let me pass, instructing me to get my things and clear out. "Ye can take your bed and the door of your cell. The rest belongs to the king."

I nodded. My throat was too constricted for words. Soldiers and monks crossed the yard, all hurrying on urgent business. A strange dog slunk around the corner of the Lady Chapel. The peace of the abbey had evaporated.

"Colin!" I turned to find Brother Arthur at my elbow. "Brother Urban is looking for folks in the town who will take in those too old to travel. We need your help to carry them there."

Roger was already in the infirmary. His tall, muscular frame bent over an elderly monk, and he spoke in soothing tones. He smiled when I came in.

"Roger, excellent!" Brother Arthur exclaimed. "Brother Urban has found a place for Father Anselm at Dame Goodman's, just past Saint John's Church. You and Colin can carry him on his bed. It won't be far by the north gate."

We used Father Anselm's simple bed as a litter and carried him across the grounds and out the narrow gate into the High Street.

"I'll take me pay now," demanded Dame Goodman when we had put down the bed in the corner of her front room. Her thin body was all bones and elbows. "Nursin' an old man is work, I tell ye."

"He'll have a pension from the king," Roger assured her. "Five pounds a year. But we don't have it yet. Brother Urban promised you the bedstead."

"Humph." She looked unimpressed. "Beds don't bring the price of firewood today. Time he's gone, I'll be wantin' more than that, won't I?" She jerked her head toward Father Anselm, who squeezed his eyes shut as if to block out his surroundings.

Roger sighed. "By the time he's gone, the bed will be worth more than firewood."

"Where's Brother Urban?" the old man in the bed whimpered. "I need my medicine."

"It's here." Roger caught up the bag we had carried with the patient on the litter and began to explain its contents to Dame Goodman.

"I'll get me money or he's out," she reminded us at the door.

Heading back up the street, I turned to Roger. "What have they done with the abbot?"

Roger studied his strong hands as though reluctant to reply. "They took him away this morning," he said at last. "To the Tower."

"The Tower—in London?" The muscles clenched in my chest. The

Tower of London was where Anne Boleyn had awaited her execution. It was where Thomas More had bled out his life for defying the king. Countless traitors, guilty or not, had spent their last days and hours inside those thick walls. I had never seen London, but everyone knew of the heads stuck on pikes on the walls of the Tower as a warning of the penalty for treason.

"The abbot is no traitor!"

"Tell Richard Layton," Roger said. "You see the people lining up to testify against him."

I felt cold and sick despite the warm sunshine.

Roger laid a hand on my arm. "They questioned him through the day yesterday and half the night. Yet, there was a peace about him this morning as they led him away—and a presence. He was not the tired old man who went to Sharpham."

"No. I'm sure of that."

Roger gave me a curious look, but I said no more. My hand groped for the cup in the pouch at my belt. It was safe.

"Will you go to Bristol?" I asked as we walked, knowing he had a younger sister there.

"Father Aidan is staying with the vicar of the Parish Church of Saint John to keep the school," Roger said. "I'll stay and help him." He flashed me his usual delighted grin, and then his look turned serious. "I gave my life to God when the plague came to Bristol and took my family. 'Twas I first took sick, so the curse that brought the death was mine." He bowed his head. "When I knew that I would live, I asked God to leave me one of my own. He spared Molly—my favorite sister."

He raised his head and his face wore its familiar smile. "They say we are released from our vows." He shook his head defiantly. "I made my vows to God, and not to King Henry. I'll not leave Glastonbury."

We walked a short way in silence. He looked at me. "And you? Will you go back to your father?"

I opened my mouth to answer, but no words came out. At the back of my mind I had the thought that at last I might go to Oxford. I didn't want to go home to face my father. If I returned to Wales, would I go back to being a sorry hound, panting for the crumbs the master might toss my way? Yet it was to Wales the abbot had bidden me go. I knew what he was asking of me—to make peace and forgive him who murdered my mother.

"I . . . I have not thought it through."

We moved another elderly monk to lodging. Brother Urban had arranged and paused to hear Mass at Saint John's. No Mass would be said at Saint Mary's in the abbey. Had there been another day in the last thousand years when Mass was not said there? But Layton's men were already pacing the church and calculating the value of its lead roof. They had called workmen from the town to discuss the most efficient way to dismantle it.

We had just returned to the abbey through the north gate when a clawed hand gripped my arm. "Do you have it? Is it safe?" Father Bede's breath was hot and foul in my face. I took a step back, but his fingers dug into my flesh. "You heard me, boy! Do you have the—" He broke off abruptly and glanced wildly around. His voice became a hoarse whisper. "—the Grail?"

I could only gape at Father Bede's disheveled state. The gray hair that ringed his tonsure stood up wildly. His cassock and surplice were dusty and disordered, and he smelled of human waste. His sharp nails poked through the wool of my sleeve. He cast a glance back over his shoulder to where a soldier stalked toward us across the lawn.

"Father—" Roger tried to release the monk's grip on my arm. "He spent the night in the punishment cell again," he explained to me.

"You must give it to me," Father Bede cried. "The abbot left us. The prior has gone over to their side. Only I stand for Glaston and the Grail! I alone can return her to her glory!" He no longer whispered. His voice rose to a shriek as the soldier reached us.

"Here, here, old man!" the soldier cried. "None of that. Ye were let out of the cell and told to leave the grounds." He pulled the librarian roughly away. "Best go, lads. The old man is mad." He dragged Father Bede toward the gate. "Go home to your family. There's no place for ye here."

Roger and I watched in horror as he thrust Father Bede through the north gate and into the street. When Roger turned to look at me, his face was pale beneath his bright hair.

I stammered. "Has Father Bede—has he been quite all right these last few days? I mean, since we left for Sharpham?"

"He's quoted Scripture a lot, if that's what you mean," Roger replied. "Long passages from the Apocalypse about trumpets and riders on horses."

I shivered at the memory of the rider in the valley of the White Spring. "Roger." I gripped his arm. "That day at the Chalice Well, what did you see? It wasn't a stag, was it?"

The color had begun to come back to his face, but now it drained again. "I'm not sure what it was." He twisted his hands in a worried fashion.

"It was a man with the head of a stag, wasn't it? A man who rode a black horse."

Roger was taking short quick breaths now, and I feared he might faint. He crossed himself. "I don't know, I tell you. It was through the trees. The shadows were deep. It must have been a stag."

"So close to the town?" I asked. "How would a stag in these cultivated lands not be caught and killed?"

"I don't know." He sounded defiant, as though he didn't want to believe in the reality of evil.

"I saw him again—last week," I said quietly, "at the source of the White Spring. But he wasn't alone. Father Bede was with him." I couldn't bring myself to say that the old monk had seemed to be worshiping the ancient god of the underworld.

Roger stared at me, his lips drained of blood. He crossed himself again.

∾

I made my way to the abbot's house. I should report to Brother Basil before I claimed my bed and door to sell for the price of firewood. I would start today for Oxford and be done with this place as soon as Brother Basil released me.

Voices came from the abbot's study when I entered the anteroom. "But this is highly irregular." Prior Robert's words trembled. "The abbot has not yet been tried. We hardly know what the charges are." He did not sound like one who had gone over to the other side.

Layton laughed. "Now don't you worry about the trial. We'll find enough to convict him. Treason, I'll warrant, and the penalty will be death. Few men leave the Tower with their heads attached to their shoulders."

"Colin?" Brother Basil's quiet voice called from the door of the study. "Is that you? I need your help." I entered the study as Layton strode out.

"Father Abbot said I was to ask you to stay on," Brother Basil whispered. "They are determined to look through all Abbot Whiting's papers, and if we do not look after them, everything will soon be in disarray."

I didn't go to Oxford that day or the next. I moved to a bed in the abbot's lodging and ate at the refectory table while others were turned out. Brother Basil and I took our meals in silence as ever, but the food turned sour in our mouths when our accustomed reading was replaced by crude laughter and cursing.

Occasionally I saw Roger, who stayed at Saint John's and steadied the schoolboys, who were easily excited at all the changes. Brother Arthur flitted here and there, looking after the scattered monks as he had once looked after the treasury. Invisible cords bound them both to Glastonbury.

Father Bede haunted the abbey grounds as often as he could slip by the guards. His habit hung loosely from his gaunt shoulders, more stooped now than ever. His pallid face showed blue around his lips and eyelids. His gray fringe became a ragged ring about his unshaved tonsure, which bristled with new-grown hairs. It was now nearly as white as the abbot's, and crumbled autumn leaves caught in the tangle.

"Father Bede, where are you sleeping?" I asked when I found him hovering near the door to the abbot's kitchen one morning. A dirty white hound lurked nearby, and the smell of the cur made me want to vomit.

"The cup! Where is the cup?" He gripped my arm with a strength that seemed beyond such a feeble body. I would have drawn back if I could have broken his grip without drawing attention. One of Layton's men leaned against a nearby wall.

"The cup is safe," I assured him. "But you! Have you no place to go? You mustn't sleep in the open. You'll catch your death!"

He shook his head and gripped harder. "Fool boy! The cup is the glory of Glastonbury! Where is it? You and I—we have the power to restore this place to what it was!" He shook my arm with more force than I would have thought him capable of. "I know the place," he hissed in my ear, "the secret entrance."

My efforts to avoid attracting attention had done no good. Layton's man was on us. "Old man, ye don't belong here. Move along now." The young man reached for Father Bede, and the dog snarled. The guard looked around for a stick and finding none, threw the dog the last of the meat pie he had been eating. The emaciated animal pounced on it, and crouched over the prize, watching, as the guard escorted Father Bede toward the front gate.

Layton's men systematically read every document and studied every ledger. They did not know what they were looking for—but that only intensified their belief that something incriminating was being hidden from them. What did not look promising was relegated to the fire. The abbey's past was being erased.

The great library was sold, piece by piece. Few outside the abbey valued reading, and one day I saw customers leaving the fishmonger's with purchases wrapped in an illuminated missal that had been laboriously copied before their great-grandsires were born. I moved through my days numbed by the horror of what was going on around me.

Scaffolding was erected in the Church of Saint Mary of Glastonbury so workmen could begin to dismantle the roof. Rather than bundle the heavy pieces of lead roofing to take to London, Layton found it more convenient to pull down the carved quire screen and quire stalls to fuel a fire in the chancel itself to melt the lead. He had it poured into ingots that would ship more easily.

Ten days had passed when Layton sent me to the church with a message for Master Pollard, who had charge of the dismantling of Saint Mary's. The sounds of tools and voices of workmen echoed from the high walls. I stumbled across the uneven floor of the nave where glazed tiles hundreds of years old had been pried loose and sold for some other building. Workmen using crowbars were busy removing more, oblivious to the empty side altar nearby. Everything of value would go, from the roof to the floor.

Without the quire screen, the view was uninterrupted from the door of the Galilee Porch where I stood to the entrance of the Edgar Chapel in the east. A large stack of broken pieces of carving rose near the Chapel of Saint Thomas in the north transept, and the scent of burning wood and hot metal reached even here. Smoke rose through a large opening already made in the chancel roof, so that the church was flooded with more light than it had seen in centuries.

I picked my way through the rubble. Even the Great Fire had not destroyed so systematically.

"Master Pollard?"

The man turned from examining a list with one of the workmen. "What is it?" His voice was curt and impatient.

"Master Layton—" I began, but I was interrupted.

"Master Pollard, come quick! We've found summat." A breathless workman emerged from the Edgar Chapel.

Master Pollard gave me a cursory look and strode after the workman. I followed. The Edgar Chapel had been stripped of gold and silver. No ornament decorated the bare altar. Broken pieces of wood cluttered the floor, but the roof was intact, and the windows rose high over our heads in their delicate stone tracery. Tiny pieces of glass glittered in the morning sunlight, held together in intricate shapes by thin strips of lead. Even in death the place was beautiful. Roger had a right to be proud.

"See here, behind this paneling." Horror gripped my bowels at the workman's words. I had no doubt what he had found behind that panel.

"Can you get it open more? I can't quite see," Pollard said. I wanted to flee and warn Roger and Brother Arthur, but my feet would no more move than if they had been sunk deep in the bog. Men crowded around the panels. There came the cracking sound of splitting wood.

"What have we here?" Pollard raised a golden goblet to the light, clearly admiring its beauty. The workman handed him a pair of silver candlesticks studded with jewels. Pollard gave a delighted chuckle.

"It appears someone has been robbing the church." He seemed more pleased than shocked. "Can you tell me who?" he demanded, turning cold dark eyes on me.

"I . . . My responsibilities were in the offices of the abbot," I stuttered. Anger was bitter as bile in my mouth.

"Where is the sacristan?" Pollard demanded of one of the workmen. "Is he not still in town? No doubt he is behind this."

A sweat broke out on my forehead although my blood had turned to ice water in my veins. Brother Arthur—they would find him! He would not even know to run away. Pollard sent someone to call up the guard and went to inform Layton of the development. I edged toward the door, my message to Pollard forgotten. If only I could get to Brother Arthur in time to warn him. The others drifted back to their work, talking of treason and the fall of the mighty.

Pollard grabbed the shoulder of his foreman as he left and pointed to the windows. "Someone should start taking those down. We can melt the lead and send it to London with the roof." He disappeared into the nave with the chalice and two candlesticks.

I slipped into the church and out through the north porch.

CHAPTER 25

I HAD TO WARN ROGER AND Brother Arthur. It was the hour of High Mass, and Roger, Father Aidan and the schoolboys were no doubt at Saint John's. I hurried through the small gate into the High Street and made my way to the parish church.

The church of Saint John the Baptist was small compared to Saint Mary's of Glastonbury. I burst through the heavy oak doors and stood gasping for breath. The sharp scent of incense filled my nostrils with the assurance that this church still lived. The roof was whole, the walls intact and the ring of the ancient words of the Mass belied the vivisection that was taking place a few hundred paces from where I stood. Several schoolboys looked my way and sniggered behind their hands.

Miserere nobis—Have mercy on us.

I joined the chanting of the *Agnus Dei* with the worshipers as I made my way to where Roger knelt among the boys. Over the sound of the chant, I hurriedly told him of the workman's discovery. "They will look for Brother Arthur," I explained. "We must warn him."

"Of course." His lip trembled. The silent communion prayer of the priest had begun when he made his way to Father Aidan to excuse himself. All the boys turned and stared as we crossed the nave and slipped out the doors.

"He will be hearing Mass at Saint Benedict's." Roger swung the door closed behind us. He started off with a determined stride past the tribunal, past the George and Pilgrim Inn, to the market cross that stood over the square a hundred paces from the abbey gates. There he stopped, facing the narrow street that sloped down to Saint Benedict's. Up the street from the church marched a troop of soldiers. A bound prisoner walked in their midst.

"We're too late." I grasped the market cross for support, but Roger threw back his shoulders and stood taller than ever I had seen him since I whispered that the chalice and candlesticks had been found.

"Where are you going with that man?" he demanded of the soldiers with all the authority of the abbot himself.

The soldiers stopped abruptly and looked at one another. The master of works in charge of dismantling the abbey church led them, and it was he who spoke. "He is under arrest for robbing the church." The man's voice, hard and defiant, dared Roger to challenge him further.

"Let him go," Roger said. "He is innocent."

"Roger!" I reached a hand to his sleeve. Even though this was no market day, the square was crowded with those bartering for the bones of the abbey or looking for some other windfall from its demise. We quickly drew a crowd. Roger made no sign that he heard me or felt my touch.

"What do you know of this?" the master of works sneered. "The judges will decide guilt or innocence."

"But I do know something of this, and I know he is innocent," Roger affirmed again. "I am the man you want. I hid the chalice and candlesticks in the paneling of the Edgar Chapel."

A gasp ran through the crowd at the audacious young man. I shared it with them. The master of works drew back his head as though Roger had moved against him, but Roger stood as still as the stone cross above us. Only his russet curls fluttered in a slight breeze off the moors.

"Seize him!" The man fell back among the soldiers and pointed an angry finger. "He is an enemy of the king!"

Two soldiers strode forward and grasped Roger's arms. They seemed uncertain how to treat a man who gave himself up to their charge and made no move to defend himself. They bound his arms efficiently and began to push through the crowd toward the tribunal.

I climbed onto the base of the market cross to see over the heads of the crowd. "Will you not let Brother Arthur go?" I called. Surely if Roger took the blame, they could not hold Brother Arthur as well.

"The judge will decide," the master declared. The troop of soldiers moved up the street, both monks bound in their midst.

The crowd began to disperse around me, returning to bargain for abbey furnishings or to the table where Thomas still sat in Spital Street taking testimony against the abbot. I stepped down from the stone platform and made my way back toward the abbey gate.

"Thief!"

I was not yet free of the press when the cry caught my attention as it did everyone else's.

"Thief!"

I turned to see Father Bede standing on a raised block, his long white finger pointing over the heads of the crowd straight at me. His face was gray as newly washed wool. His eyes were red and wild. His hand shook as he screamed, "He has stolen the Holy Grail, robbed the house of God!"

"Get him!" cried a stocky workman in leather leggings. Hands grasped at my clothes.

I twisted away, swinging elbows in every direction. "I've stolen nothing!" I cried. "The man is mad!" Someone pulled at my cassock. I twisted again.

"Umph!" My assailant crashed against my legs and nearly tripped me as he fell.

"Colin! This way!" A friendly hand plucked at my sleeve. "Come on!" Wil's face peered between surging bodies.

"Don't let 'im escape! He robbed the church same as the others. Bad as treason!" someone cried. I didn't know what he thought the whole crowd of them was doing if not robbing the church with their paltry prices.

At the cry of treason, the uproar increased. I nearly tripped on two boys who grasped at my clothes. I picked up one and tossed him into his companion. They both fell in a tangle of arms and legs, blocking the onrush for a moment.

I darted after Wil. He slipped quickly into a smaller lane off Benedict Street behind the church. I followed. Those who belatedly gave chase did not see us at the turn and so raced on down the main street. Most of the crowd seemed more interested in what bargains they might find in the square than in catching a thief, even one said to have robbed a church. We pressed up against the back of Saint Benedict's and caught our breaths.

"Thank you, Wil."

He shrugged off my thanks. "Ye'll come stay with us."

I gave him a sideways look and shook my head. "Your father won't have me."

The boy cocked his head to one side. "Why not?"

"He blames me for . . . He thinks I . . . I did. I betrayed him without meaning to. I delivered letters that accused him."

Wil shook his head vigorously. "Alice told how ye meant naught but to warn us. She talked loud to Granfy on it. Alice does that sometimes. Besides, Jesus says to forgive even if ye did it seventy times seven times. Father read that in the Holy Writ. I don't know how much 'tis, but 'tis more than all the houses in Meare. Maybe more than all the houses in Glassonb'ry." He scraped his bare foot thoughtfully in the dust. "And tha's what the holy writin' says."

I looked at his frank eyes. This child knew more Scripture than I did. An English Bible, read daily, had wrapped itself around his heart more than all my Latin Masses and rote prayers.

Wil pulled at my sleeve. "Please, Colin. I been here lookin' for ye near every day. They wouldn't let me into the abbey." He pulled at my hand as if to lead me from our hiding place. "'Tis a'right. Come on."

The noises of the crowd in front of the gate reached us even here. My mother's cross was around my neck. The cup was at my belt. Nothing was left for me at the abbey except a few pennies' worth of bed and the hateful duty of helping the abbot's enemies.

"I'll come," I said, "Perhaps if your father won't have me, there'll be someplace else for me to go."

At dusk we climbed the slope from Meare Pool to the village. The manor house where I had once stayed blazed with light. Layton's men were no doubt in residence. I wondered if James Toogood still lived there, or if he too had been evicted. The inn was crowded with those eager to discuss the events of the day. The street beyond was quiet. I hung back as we reached the last house in the row. A thin carpet of new grass had grown over the charred place where the family's goods had been burned.

"'Tis a'right. Ye'll see," urged Wil once more. He pulled at my hand and pushed through the door. I didn't enter but stood awkwardly in the doorway. The room was more sparsely furnished than on my first visit. A thin mattress and a pile of blankets were spread in place of the old bed. Wilfrith sat on a stool near the fire. His hair looked whiter and his shoulders more rounded than when I rode with him in his cart. Was it scarce a year ago? Alice set a steaming trencher on a bare board laid on trestles that looked newly made.

"Wil, ye're safe!" His mother rushed to throw her arms around him. Nicholas looked up from where he was seated pulling on his boots. A fresh scar marked his cheek. He sighed with obvious relief.

"Where ye been so long?" Matilda demanded. "I wasn't half worried! They're taking monks for doing terrible things, and ye out in it and not come home! Your father was goin' to look for ye. Ye frightened me so!" She squeezed the boy again, and he gave me a helpless look. The smell of lentils with herbs simmering on the fire filled the room.

Nicholas stood and tousled his son's hair. "'Tis a'right, Matilda. The boy's safe. I told ye he was."

"Father, I brought Colin."

All looked toward the door and noticed me for the first time. Matilda clasped Wil more closely to her. Nicholas turned a little pale, and his eyes held remembered pain. Alice stood against the wall, darting glances from one to the other, waiting.

"I shouldn't have come," I said. "I thought . . . since you sent Wil to warn the abbot . . ." I trailed off. It had been foolish to think they might forgive.

"Sent Wil?" Nicholas looked inquiringly from me to the boy.

"Ye said the soldiers was comin' for the abbot. . . ." Wil's voice was strained.

"And ye went to warn him?" His father's jaws clenched, and the air of the room pressed down on us like a low winter's sky before a storm.

"I'll go." I turned to leave.

"Where will ye go?" asked Alice in a small voice.

"I'll find somewhere." I thought of a tumbled down hut between here and Westhay. It would do for a night or two.

"Father?" She fixed him with those blue eyes that had filled my dreams and made me unsure of my calling. Wilfrith said no word, but stared into the fire. Nicholas searched the floor as if there he would find the words that eluded him.

I paused with my hand on the doorpost. My lips felt dry, and I ran my tongue over them. I spoke to the doorpost, ashamed to turn again and look into their faces.

"I didn't mean to hurt you, but I carried letters . . . the letter from Toogood to the Abbot accusing you." I shook my head with regret. "If I'd been thinking of you instead of my own fears, I might have realized. . . . I meant no hurt, but I brought hurt all the same. And when I knew that you were threatened, like a coward I neither warned you in time nor spoke in your defense."

I could hear Alice move to her sister's side, and Matilda's quiet crying. I turned and faced them. "You are just to send me from your door. No one deserves what was done to you—not for seeking God's truth."

I looked with longing on these people I loved as family. Then I turned and walked into the growing darkness. Behind me I could hear Wil's voice, trembling with uncertainty.

"The Bible says to forgive. Seventy times seven—tha's what ye read, Father."

A crisp wind blew off Meare Pool, and I wished for the cloak I had left behind at the abbey. A tiny cloud on the western horizon still caught an edge of golden sunlight. I started when a hand fell heavily on my shoulder.

"Colin."

I turned slowly and faced Nicholas. At this moment he looked nearly as old as his father-in-law.

"Trust and forgiveness—they don't come easy for me. I know ye meant no harm, and I know God wants me to forgive ye. But it comes hard." His chest rose and fell in a deep sigh.

"It's all right, Nicholas. I don't deserve forgiveness. I wouldn't have come but for the boy."

"No, 'tis not a'right," Nicholas responded. "'Tidn't about deservin' or not deservin'. Tha's what Wil and Alice both been sayin'. 'Tis about me livin' like a citizen of the kingdom of heaven."

I stared at him.

"Please," Nicholas said quietly, looking at the ground. "Stay the night. Ye owe me that."

"Owe you? I don't understand."

"If ye stay, perhaps He'll give me what I be needin'."

CHAPTER 26

WE ATE A SIMPLE SUPPER IN SILENCE. Elwina and John came to the door shortly after, but Alice met them there and shook her head.

"Not this night," she whispered, and glanced over her shoulder to where I sat alone on a stool in the corner, nearly crushed by the terrible changes of the day. Elwina and John must have told the others, for no one else appeared.

Nicholas sat late at the trestle table, reading by the flickering light of a wick in a dish of oil. The pages of the book were crisp and new.

"'Twas not our coins alone that went to buy it," Alice said when she saw me staring.

The next day Nicholas and the other family members went about their duties on the farm. Only Wil spoke more than a few words to me, and he seemed much effected by his elders' silence. I stayed hidden in the house, lest someone else take seriously Father Bede's accusation of theft. The cup rested safely in the chest with the new English Bible.

The second night neighbors gathered for evening prayers, and Alice didn't turn them away. I helped Nicholas move boards from the table to form benches. We didn't speak, but he didn't refuse my help. There were more worshipers than I'd seen before. Possibly the fall of the abbey had given them boldness. Most avoided looking in my direction, and I stayed off to the side. Only William's wandering eye seemed always upon me.

"Colin has been falsely accused," Wilfrith explained at the beginning. "'Tis our duty to shelter him and to say naught, so his place isn't known to those at the manor."

Several nodded agreement. They seemed to accept the soldiers who had invaded their village as their natural enemies, and expect no justice from them.

Alice read that night. I was not the only one who enjoyed listening to her sweet voice rise and fall with the power of the words. Nicholas seemed to have selected the passage with a particular thought in mind. He listened quietly, head bowed, as she read from the Gospel of Matthew, chapter 18.

> Therfore is ye kingdome of heven lykened vnto a certayne kynge which wolde take a countis of his servauntis.

Jesus was speaking. He told a story about a servant forgiven a huge debt who refused to forgive one who owed him a pittance. The king had the unforgiving servant thrown into the debtors' prison. It must have been the number of bodies cramped into the small room, for although the night was chill, the room seemed uncomfortably warm. Alice concluded the section:

> So lyke wyse shall my hevenly father do vnto you, except ye forgeve with youre hertes eache one to his brother their treaspases.

I expected Nicholas to say a few words, as he had the night of my last visit to Meare. The others seemed to expect it too, but he mutely stared into the coals that glowed on the hearth. Once he looked my way, and his jaw grew tense. I thought he might expose my betrayal to the others, but he said nothing. He bowed his head again, and although his eyes were closed, a single tear glittered on his cheek.

Some of the neighbors shuffled their feet nervously in the rushes of the floor. A child whimpered.

At last Wilfrith spoke. "I 'spose we best say a prayer."

The people slipped from their stools and knelt in the straw.

"God, have mercy," Wilfrith began. His voice broke. When he mastered himself and began again, it was with the memorized words of Our Lord's prayer. They were slow and broken at first, but as others joined in, they gained strength.

> Give us this day our daily bread, and forgive us our trespasses . . .

I stopped. I couldn't say the words. I had no right when I had not forgiven my father.

"Even as we forgive our trespassers," prayed those around me. A muffled sob escaped Matilda.

As the prayer ended, I heard Nicholas's voice, rising above the others:

> For thine is the kingdom, and the power and the glory forever.

His voice was fierce with determination. I looked up, as did several others. His head was thrown back, his face tilted toward the roof, but I knew his heart soared above it.

"Amen." The word had all the finality of Abbot Whiting's last Mass at Sharpham.

"Amen," I murmured.

When the others had gone, Nicholas extended his hand to me. "Forgive me, Colin."

My mouth gaped. "Forgive *you?*"

"Our Lord has forgiven me. I been wrong to hold this against ye."

In his face I saw a holiness as great as in Brother Fergus, who had given his life to the Church and the poor and had died for what he believed.

"Aye, Colin." Wilfrith rubbed his chin. "I be askin' your forgiveness as well. I told ye to git, and I damned ye to hell. Tha's not our

Lord's way . Ye're welcome to stay as long as ye choose." He embraced me like a son, and tears flowed from us both.

❧

Wilfrith spent the next afternoon with the old men on a bench outside the inn. Among all the gossip, nothing was said of the missing cup or any search for other monks. He did hear that one of the monks was staying with a brother at Godney, on the far side of the pool. No one seemed to know the monk's name or anything about him, except that he had come from Glastonbury and was brother to the bailiff. That was as certain as any story passed over a flagon of cider could be.

Wil carried a message from me to Brother Basil, explaining my absence. He brought back a bundle that proved to be my cloak and the clothing I had used when I traveled to the estates. It would be less conspicuous in Meare than my white cassock. He also carried a note saying Layton and his men were preparing to return to London, their case complete. Brother Basil would soon be taking a position as steward for a landowner in Exeter. There was no need for me to return to the abbey. I breathed a sigh of relief. What excuse he had made to Layton's men for my absence I could only guess.

The last sentence penned in Brother Basil's careful hand read, "You will want to know that Brother Arthur and Brother James"—the name Roger had taken at his vows—"have been removed to London to join Father Abbot. Pray for their souls."

❧

The next day I ventured out to help Nicholas turn the thatch that was drying in the yard. The long strip fields of barley and oats that he worked with Wilfrith had been harvested, but there were still apples and roots from the garden to be picked and stored, and long winrows of black peat turves to be turned regularly so they would dry evenly. For a farmer, whether in Somerset or Wales, autumn is a busy time of year.

"Fortnight ago Tildy said there'd be nothin' from the garden this year." Wilfrith laughed. "Too much rain was rottin' the vegetables afore they was pickable, she said. But look how the herbs have revived. Every onion Alice pulled this mornin' double, and I never seed so many tubers. We'll have enough and to spare the winter."

I didn't mind the work. It kept my mind off my friends in prison and my own uncertain future. Once I glimpsed a stooped figure on the moor wrapped in a black cloak like those of the abbey. His hair was shaggy and unkept, and by his side was a hound. By some trick of the light, the animal looked a shimmer of silvery white across the water-logged waste.

I gazed often across the moors toward the Mendip Hills where the road to Oxford began. It was a long road—as long as the way to Brecon.

"We're not amind to push ye out the door," Nicholas said one afternoon as we stacked dry turves into cones higher than my head that Wilfrith and Nicholas called "ruckles." Their shape would shed the winter rains like a haystack and let the peat continue drying until it was needed for fuel in the coming months. He stood up straight and rested his back.

"—But if ye're fixing to see your father in Wales, ye best go afore winter sets in."

I stiffened. "My father . . . ?" My voice sounded hard even to me. I had put the man out of mind, along with Abbot Whiting's last instructions.

"I see," Nicholas said. He returned to his work. "Seems ye have some forgivin' of your own to do."

"You don't understand," I burst out. "You don't know what kind of man my father is."

The scar on his cheek from his day in the stocks quivered. He nodded slowly but didn't say anything more.

Nor did he need to. Wil's voice pounded at my conscience. "Seventy times seven . . ."

I threw down my turf and stomped across the moors.

The path I chose in my blind haste skirted a copse of withies by a stretch of open water. The soggy land between the two was thick with the thatching reeds that Nicholas and Wilfrith harvested. They swished in the wind like the silks of my mother's skirt and brought tears to my eyes. How long ago her death seemed. I'd lived a lifetime in the year since, and yet waited, like a babe unborn, for another life to begin. Where and what that life would be, I did not know. My thumb rubbed the thick line on my wrist, the scar my father had given me.

Of one thing I was certain: I would not return to Wales to forgive the killer of my mother.

The setting sun colored the sky orange and pink and glittered in places where the swamp grasses were sparse and water showed through. A lone swan pumped his wings with steady power that carried his heavy body over water, grass and trees. I rotated slowly, watching his progress until he passed in front of the Tor, silhouetted against the sky.

"Cursed hill!" I muttered. I wrapped my arms around myself against the evening chill and turned my back on the Tor. Far off, beyond an expanse of water that reflected the evening sky, a figure in black stood where the withies ended and the moors began. He was still as the trees that grew beside him, and at first I took him for a tall stump broken off in some long ago storm. But when I looked again, he was gone.

A flock of birds swooped overhead, a whirr of wings. They dipped and rose, stirring the tops of the reeds with their passing. There were hundreds of them, moving as one. The mass dipped and rose together, stretching and compacting, now a broad scatter of dark birds against a pale blue dusk, now compressed into a single blot, staining the sky. The flock shifted direction and swirled to my left, divided, scattered and returned to one.

Alice skipped from the trees behind me. "The starlings!" Her cheeks were as pink as summer's last blooms outside the cottage door. She threw back her head and spread her arms as if she wished to join the dance of the birds. A second flock flew over. They dipped under the first, then rose to join it, swooped away to the right and returned.

The two flocks mingled in a dance as intricate as any courtier might devise, flew apart and rushed back to one another once more.

Alice's joyful laughter rang in my ears. "'Tis a wonder!" She whirled around, arms outstretched, her petticoats twirling about her. "I love the starlings!"

A third flock arrived from across the moors to join its brothers. Now thousands of birds bowed and turned over our heads. My heart rose up in me, until like Alice, I wanted nothing more than to fly up into their midst and leave behind my earthly troubles.

When Alice turned to me the joy in her eyes seemed lit by a thousand candles. I bowed. I had felt awkward when my mother made me practice dances at home. At neighborhood gatherings I had hovered near the musicians, trying to imitate their skills on my lute rather than catch the eye of some female who might expect me to lead her to the floor. But here in the twilight of an autumn evening, while starlings danced to the music of the waving reeds, I offered Alice my hand.

She grew serious and still, lowered her chin, and looked at me from beneath lashes darker than her flaxen hair. She placed her fingers shyly on my palm and curtseyed low as any graceful lady at court. She met me as we stepped together. I'm sure no one had taught her to dance except the starlings, but we bowed and turned and stepped as neatly as any dancing master might wish. When we stopped, the starlings had settled in the reeds and the trees had lost their color to the gloaming. I was reluctant to drop her hand. It felt warm in mine, and I stood for a long time looking down at her blue eyes and slightly parted lips, wondering what it would be like to spend a lifetime with someone so full of fire and joy.

Alice drew a long breath. "Tildy sent me to find ye. She saved ye some dinner."

I was silent.

"Ye're fearful about your friends?" When I didn't answer right away, she went on. "They cassn't think the abbot guilty of treason."

I looked out over the reeds turning dark in the fading light, relieved that she knew nothing of my father and the wrestlings of my heart.

"Abbot Whiting is guilty of not giving King Henry what he wants. If that be treason, then he is guilty."

Alice's strong sense of fairness clouded her face, and she dropped my hand as she turned in exasperation. "Is there no law in England?"

A light seemed to flare up in my mind. It came from the cup, but it shone on a book.

"It will come, Alice, when more men and women like you and Wil know how to read; when we search the Scriptures and seek God's wisdom to think for ourselves instead of blindly accepting what we're told; when more men have the courage of Nicholas to speak the truth aloud. Then will come the rule of law."

I stopped, embarrassed by my presumptuous prophecy. I swallowed and fought to steady the thumping of my heart.

"May it be God's law that governs us and not merely the laws of men."

CHAPTER 27

WE WALKED BACK ALONG THE ridge between the withies and rushes. Our hands brushed once, and I stepped shyly away. She turned to look at me, but I couldn't read her face in the fading light.

"Wha's that?" Alice pointed along a smaller track that joined the low ridge we were following.

I squinted into the gloom. "I don't see anything."

"Looks like a useful bit of cloth." She started forward to where something dark showed among the reeds, half submerged. "Tildy might make a warm cloak for Wil."

A snarl came from the grasses that lined the track, and she let out a little cry. Two red eyes burned like coals. I jerked her toward me. A silvery white hound stepped from the reeds. His lips were pulled back to show sharp teeth, and he smelled of dung and rotting meat.

"Back away, Alice. Slowly. We mustn't startle him."

"But Colin . . . ," she planted her feet. "Look."

A sandaled foot showed beneath the water-soaked cloth in the bog. It was a man. "We cassn't leave him there."

I thrust her behind me, and reached for the fallen branch of a scrubby tree by the path. Holding it in front of me, half shield and half lance, I stepped toward the dog. He snarled and snapped and leaped at my flimsy defense.

Alice screamed.

The smaller twigs crumbled and broke, but the main branch held. I shouted and thrust it again and again at the pale hound, forcing him up the track, away from Alice. His snarling and snapping never ceased, and the unholy light that burned in his eyes filled me with dread.

At last he gave the field. He snapped a final time at the thrusting branch and retreated several strides. I had no desire to be led away and lost in this watery waste at night. When I failed to follow, the hound paused. He turned his head and looked at me. The eyes glowed with hellish fire, and he slunk away into the reeds.

"'Tis a monk," Alice said when I returned to her. "Poor man."

I stepped off the firm ground into the muck. Alice pulled at his feet as I sloshed in cold water to my thighs trying to get around the reeds and reach his shoulders. His head was held above the flood by the thicket of plants.

"He isn't drowned," I replied, "but he'll soon be dead of cold." Wet gray hair plastered his face and hid it completely. I gripped his thin shoulders and lifted him toward firm ground. My foot caught in the tangle of weeds beneath the water, and I fell, heaving the man before me.

"Oh!" Alice cried as she sat with a thump. I pulled myself upright and pushed the body toward her. She scrambled to pull him clear of the reeds.

The smell of dung and rot caught in my throat. There was a sound of rustling grass that was not the wind. A twig snapped. I turned. Not more than two cart-lengths behind me a pair of fiendish red eyes glowed.

Alice caught her breath. She had seen them, too.

I glanced around for another branch, but found nothing to protect myself where I stood, deep in the bog.

The demon dog leaped.

"*Jesu*, save us!" Alice cried.

The dog yelped and twisted in midair. He landed on the body of the man, only a breath away from Alice. He sprang again without pause, his claws ripping the monk's habit with the force of his leap, and disappeared into the darkness.

Alice let out her breath in ragged sobs and murmured a prayer of thanks as I slogged out of the bog onto the soggy meadow.

She wiped her eyes and smoothed the man's habit. Her hand came away wet with blood. She wiped it on the black wool and bent her ear to his chest. "He lives," she said, "but he's so cold." She rubbed his pale hand between her own and brushed back the hair from his face.

I gasped.

"What is it?" She looked at me.

"It's Father Bede." My innards were slowly turning to ice. "He's . . . He's the one who had Nicholas put in the stocks." I hung back, not wanting to touch his cold body. "He must be the monk we heard about, the one at Godney." I knelt beside him. "I'll take him there."

"Colin, he's much too sick for that! We'll take him home and get him warm."

Before they took me in, I would have scoffed at her. After all this man had done to them and tried to do to me? But I had seen their commitment to forgiveness no matter the cost. Why couldn't I do the same?

Seventy times seven, came Wil's voice in my head once more.

So likewise shall my heavenly Father do unto you, Alice had read, *except ye forgive with your hearts each one to his brother.*

I clenched my teeth. It was not my brother that I needed to forgive.

Alice had not stopped straining to lift Father Bede, but he was too heavy for her. She rested her hands on her hips. "Well? Ye goin' to help me—or must I fetch Nicholas?"

I said nothing. I couldn't let her see the confusion of my heart. I bent and swung the monk onto my shoulder. He weighed no more than a couple sheaves of thatching reeds. No, we couldn't let him die out here, whatever his crimes against the Thatchers or me.

❧

We made our way out of the copse and onto a track that led to the village. My boots squelched uncomfortably, and I stank of rotting vegetation, though not so badly as Father Bede.

Alice ran ahead. When I lugged my burden through the door,

Matilda was ready with a dry sack for a towel. Nicholas looked up from setting a warming pan in a heap of bedding.

"Lay him here by the fire," said Wilfrith, "and we'll get the wet clothes off him."

Matilda tried to spoon warm broth into his mouth, but it only dribbled down his chin while Wil rubbed his icy feet to get the blood moving.

"His name is Father Bede," I explained. "He must be the one living with the bailiff in Godney."

"Well, he be too sick to go there tonight," Matilda said. "We'll send word." She looked to Nicholas, who began pulling on his heavy cowhide shoes.

"Ye stink," said Wil, screwing up his face at me.

"I'd better wash."

"And put on dry clothes," Alice called as I made for the bucket to fetch water for washing. "We don't need anyone else takin' sick."

Wil was just slipping back in through the front door when I entered from the back, having scrubbed the bog scum from my head and body.

"I sent him to warn the neighbors not to come for prayers," Alice whispered.

Father Bede lay on the pallet that was all Nicholas and Matilda had left for a bed. He was wrapped in blankets, his face pale as the bed linen and his wispy hair a mere shadow on the cushion. Before Nicholas returned, Father Bede's chill had turned to fever. Alice bathed his brow and cooled his body with wet cloths while Matilda brewed a concoction of herbs over the fire. He stirred restlessly in the bed when I bent near.

"The cup!" he whispered urgently. "Where . . . ?" He gripped a handful of my shirt in a powerful fist. His eyes were wide open, yet I wasn't sure it was me he saw.

"Hush now," Matilda soothed him. "Ye must rest." His fingers relaxed, and he lay back on the cushion. I began to breathe again.

"I must find it." He was quiet for a few moments, then laughed. It was a coarse sound I had never heard him make. "The fools! What do they know?" His gray face twisted into a sneer, but his eyes remained closed. "They have never studied the books I have. They don't know where to find the gate. Only I can unlock the secrets."

Matilda drew back, crossing herself. "'Tis the fever. He dassn't know what he's sayin'." She sniffed. "Wha's that smell? Never knew the bog to smell so bad." She dipped a fresh cloth in water and laid it on his forehead. The monk shook it off impatiently and continued muttering words I couldn't quite catch.

I glanced at the front door. It was securely barred, as was the door to the garth. When the others were occupied, I checked the shutters on the two small windows, to be certain they were latched. A faint odor of dung and rotting meat seemed to seep around their edges. I had come to fear that dog as more than a common cur, and I worried for Nicholas outside with him.

"God protect us," I prayed.

At times Father Bede quieted. Nicholas returned safely without seeing the animal. He and Wil climbed to the rude loft of the cottage to sleep. Alice stayed below to help Matilda. Wilfrith stretched out on his pallet, and I lay by the fire and dozed. At some point I heard Alice climb to the loft.

I dreamed again of the strange cavern I'd first entered on the night my mother died. Now the flowstone in the cave reminded me of formations around the White Spring, but those were weathered and covered with mosses and green, hillside plants. These glistened whiter than bones. My father was in that dream cave. I wrestled with him, but in the way of dreams he changed, and it wasn't my father but Father Bede against whom I struggled. After a long time I found I was locked in combat with neither my father nor the priest, but the stag-headed god, Gwyn, himself.

"Power!"

The shout woke me, as it did Matilda. She had been sleeping on her stool, pressed against the wall, and now she startled, overturned the stool, and sprawled onto the floor.

Father Bede sat up. "The power—it is mine by right!" His eyes were open and filled with as much pride as I had ever seen in him. I helped Matilda to her feet, but could not stop watching those pale eyes that looked beyond us at something we couldn't see.

Suddenly he cringed, shrinking into himself like a frightened child. "No, please!" He whimpered and raised an arm in front of his face, as if to fend off some attacker. "Please, I'll do anything you ask. Anything! Don't . . ." The rest was lost in sobbing. I rubbed my nose. The scent of dung and rot had returned.

Matilda put her arms around the old man's shoulders. "There, there. No one's goin' to hurt ye. Go back to sleep." My hands trembled as I helped ease him onto the cushion.

Toward morning the fever broke, and Father Bede fell into a quiet sleep. I rose and went to the byre to help Nicholas and Wilfrith with the morning chores.

"The cow be givin' nicely," Wilfrith said as his fingers gripped her teats and a steady stream of milk squirted into his pail. "Afore Michaelmas I thought she was goin' dry, but now she's givin' good milk aplenty."

He laughed. "Martin Fletcher thought she was pas' her prime. Sold her to me for a good price, he did." He patted her side affectionately. "Tildy be happy for the butter and cheese, and a growin' boy like Wil needs milk." He flexed his fingers and eyed them thoughtfully. "Me hands be gettin' strength with the milkin'. They pained bad in September, but look now." He pulled firmly on a teat. "They's near as good as Nicholas's. No more back pain neither. Havin' this old lady about is makin' me feel a young strapper." He patted her again.

I pitched some hay into the slatted box that was fixed to the end of the shed where the cow was tied. She pulled dried and cured grasses into her mouth with a contented air.

Perhaps it was Father Bede asking for the cup in his fevered dreams that put it in my mind. Was there some special virtue about that cup for those it came near? During the months it was in the infirmary with Father Dunstan, people seemed to get better faster. No one died until after the father breathed his last and the cup was moved to the abbot's lodging. Things thrived in this home now. The cow and Wilfrith were likely good medicine for each other. But there was also that hardy primrose that Alice had found in the woods and planted by the door. It bloomed long after other flowers in the village had faded.

And Matilda's garden—the harvest had been more bountiful than anyone had a right to expect after a cool, wet summer.

Father Bede was sitting up by the fire when we returned to the house to break our fast. He was wrapped in a heavy mantle, but his gray face looked as healthy as I had ever seen it.

"'Tis a miracle!" Matilda told us. "I never thought he'd last the night, and here he is, talkin' of walkin' home to Godney hisself."

Father Bede truly looked like a different person. How could he have recovered so quickly from the near corpse we had brought in from the heath? It was almost like Father Dunstan's return to strength. I glanced at the chest where the cup lay and wondered.

Father Bede eyed us. "Nicholas Thatcher, isn't it?" he said. "So it's your house I've been brought to. And Colin—" He waved a finger at me. "You sly boy, you made me think these folk were unknown to you." His Oxford accent had slipped away in the weeks home with his brother in Godney. His cheeks stretched into a forced smile, but his cheerful, friendly words didn't match something I saw in his eyes.

"I'd only just met them when I came to the Abbey," I assured him. He looked around the room, and I noticed how his glance lingered on the crowded shelf that held the family's cups and eating utensils.

"It does not surprise me to find you here among them, nor that I have been brought here."

"Colin and Alice found ye in the bog," Wil explained. "'Twas Colin carried ye home."

But that was not what Father Bede meant. He eyed the trap door leading to the loft. Alice brought him cider in a wooden cup. Father Bede took it, and a faint smile turned up the corners of his mouth. "Has Colin shown you his cup?" he asked Wil.

Alice laid a firm hand on her nephew's shoulder.

"Ow." Wil frowned and shrugged her off. I held my breath, willing the child not to reveal the secret.

"Colin has a very old cup," Father Bede continued, holding the small boy with his eyes. No one said a word. Matilda bit her lower lip and turned to stir the pot of porridge on the fire.

"'Tis a valuable cup, and I'm sorry to tell that Colin did a wicked thing and stole it from its rightful owners."

I drew in my breath sharply, but Wil gazed at Father Bede with all the fascination of a mouse hypnotized by a snake.

The monk curled his lips in a smile. "I expect a fine young man like yourself knows where a cup like that would be hidden." Wil swallowed so hard he blinked. The boy's eyes slid for a moment toward the chest before he jerked them back.

It was enough to tell Father Bede what he wished to know. He turned his pale eyes upon me. I shivered, wondering if I had been caught with what folks called "the evil eye" and would be cursed, but he continued to speak to Wil. "Colin knows he must return the cup or he will die in his sin." Then I knew he had given me the evil eye. I couldn't move, even to draw breath into my lungs.

It was Matilda who broke the spell. "Porridge is ready." Using her apron to protect her hands, she lifted the heavy iron pot and swung it away from the coals.

"You shouldn't be doing that," said Father Bede. "Not a woman in your condition."

Nicholas glanced up quickly. "Condition?"

Father Bede looked slyly at Matilda from under half closed lids. "Your wife didn't tell you she's expecting a child?"

Nicholas looked quickly from Matilda to Father Bede and back again. "A child?" His face lit with expectant wonder.

Matilda blushed like a summer rose. "I dinne want to tell ye until I was certain. I dinne want ye to be disappointed like—"

Nicholas cut off her words with a strong embrace. "God has blessed us with a child!" He lifted her off the floor and both of them laughed for joy. Alice slipped an arm around Wil, who stood open-mouthed as his parents behaved like giddy children. Father Bede looked on with an expression I'd have taken for benevolence had I not known him better, and I stole a hard look at the chest in the corner.

❧

The cup itself was not mentioned again. When the autumn sun shone strong at midday, and Bede sat outside the door for an hour or so, I sent Wil and Alice to occupy him while I opened the chest. It was nearly empty now. The linens Alice had prepared for her marriage had been looted by the mob. There was nothing left but the Bible and a worn cloak in the bottom and, beneath it—the cup. I hid the cup under one of the ruckles of drying peat in the garth. That night I pretended to be asleep until Father Bede rose and tried the lid of the chest.

I sat up and asked innocently, "Do you need something, Father?"

He kicked the chest with his bare toe in his surprise and muffled a curse. "A cup of water, if you please," he said with hardly a moment's hesitation.

I blessed Matilda for the pail and ladle she kept near the fire. "I'll fetch it for you." I brought him a drink without once taking my eyes off him until he lay back down.

He stayed three days, recovering his strength, although it seemed to me he was as strong as ever the day after his illness. I resented that he was wheedling his way into this family I almost considered my own. By the morning of the third day, he had no excuse to linger. "Colin will see me safely home, won't you, lad?"

"Of course," I murmured after I succeeded in swallowing the bread that stuck in my throat. "If Nicholas and Wilfrith can spare me." Wilfrith nodded as he chewed and then washed the mouthful down with cider.

Nicholas raised his eyebrows as though surprised I would seek his permission. "Go. I won't be stoppin' ye."

Father Bede took my arm as though for support as we left, but before we reached the abbot's fish house at the other end of the village, he was striding confidently along.

"We must make our plans, Colin."

"Plans?"

"To use the Grail to restore the power of Glastonbury, of course."

If I had felt stupid in his presence before, now I felt doubly so. I stopped still in the lane where the drove to Godney turned off from the main road.

"Come on, lad. Don't be a fool. We have the power, you and I. Why do you think I recovered so quickly? It was the Grail. I was near to death when you found me, but lying all night with the Grail in the chest at my feet restored me. You moved it, but it was there."

I looked at him sharply.

He pushed his face close to mine. "You have seen what the Grail can do. It is a power greater than this land has known." He drew back. "You have the cup, but I have the knowledge. I have studied the secret books in the library at Glastonbury, ancient books that tell how to call powers of earth, air, fire and water to our bidding."

"That's witchcraft!"

"Power, Colin! It's the power to restore the abbey to its glory as the most ancient and holy church in all of Britain."

I hung back. Was he completely mad?

"Power, Colin! You've felt the cup; you know the tingle to the tips of your fingers. I know you do, but you don't know how to use it. When I raise the Holy Grail and call upon its power, all men will fall at my feet and worship! The abbot will be released at my command. He is too old and ill to rule at Glastonbury. I will allow him to live out his days quietly, while I make of the Holy House at Glaston all that the gods intended it to be!"

I trembled at his blasphemy.

He turned and strode off along the twisting path through the marshes with an assurance that said he had walked this way before.

"The trial has been delayed," he called back to where I stood. "The king awaits the arrival of his new queen, the German princess Anne of Cleves."

I wondered how he knew. Then a white hound stepped onto the path behind him. It turned its red eyes on me, and the stench of dung and rot reached across the moor.

CHAPTER 28

AFTER THAT MY EYES OFTEN searched the moors for a thin shape in a long black cloak. Some days I felt his gaze upon me, but I never saw him. Nor did I see the pale hound that had attacked us on the moor, although I made sure that neither Alice nor Wil strayed from the village alone.

The cup stayed beneath the ruckle of peat in the garth. I checked it once or twice. It was dry enough there, and neither Wil nor anyone else could accidentally give away its hiding place.

As November came, the mists hung thick as a fleece along the man-made channel of the Brue. I had determined to climb the Tor once more and pray for Roger, Brother Arthur and the abbot in prison.

It had been a year since last I climbed. Next week the year and a day of my novitiate should have been completed. "I'm glad you never took your final vows," Abbot Whiting had said. Was I?

At full light I ascended the slope off the moors and into the town.

"Little Jack Horner sat in a corner, eating his Christmas Pie." Chanting voices of children already sounded in the street. I knew of whom they sang. John Horner had been sent to the king with a meat pie stuffed with the titles of a dozen abbey manors. I remembered well the day the abbot sent him. "Perhaps now our troubles will be resolved," he had said. But if rumor was to be believed, the pie arrived one deed short. Was that what brought down the king's wrath on our heads? Now Horner had charge of all the abbey estates, and I had no doubt he would keep the plum for himself.

There seemed to be an unusual number of stray dogs about Glastonbury. One cowered near a doorway where a mother slapped her child. Another peeked a head from an alley where a beggar searched for something to eat. The smell of rotting garbage seemed worse than usual even in this crowded town.

I took the footpath behind Chalice Hill and climbed above the mists to the Tor. By that route I did not have to go along Spital Street past the abbey gates. But even here the stench lingered. I came upon a peddler, beating his thin, overloaded packhorse. From the prickly shelter of a gooseberry bush, one of the pale hounds peered out, watching with unnatural red eyes. I shivered and hurried on.

The way was steeper on the north side of the Tor, crossed with ridges of ancient terracing. I knelt in the dewy grass and prayed for my friends. I wished I had thought to bring the cup. Its presence would have been a comfort. It glowed on the backs of my closed eyelids, but instead of the voice of Abbot Whiting reciting Mass, I heard Wil's voice, young and innocent.

Seventy times seven. Tha's what ye read, Father.

I pushed the thought aside and climbed to the first terrace. There I knelt again to pray. Again I saw the glowing cup before my closed eyes. This time it was Alice's voice I heard.

So likewise shall me heavenly Father do unto you.

"This cursed hill!" I muttered, knowing I could curse neither God nor Alice.

The bank grew steeper, and I climbed nearly hand over hand. I knelt on the next terrace, where I suddenly heard Father Dunstan's voice in my mind.

This is the way of Christ, Colin, the way to which He has called us.

I didn't try to pray again. I climbed straight up the steep hill and reached the back of the church of Saint Michael, flushed with exertion. The abandoned church didn't have the empty feel I expected. For some distance I had been hearing the sound of hammers and shouts of workmen. I rounded the church and stood where the path stretched down to the fair field and the abbey barns.

The Stations of the Cross were gone. Papist trumpery, Chancellor Cromwell had called them. In the hollow before the tower, where the twelfth Station had stood, was a pile of hewn logs. Workmen had constructed a platform of the sort on which nobles sit to watch a spectacle. Three laborers struggled with pulleys and tackle to raise a heavy beam and drop it upright in a hole. Their shouts reached me as if from far off. I hardly heard the words for the blood pounding in my ears.

The foreman approached me. "Comin' to see the hangin'?" he asked.

"What hanging?" I managed weakly.

"Why the Abbot of Glassonb'ry and his cronies. Ye're wise to come today. Won't get so close later with the bishop and all the judges. We be puttin' up the gallows now." He pointed proudly to where his men struggled to raise a second post.

"They haven't been tried yet!" I protested.

"Bringin' them to Wells tomorrow for the trial. The next day they'll bring them to Glassonb'ry by cart, chain them to hurdles and drag them up here." He gestured to the path Father Dunstan had said the abbot would climb once more.

"But the verdict hasn't been given."

He looked blankly at me. "What difference does that make?"

"If they're found innocent . . ."

He laughed. "Innocent? The king don't send folks to trial to be found innocent."

There was nothing in my stomach for I had chosen to fast that day, but I wasn't sure I wouldn't retch anyway. I could see the man beside me, pointing and explaining. His mouth opened and closed, but I heard only a muffled roar.

If the king wanted to strike terror in the hearts of any who might think of resisting his will, why not do it in the town or on the fair field or in the larger city of Wells? The steep sides of the hill would keep all but a few from witnessing the deaths. Here, suspended between heaven and earth. . . .

Or was it between heaven and hell? I smelled the scent of dung and rot before I saw the dog. It sauntered around the pile of wood and looked at me across the hollow with its evil, glowing eyes. The tales of Annwn came rushing back upon me, every tale that Llwyd had sung or Brigit had told of Gwyn ap Nudd and his hounds who carried doomed souls to hell. A workman threw a stone to drive the hound off, but he only backed a few steps and raised his head to howl.

His call was answered by a chorus of baying hounds that echoed deep inside my head. Or did the sound come from some chamber beneath my feet? I stared at the grassy hilltop between my boots. Flickering light in a faery cavern . . . a blood-red cloak, the head of a stag and a horse as black as a moonless night. I clutched my cloak around me and fought for breath. The stench that seemed to emanate from the dogs filled my nostrils.

"The heads'll go on the abbey gates," my guide continued without seeming to notice my discomfort. "What else can ye do with a rebel abbot and his pack of thieves, I ask ye now?"

Whether he expected an answer, I do not know. I fled.

ᐁ

I strode quickly the six miles back to Meare. The shirt and hosen I wore made the walk easier than it would have been in my novice cassock. I must think what to do, but my mind was empty as a new ledger book.

Wells. The seat of the bishop, long-time enemy of the abbots of Glastonbury. It was not so far. I would go there. Perhaps I would be allowed to see my friends. If I took the cup, the abbot might be permitted to celebrate one last Mass with it, and so be encouraged.

My head felt light and my hands as cold as ice. A misty rain had started to fall by the time I reached the cottage. The brief sunlight of a November day was fading. I stumbled through the apple trees to the ruckle where I had hidden the cup. Lying on my chest, I slid my hand between the turves of the lowest round. It touched only dirt. I slid forward and reached further in until I could feel all the way around the small dry space. Nothing.

"No!" I leaped to my feet, flailing my arms and collapsing the turves. "No!"

"Colin?" Alice stood in the back doorway of the cottage. "Wha's wrong?"

"It's gone!" This could not be true. "The cup is gone!"

She was by my side in a moment. "Are ye certain this be where ye hid it?" Nicholas followed.

"Yes, I'm certain."

"Could it of been this one? Or this?" She knelt on the damp ground and felt under the nearest ruckles. I dug wildly into them, but there was nothing there.

"It's gone! Father Bede took it."

"Colin, ye can't be sure." Nicholas had joined us and shook his head.

"I am sure." I kicked at a fallen turf. "I hate him! If I burn in hell for it, I still hate him. And I hate my father!" I said it deliberately to hurt Nicholas who wanted me to forgive. In my anger I must hurt someone, and he was the only one near enough except Alice. It must have hurt her, too.

Nicholas began patiently to restack the turves. Alice stooped to help him. I looked off across the pool in the direction of Godney. "I have to find him and get it back."

❧

The path that led from Meare to Godney in the summer and early autumn was under water now that the winter rains had come. Nicholas rowed me across the pool. His flat-bottomed boat floated through the twilight mists that hid the surface of the water. The oars swished across drowned grasses in the shallows before we stuck fast. I jumped out onto the soggy ground and pulled it safely onto the shore.

As I turned quickly for the village, Nicholas laid a hand on my arm. "Colin, calm yourself." I gritted my teeth. He walked silently beside me.

For the most part the houses of Lower Godney were smaller and poorer than those of Meare, save one, which I took to be the house of the bailiff. My hand trembled with anger as I knocked.

I spoke harshly to the middle-aged woman who answered. "I'm

looking for Father Bede." Her plump face was ruddy, and she held a long wooden spoon as though she might rap my head with it if I displeased her.

She snorted. "Gone to the Devil for all I care. Nothin's ever right by him. Bread too coarse, wine too crude. Fish not to his likin'—and that straight from the pool what sends it to the abbey—or did afore this business of the traitor abbot."

Conscious of Nicholas behind me, I clinched my fists at my side and refrained from defending Abbot Whiting. "Where is he?" I demanded.

But she hadn't finished her tirade. "We're not good enough for milord, who should of been abbot or at least a prior, to hear him talk. The man says his prayers at midnight in a voice to wake the dead." She shuddered at the thought. "I won't be sorry if me husband finds him floatin' facedown in a rhyne. He fell in once before, ye know."

"I know," I said. "I repent of having pulled him out." She gave me a startled look, but I went on. "So you don't know where he's gone?"

She looked wary. "No. Out all day. The man does that sometimes and 'tis a relief to me, I tell ye. Eats no more than a mouse, for all his complaining. Fastin', he says, for the glory of Glassonb'ry. There be a light of devilment in his eyes, I tell ye." She leaned close to whisper these thoughts, close enough that I could smell the rotting teeth in her mouth.

I backed away. "Thank you, missus. I'll call again if I don't find him."

"And I hope ye don't!" she called after me.

Out all day. So he hadn't been home since he stole the cup. He must have seen me from across the moors one of the times when I checked the hiding place.

"Colin." Nicholas spoke beside me. "Let's go home. We'll find him tomorrow."

I shook my head, fearing I would be too late. "No. He's gone to Wells to use the cup as magic. I must find him before he does something terrible." To return to Meare would take me in the opposite direction.

Nicholas shook his head. "The marshes are dangerous in winter. Sure, there's a way to the Wells road, but places ye could pass in summer are under water. Ye'll lose yourself."

"I must try."

Nicholas made a sound of exasperation. "Colin, no cup's worth this. Ye'll drown and your bones'll not be found till spring. Why do ye think they call this the Summer Country?"

I turned from the pool. "Go home, Nicholas. Matilda will be worried. I know what I have to do." That wasn't completely true. I had no idea what I would do when I found Father Bede, but I had to find him.

He must have seen he could not change my mind. "Ye'll need a torch." He cut a handful of dry reeds at the shore and twisted them deftly into a knot. We lit it at the hut that passed for an inn in the village.

I reached for the torch, and our fingers touched. "Nicholas, whatever happens, I . . ." I had no idea what lay ahead in Wells.

"Go with God," he said in a voice of resignation and turned back toward the boat.

A well-worn track led to Upper Godney, smaller even than Lower Godney, but from there the track twisted and turned, seeking the firmest way across the peat bogs. The mossy earth squished and oozed beneath my boots. A fine white mist reached long fingers from the bogs on either side as if to grab my ankles and pull me into the black waters. I had to wade short distances, fixing my eyes on the gap in the grasses that showed where the path continued at the edge of the ring of torchlight. Logs and branches had been laid down to bridge the softest spots, but sometimes even those disappeared beneath the mists and water.

Twice I followed trails the livestock must have made in summer that now ended in misty pools rimmed with deep mud. I lost precious time turning back to find where I had gone wrong. The night wore on. The fog thickened. I was cold and tired and despairing of ever getting out, much less of finding Father Bede.

"Nicholas was right," I muttered as my feet splashed once more in water to my ankles. "I was a fool to try this. What can Bede do before morning?" I held the torch high and peered into the darkness. A gap showed in the grasses to the left inviting me that way. There were no logs laid down here, and I was not altogether certain I was still on the path.

I felt my way forward into the shallow water step by step. The light of the torch reflected from a low blanket of thick fog. I could see neither the surface of the water nor any snags beneath it. The ground sloped gradually, and water rose halfway to my knees. A way led through the grasses to the left. It was not so wide as the path that had brought me here, and I began to wonder if it had been made by ducks and other water fowl rather than residents of Godney making for Wells or Glastonbury. I took another step, and my boot sank in the mire. I must turn back. I tried to pull my foot out, but the mud sucked at it like a living thing.

Panic gripped my chest. My breath came fast and shallow. I tried to shift my position for more leverage, but my feet found no solid ground. I grabbed for a branch of an overhanging shrub, but twisted, caught my foot on an underwater root and fell with a loud cry. The torch flew from my hand. For a moment it lit the shroud of mist before it extinguished itself in the hidden pool. Darkness dropped over my eyes like a hangman's hood.

I clung to the shrub beside me. I must not lose my direction, but I gripped so tightly that the thin twigs broke off in my fingers. The branch sprang back out of reach. I swore all the oaths I had ever heard my father use while my hands splashed frantically, feeling for the firm ground I had been standing on a moment before. But I only stirred up the thick stew of the bog.

I forced myself to stop. I must think and not exhaust myself in useless struggles. A fish nibbled at the exposed skin of my calf where the legging had come away from my boot. I shrieked as a vision of exposed white bones not found until spring flashed through my brain. Again I struggled against the sucking mud.

"Not that way, you fool." An irritated voice spoke through my splashing. I looked up. My eyes had grown accustomed to the torchless dark. The black form of a man hunched against the star-pricked sky. "Go slowly now." He reached out his hand and pulled me backwards by my shirt collar until I felt firmer ground under the shallow water. My feet stretched in front of me, still captive to the bog.

"Ease it gently," the voice commanded, sounding vaguely familiar. "Ye don't want to lose your boot. We've a long way to go."

It was Father Bede. How had he found me when I was seeking him?

Slowly I eased first one boot then the other free of the muck. I was cold and wet and the pungent smell of fear and rotting vegetation nauseated me. Or was it the smell of demon dogs? I fought to control the heaving of my stomach. At last I was free, and the old man led me shivering and humiliated back along the way I had come.

I was even more humiliated when I saw how clearly the path I had missed led off to the north only a few strides from where I had nearly lost myself forever.

"The mists hid it," I told myself angrily and clutched my wet cloak around me. My boots squelched with mud and water, and I bent to remove a sodden reed that tangled around my foot. "How did you find me?" I asked sullenly.

"Ye made enough noise to bring the bishop's men from Wells." He stopped under a yew tree where the ground was firm and nearly dry and drew himself up in his usual posture of command. "Now spread your cloak on the branches to dry, and get some rest. We must be in Wells in time for the trial."

My chin dropped. "So you *are* going to Wells." I wrung out my cloak as best I could and spread it on the branches. Water dripped from my soaked clothes, and I rubbed my arms to get warm. "You stole the cup, didn't you?"

"I didn't steal it. You did. It belongs to the abbey. Abbot Whiting is in prison. Prior Robert has joined the enemy, and as third in rank, I alone represent the Holy House of Glastonbury. It falls to me to restore her glory. You are an impudent boy without the courage of a water rat. You had in your hands the Holy Grail, but you have neither the knowledge nor the will to use it. I have both."

I stared at him, fascinated by his madness. I longed to escape, but we stood on an island of green in a sea of white mist, and I feared to lose my way again.

"Instead you fraternize with heretics who break the laws of God and man and bring down judgment on their heads." He took a step toward me, his eyes beneath their bristling brow as sharp as the finger he pointed at my heart. "I tell you, when the power of Glastonbury is restored, when I sit in the abbot's chair, Nicholas Thatcher will not get off with a day in the stocks. I will light a fire on the Tor that will be seen as far as London and burn every man, woman and child who listens to his teaching and does not bow to me!"

"They saved your life!"

"Don't think I don't know that he still hides the heretics' Bible. That girl reads it and entraps men with her siren's song and draws them into sin with her filthy female ways. She will be the first to burn in hell."

I wasn't aware of handling the knife in my belt, but suddenly it was there in my hand, and my grip was not to cut meat at table. I held the sharp blade like a sword—my brother's sword, which I had used against my father.

A pair of red eyes gleamed in the darkness beyond the yew tree, and the stench of rot reached me, but I ignored it. I took a step toward Father Bede. He raised his chin and watched me from under his thick gray brows.

"You will not harm my friends. Do you hear me?" My voice rose in a shout and then quieted menacingly. "You will not touch Alice." I was less than two paces from him. The muscles of the arm that held my knife tensed in readiness. Everything in me wanted to thrust it forward and end his life. The red eyes blinked, and instead of dung I smelled cinnamon.

Father Bede did not move. He looked disdainfully at the knife in my hand. He thought no more of me than an insect to be squashed under foot. But was that all I was? Had I learned nothing since fleeing my father's house?

Seventy times seven. Tha's what ye read.

I licked my lips and pressed them together to stop their trembling. I swallowed hard and slowly lowered the knife.

A sly smile spread over Father Bede's face. "Didn't I say you hadn't the courage of a water rat?"

I raised the knife again. "It takes a different kind of courage to do what is right when everything in you wants to do what is wrong."

The red eyes no longer glowed at the edge of the clearing. The fiendish creature must have gone, for the smell was not so strong.

Father Bede lost his smirk. "Put the knife away, boy." He didn't sound quite so confident. "We must be in Wells in the morning if we are to save the abbot. You do have courage for that, don't you?"

"Where is the cup?" I demanded. He patted the pouch at his waist. "Give it to me." He hesitated. I raised the knife only a little. I knew I wouldn't use it, but Father Bede could not be sure. He drew the cup from his pouch. I took it from him, never letting my eyes leave his. Only then did I put away my knife. "We will rest as you say. It must be nearly morning."

I slipped the drinking bowl into my shirt. It felt smooth as silk against my skin, and the chill of the night no longer cut as deeply. Father Bede eased himself to the ground and rested his back against the tree. I sat down a few strides away, took off my boots and dumped out the water and muck that had puddled there. By the time I had finished scraping off the worst of the mud, his eyes were closed, and his breathing was slow and even. I pulled my damp cloak around me and curled on the ground, cradling the cup to my breast.

I did not intend to sleep. I wanted only to rest my eyes, but the struggles through the bog after my long walk to Glastonbury and back had worn me out. I dreamt my mother bent over me and adjusted the coverlet to keep me warm, but it was not her gentle hands, and there was no warmth in the touch.

When I woke, the sun was well up. Shreds of vapor weaving in and out of the reeds were all that remained of last night's fog. The Tor shimmered in a golden mist, and a cart lumbered toward Glastonbury on what I took to be the main road a scant 100 paces to the east.

I was alone, and when I felt for the cup, it was gone.

CHAPTER 29

"CURSE HIM!" I MUTTERED as I struggled to my feet. *How could I have been so foolish?* I splashed my face with water from a pool and shook my head vigorously to clear the web of sleep from my brain. The sound of bells from a village across the water proclaimed that it was already the hour of morrow Mass, and I still had two hours' walk ahead.

I sprinted to the road and dashed toward the oncoming cart. "Did you see a monk on the road to Wells?" I asked.

The driver rubbed his chin in a gesture much like Wilfrith's. "Aye," he said slowly.

"How long ago?"

He turned and gazed up the road with maddening slowness. "Some way back," he said at last.

I bit back the impatient words on my tongue. I was wasting time. "Thank you," I said and started off at a brisk clip.

❦

The sun had dried my cloak by the time I reached the city walls, and I paused at one of the public wells that gave the town its name to clean myself as best I could. Surely Father Bede had passed this way. The crowd was festive, laughing and shouting bawdy comments on the fate of those to be tried. Hawkers passed to and fro carrying trays of sweetmeats and fresh-baked bread. I bought a piece and ate it, scanning the crowds for a glimpse of a gray head and a black habit.

The press of people drew me through a fortified gateway toward the bishop's palace. The bare trees of his garden rose over the wall and were reflected in the moat that separated the city from her spiritual rulers.

I passed the drawbridge onto the grounds and entered the bishop's hall where the court was already in session. Eight great windows with high pointed arches in the gothic style lit the hall. It was large enough to banquet 200 men, and the crowd that filled it laughed and ate as if they had come to see a play instead of men condemned to death. The chief freemen of the city sat as jurors on the raised dais at the front of the room. I clenched my teeth in anger when I recognized Jack Horner of the children's rhyme among them. They fined a wool merchant for misrepresenting his goods, and sent a common thief out to be hanged, much to the crowd's delight. There was no sign of the prisoners from Glastonbury or of Father Bede.

At last the bailiff called the case of "Richard Whiting, formerly abbot of Glaston, and his accomplices, John Thorne and Roger James." Guards hustled the prisoners through a small door at the foot of the dais. Roger drew back when he saw the crowd, and Brother Arthur looked around, baffled. His cheeks had lost their roundness, and his cassock hung loosely. Was it possible they had not realized they were being brought to trial?

By the smirk on Layton's face as he led the guard, I could well imagine that he had let them think he was escorting them home.

Their faces were worn and tired, and I suspected they had only just arrived, with no time to rest or refresh themselves. Abbot Whiting kept his dignified gaze fixed on the judge, whatever thoughts may have confused his mind.

The judge read the charges. Treason was not among them. It seemed to be already assumed, although no proof was shown. They were charged with the theft of a golden chalice and certain other items of value.

"Curse you, Father Bede!" I muttered. Why had he put it into their heads to hide those pieces in the wall of the Edgar Chapel? Yet I knew

that Chancellor Cromwell would have found some other excuse to destroy the abbot. But Roger and Brother Arthur might have survived.

The crowd was thick, and the court was calling disgruntled tenants to testify against the abbot. The abbot blinked several times at
their lies and once stepped forward as if to defend himself.

The judge looked sternly at him. "You will keep silent. No defense
is permitted." He returned to questioning the witness, who told one
lie after another, twisting the truth until the falsehood must have
been obvious, but the verdict was already determined.

I wondered what reward the witness expected for giving the king
the verdict he sought. I edged along the north wall of the hall, trying
to get near enough for my friends to see they were not alone in this
hellish place.

A scuffle broke out near the front.

"Hoc est corpus meum!" To the right of the dais, Father Bede raised
the cup over his head and shouted the words of the Mass. Roger turned
and looked at him. At first the joy of recognizing someone from the
abbey crossed his face, but his expression soon turned to horror.

"What hocus pocus is this?" murmured a merchant beside me. "Is
the man mad?"

Indeed, that was clearly the thought of all. I pushed forward more
desperately. "Let me through!"

Abbot Whiting wore a look of compassion. He stepped toward
Father Bede and the raised cup before a guard jerked him back.

The cup did not show its power as Father Bede had expected. It
did not cast its light on the darkness of the court. Instead of falling
at his feet in worship, a crowd of onlookers rose up to assist the guard
in subduing a mad priest, and the aisles were so jammed with shouting people that I could not get near. Long before I reached the place,
Father Bede was swept out the door at the foot of the dais amidst the
laughter and mockery of the citizens.

The trial was already drawing to a close. The judge's voice rose over
the babble of the crowd.

Richard Whiting, you and your accomplices are found guilty
of the theft of these items. Tomorrow you will be taken to

Glastonbury, bound to hurdles and dragged through the town to the top of the local Tor. There you will be hung, and drawn and quartered. Your heads will be placed on the gates of your former abbey as a warning to all who would commit such a crime. Parts of your bodies will be exhibited in Wells, Bath, Ilchester, and Bridgewater. Let all men fear to break the king's law!

CHAPTER 30

"No!" I SCREAMED. "They have done nothing!" But the jeers of the crowd drowned out all other sound. Roger's face was pale beneath his red hair, and his tall frame swayed. Brother Arthur raised his chin defiantly. They did not beg for mercy, but followed their guards meekly from the hall while the bailiff called the next case.

I pushed through the crowd and out the door at the foot of the dais. "Father Abbot!" I cried, but a grizzled soldier gripped my coat.

The prisoners were being marched toward a small tower a hundred paces away, built into the wall overlooking the moat. They paused and looked back. Brother Arthur's lips parted in surprise at sight of me, then he nodded and pointed heavenward as if to say they were trusting in God. The abbot raised his hand and began the sign of the cross before he was roughly shoved into the tower.

"Father Abbot! Forgive me!" I fell to my knees, sobs shaking my chest. I had failed him. I had not gone to Wales. I had not been reconciled to my father. And I had lost the cup he entrusted to my care.

"Forgive me," I whispered again, reaching my hands helplessly across the courtyard.

But I felt no forgiveness. I had not forgiven.

"Ye'd best be gone," the soldier said, dragging me to my feet. He pushed me toward the palace gate. "You and that madman."

I stopped so abruptly the guard walked into me. "The madman! What became of him?"

The man jerked his head toward a formation of soldiers preparing to cross the drawbridge. "Got away for now, but don't ye worry. They'll bring him back." I watched warily. "Screamin' curses on King Henry, he was. Another gallows on the Tor tomorrow. He can hang with the rest of them." The old soldier looked narrowly at me. "Ye're no friend of his, are ye?"

I thought to call him "enemy," but only said, "He has something that belongs to me."

"Well, be gone with ye now."

I glanced once more at the tower where my friends were imprisoned and slipped across the drawbridge in the crowd. I followed the contingent of soldiers through the gateway into the market. A cry went up as they began to search for Father Bede among the stalls, overturning some in their zeal, and bringing the tradesmen's wrath on their heads.

The sergeant questioned bystanders, and a vendor of leather goods pointed toward a porch between two buildings. I darted in ahead of the nearest of King Henry's men and nearly tripped over the extended leg and crutch of a beggar there.

"Alms!" he cried. "A penny for the poor!"

Two ragged children thrust grimy hands at me from a dark corner. "Please, sir."

I hesitated with my hand on my pouch, but sunlight glittered on the approaching armor of the soldiers in the market. They were after Father Bede and not me, but I had every intention of keeping out of their way. I fled out the other side of the porch.

A vast green spread before me, dotted with people and grazing sheep, and ringed by the yellow stone of cathedral buildings. To my right rose the ornately carved West Front of the great church. The echoing voices of soldiers shouted the beggars out of the way in the porch behind me. My quick glance caught no sight of Father Bede on the green, and I thought it far more likely that he would hide himself in the church. I slipped through the nearest door as the first soldier emerged from the shadows of the porch.

The south aisle of the cathedral was dimly lit. Its shadows were chilly after the warm sunshine. The heavy steps of soldiers echoed from the vault above me. I must find Father Bede before they did—and I must not be found!

I pressed my back against a broad pillar, sliding around it to keep its bulk between me and two of King Henry's men. On the far side, I came upon another. He was scanning the nave, and I dropped to my knees, feigning prayer before the lighted candles of a chantry chapel built into the arch until he passed beyond me. A shiver ran from my scalp to my toes, whether from fear or the cold floor, I could not have said.

When at last the soldiers made their noisy exit from the cathedral, I continued my quieter search of its darker corners. Perhaps with the danger past, Father Bede would emerge from hiding.

Whether his madness was the result of consorting with demons or merely of old age and the horrors we had all witnessed, I had no understanding. But I found that I hated him no longer. I pitied him. When I found him, I would take him home to Godney. Surely his brother would take him back, for he was kin. And somehow I must convince him to give me the cup. But I found no sign of him. Father Bede had gone, if indeed he had ever been there.

I emerged into the sunlight and followed one of the paths that crisscrossed the green, coming out beside an inn in the High Street. The smell of simmering stew and roasting meat roused my stomach, but I had no time for it.

"How little men understand of miracles," Father Dunstan had said. Father Bede thought the cup meant power. He didn't realize it was the power of God's presence and not a talisman to manipulate for gain. In the court he had tried to use the Mass as a magic spell. Would he try again? If so, where?

The abbey. It's the glory of Glastonbury he seeks; that's where he'll go.

I started to run down the sloping street, out of the town and out of the hills. It was dark before I reached the levels. I had long since slowed to a walk, but I pressed on steadily, uneasy about what the mad priest might attempt. Would the soldiers also think of looking for him in Glastonbury?

My stomach was empty. I had not eaten since the bread in the market place that morning, and fasted the day before. I wished I had taken something at the inn in Wells. But I was no stranger to fasting now, and each pang of hunger reminded me to pray for courage for my friends who would die tomorrow.

There was no moon, and if the road had not been broad and raised over the soggy moor, I might have stumbled again into the bog. When I came out from behind Harter's Hill, the shadow of the Tor rose before me, blotting out the stars over Glastonbury. The hour was late and few lights shone from the village.

It was well past Compline when I reached the northern edge of the town. The streets were dark and quiet, but I saw no sign of the demon dogs that had haunted them yesterday. I wondered warily where they had gone.

I tried the small abbey gate opposite the north porch. It was locked, as I knew it would be. The space between its iron bars and the stone arch was smaller than even Wil could fit through, but farther on, a tree hung over the wall. I dug my fingers and toes into the crevices between the stones and climbed until I reached the branches and clambered over. I landed with a thud on the mossy ground. Ahead of me rose Saint Mary's of Glastonbury like some monstrous skeleton. Stars peeped through where the roof had been. Even most of the windows were gone.

"For their lead." I spat my contempt.

I waited in the deepest shadows along the wall for several minutes. My confidence began to wane. Father Bede could not have climbed the wall as I did. And what did he expect to accomplish in this place abandoned by God?

I saw no sign of soldiers. Perhaps they were in the guardhouse at the front gate, keeping warm. I rubbed my cold fingers together. The damp chill of autumn seeped through cloak, doublet, shirt and skin to my very bones now that I had stopped my brisk walk. There would be no moon tonight.

I was here now. At least I could look. I sprinted across the lawn to the deeper shadows of the north porch. The great oak doors were gone, no doubt to lock some manor barn, and I could see straight into the ruined church. The floor was littered with rubble and broken tiles not worth carrying away.

I slipped around the corner and pressed myself against the wall of the north aisle. I could not believe that scarce two months had gone since more than fifty monks had worshiped here. I picked my way toward the chancel, stepping over a pillar that had fallen into the nave and shattered. Its loss mattered little since there was no longer a roof to hold up. Only an alcove remained where the altar of Saint Thomas had been in the north transept. The side altars were similarly stripped. The lions that graced the head and foot of the tomb of King Arthur had been chipped and broken by some careless workman, and the black marble pried from the core and stacked in the quire, ready to be carried away.

There was no sign of Father Bede. In truth I could not imagine saying Mass here. Where once the Great Sapphire had hung over the high altar, there ought to be a banner proclaiming, *"Ichabod! The glory is departed."* Perhaps some sense of the presence of God would return someday when rain and wind had softened the wounded stones that remained and a green carpet of grass had grown over the ravaged floor. But for now, this place spoke only of judgment.

I knelt a few moments where the high altar had once been, feeling exposed despite the moonless night and wondering what Henry's men would do if they caught me here. I tried to pray, but no words would come except, "Have mercy, Lord!" After a few moments I rose and made my way back along the south aisle. Through the doors I glimpsed the cloister, now no more than a yard piled with stone waiting for use in some other place. The dorter had been the first building to go lest any of us be tempted to return.

The Lady Chapel stood almost intact. Its unglazed windows stared down at me like unseeing eyes, making me wonder once again where Henry's guards were. My skin crawled. I must leave this place. It was no longer a home to me. A faint scraping sound caused me to whirl around. But there was nothing behind me except the long empty nave with its starry roof. When my heart slowed its startled pounding, I realized that the sound had not come from behind me, but from under my feet.

The Chapel of Saint Joseph! It was in a crypt beneath the Lady Chapel. Surely it was the least damaged part of the abbey. And it was Saint Joseph of Arimathea who had brought the Grail from the Holy Land. What better place for a mad priest to try to restore the abbey?

I backed noiselessly out of the Lady Chapel and passed around the outside to the stone steps to the crypt. If I could hear Father Bede, he would no doubt hear me, and I preferred to surprise him. I crept down the steps and paused at the entrance to the long hall. No sound came from the chapel. A faint light shone, and when I moved cautiously into the room, I saw two lighted candles on the altar. Their light reflected off a single window, which the looters had missed, set as it was in a well below the ground.

I stepped carefully forward. The vaulted ceiling was low, and I had to duck in places. The candlelight did little to pierce the darkness. Although I could see no sign of Father Bede, he was surely there. Someone must have lit the candles. I crept, step by step, as silently as I knew how, toward the altar. Gradually, I became aware of breathing, rapid and irregular, the little gasps of someone more frightened than I.

I grew bolder. There was no way out, save the steps behind me. "Father Bede?" I whispered, urgently.

A heap of shadows on the floor almost at my feet whirled around. My heart leaped to my throat, and I pushed against the wall of the crypt. The candlelight showed a white face that drew a long started gasp.

"Colin? Is that you?" The voice was Father Aidan's. "I feared it was the guards come to throw me out. Have you heard the news?" The novice master paused, and a small sob escaped before he went on. "They have been condemned."

"I know." I closed my eyes and steadied my breathing.

"I intend to pass this night in prayer. I'm so glad you're here to join me."

I knelt beside him and clasped his cold hands. "I'll pray with you a little while, Father Aidan, but I must find Father Bede."

"Father Bede?" He wrinkled his brow. "He is staying with his brother in Godney."

I nodded. "But he's missing. The soldiers are looking for him. He . . . he has the olivewood cup. I think he wants to use it in some rite to restore the abbey. He tried at the trial."

A look of concern passed over Father Aidan's face. "The madman they mentioned." Concern turned to wide-eyed fear. "Bede . . . he always had an unhealthy fascination with witchcraft. At Oxford there was—something. It was years ago. I don't know exactly what it was, but he was brought back to Glastonbury without finishing his degree. There were those who might have selected him for abbot, if there hadn't been questions about his past."

He shook his head. "He won't be here in the house of God to work his spells. He'll be on the Tor—or under it."

I stared at him. "The White Spring . . . I met Father Bede there a few days before the soldiers came for the abbot. He . . . He was talking with a stag."

Father Aidan drew back and crossed himself. He glanced toward the single glazed window, but the only light came from the reflected candles. "It must be near the hour of Matins," he said. "Midnight." He gripped my arm. "Hurry, Collen. You must find him. Whatever he intends to do—it must not be done."

CHAPTER 31

I FELT MY WAY BACK ACROSS the chapel and up the steps. Halfway through the ruined church I realized that Father Aidan had dismissed me as *Collen*, not the English inflected *Colin*. A year in the monastery had not turned me into a saint, but I had experienced forgiveness, and I knew I was not the same.

"God help me!" I gasped as I ran.

I climbed the tree and swung myself over the wall into the empty street beyond. My boots echoed on the cobblestones, and I gave up hope of being quiet. I darted into the shadows of the lane behind the abbey just as the watch rounded the corner of the High Street. It was easier to be quiet on the path around Chalice Hill, but harder to see the way. I wished for a torch. Banks of clouds approached from the sea, blotting out the stars as they came. A tiny flash of lightning lit the sky far to the west.

I dreaded the thought of the Tor looming above me with those three gibbets raised at the top. When I reached the entrance to the little valley, my courage failed me. Cold darkness flowed from its depths, stronger than the mingled waters of the two streams—White and Red. The blood pounded in my ears, all but drowning the sound of water flowing over stones.

Saint Collen confronted the Devil under the Tor, but he had holy water. What did I have? I didn't even have the cup. Father Bede had that. I had the cross around my neck that had belonged to my mother who loved me, and I had the Christ it represented. That would be enough. It had to be.

I strode forward into the valley. Splash! In the darkness I stepped into the stream. I jerked my foot back before the frigid water had time to seep into my boot. Just when the darkness seemed impenetrable, a flash of lightning lit the sky behind me. It threw my shadow into stark relief along the valley floor. For a brief instant I could see the red stream winding down from Chalice Well on the left and formations of calcite along the white stream. Darkness returned, and distant thunder rolled slowly toward me across the moors. I took a few confident steps before slowing down to feel my way once more, but another flash soon revealed the next steps I must take. This time the thunder was not quite so distant. Clouds rolled in and wiped the stars from the sky like a tide clearing the beach.

At the next flash, I saw the path running close beside the faery carvings at the bottom of the Tor where the White Spring seeped from the ground. Around the next corner I had seen Father Bede and the stag. I felt my way forward as the rumbles of thunder grew nearer and a cold wind began to blow straight down the little valley. I clutched my cloak around me and bent to walk against it. It was a relief when I stepped into the shelter of the ravine. The storm was nearly upon me. Large drops of rain splattered one by one on trees, ferns and rocks. They splashed like stones where they hit the water of the spring. In the distance I could hear the rush of coming rain. I felt my way forward, toward the steep hillside and the delicate calcite formations shrouded in moss and ferns that I remembered.

A bolt of lightning like the finger of God struck a yew near the crest of Chalice Hill. The tree burst with light, every branch tingling with power. The touch of heaven to earth seemed to go on and on as the crash of thunder exploded around me. I crouched against the hillside and put my fingers in my ears, gazing at the awesome sight. The tingling of the branches turned to flames. Even as the sound faded away, echoing from the hills that edged the Vale of Avalon, the yew became a torch lighting the night.

The bells of Saint John the Baptist began to ring faintly in the distance. They should have been joined by the bells of Saint Mary's, now forever silent. Matins. Midnight.

I turned back to the hillside and was shocked to see by the light of the burning tree a deep scar where the ferns and white faery stone had been ripped away. Someone had opened a gash in the hill and tossed his iron tools carelessly aside. I moved closer to see. The exposed crevice led to a tunnel from which the spring flowed. And when the rain began to fall like the waters that floated the ark of Noah, I slipped inside.

❧

The light of the burning tree did not reach here, and yet the place was not completely dark. A faint glow came from the low, damp passage that led into the hill. I felt my way along it, a hand on each wall. Thunder rumbled again, but whether it was more distant or the hill around me muffled the sound, I did not know. The splash of falling water echoed on every side. In places I had to straddle the stream in order not to wet my feet. Farther into the cavern, the light grew brighter, and I was filled with an uncanny sense that I had been in this passage before. I shook my head to clear the dreamy fog of remembrance and pushed on.

The rock of the tunnel was strangely shaped, as was everything formed by the White Spring. It appeared to flow into the darkness with the stream that formed it. The walls ahead glimmered lacy white in the light of some unseen torch. Near the end of the tunnel my feet tangled in something dark. I stumbled and reached a hand to steady myself against the wet walls. A cold dread crept up my fingers to my heart. I felt in the darkness at my feet and pulled up a soft wool garment—a monk's robe.

At last the passage opened into a great hall, as large as the abbey refectory and crowded with pillars of stone. I knew it instantly as the cavern of my dream the night my mother died. Fear brushed me like the wings of a bat. My head felt light and the cavern seemed to grow darker for a moment, but it was only the pounding of my own blood clouding my vision. Delicate columns, too fragile to hold the weight of the earth above, glittered in the light of a circle of torches. I knew well enough this was not heaven. I crossed myself and hoped it wasn't the gate of hell.

Father Bede stood naked in the center of the circle of torches. His hair, the color of ashes, was as wild as when I had seen him on the moors, and his gray body was thin and bent. A pattern of pink scars marked his breast where the demon dog had leaped. He was engrossed in a book he held and didn't appear to notice me.

The floor of the cave was cut in the same pattern of interlocking circles that decorated the cover of Chalice Well. In the center of the etched pattern sat the cup.

I started forward, thinking only to take the cup and run from this cursed place, but at that moment Father Bede stooped. He laid down the book and picked up the cup. He dipped it into a stone basin overflowing with spring water and slowly walked around the circles, pouring water on the pattern he had cut and chanting words I did not recognize.

He filled the cup once more and placed it in the center of the pattern. When he took up the book again, I saw that he held it upside down. Although I was too far to read the words, the illuminated capitals were in the wrong place. And when he began to speak again, I knew the words for Latin, but there was no sense to them—no sense until I realized he was reciting the Mass backwards.

Far in the distance I heard the baying of hounds and the call of a hunting horn. I glanced back through the passage, but I knew that was not the direction from which the sounds had come. They echoed deep inside the cavern, resounding from the bowels of the earth, like the phantom hounds of my dream. What was Father Bede doing? Did he not hear? I glanced around for some escape.

The old man went on reading backward from the book in his hands. His voice rose over the clatter of hooves that rang from the depths. The stone beneath my feet vibrated. He heard. I knew that he heard as I did, yet he read on.

"Father Bede, no!" I shouted, but my voice was drowned in the rumble of falling stone. I stared at the opening in the rock face on the far side of the hall.

Father Bede set down the book. He stood in the middle of the circle of symbols and made the sign of the cross in reverse over the olivewood bowl. It shook with the vibrations, and water spilled from it, dark as blood on the stones. The faery pillars swayed. One dropped from the ceiling and shattered across the floor. Flying slivers of stone filled the air. A piece stung my cheek, and when I took my hand away, I stared at the blood that marked my palm.

Father Bede threw back his head and shrieked with twisted joy. He bent and picked up a shard of shattered stone, long and pointed like a dagger. With it he stabbed first one palm, then the other. Blood ran onto the floor as he bent to stab his feet as well in imitation of the wounds of Christ.

"No!" I cried again.

He raised the stone dagger as if to pierce his side.

"No!" I leapt from my place beside a flowing curtain of stone and threw myself upon him. We fell to the floor, struggling.

"Stop it!" came the muffled cry beneath me. "Get off me!" He thrust me aside. "This is the moment of glory! Power comes again to Glastonbury—power not known since the days of the druids!"

Horror laid its icy fingers on my belly.

"The power of the abbey was a small thing." He stumbled to his feet, blood dripping from his wounds. He peered at me with eyes that flamed in the torchlight. "That power was easily broken by a mortal king." He drew himself to his full height, threw back his head and raised his arms in triumph. "But this power will rule all England for a thousand years!"

A mad laugh shook him. He dropped his arms and leaned toward me where I still huddled on the stone floor. "Never again will I be passed over. Do you understand, boy? Whiting will crawl to me to beg for his life. Cromwell will offer me the riches of his treasury. King Henry will lean on me as his chief advisor. I shall wield this power. So they have promised me."

"Who promised?"

"The givers of power beneath the hill."

One by one the torches fell and went out until only one remained. It lit the olivewood bowl, lying on its side, its clear water mingled with the blood on the floor like the waters of the two springs.

The noise of the approaching hunt grew louder. In a moment the silvery white hounds that had haunted the town burst into the cavern, their red eyes burning like glowing coals. A power that would rule all England for a thousand years, Bede had said. *No!* my soul cried.

I threw myself across the space that separated me from the cup. The moment I grasped it, my fingers tingled, and my heart relaxed its frantic beating. I knew what I must do. I scrambled to my feet and thrust the cup over my head.

There was a deafening rumble as Gwyn ap Nudd swept into the hall on his black stallion. His antlers brushed the nearest columns, and his blood-red cloak swirled around him. Death had come to reign on the earth.

"Stop!" I cried.

The horse reared and snorted, so suddenly did it halt. The hounds yelped and drew back, whimpering beneath the stallion's feet. A stench as of rotting meat rose from them. Behind me I heard a thump as Father Bede collapsed to the floor.

I held the cup between myself and the phantoms from the depths, and it suddenly glowed with a golden light that grew brighter and more intense. The rider threw up his arm to shield his hideous eyes. My arms trembled, and my breath came in short gasps.

In the name of *Jesu Christe*—

The hounds whined, and the horse pranced in place as though it longed to come forward, but could not beat back the light. The white walls of the cavern glittered with an intensity that cast black shadows behind every rock and curve of stone.

My mother's silver cross took on the weight of stone and pressed against my breastbone. I repeated my cry, stronger now.

In the name of *Jesu Christe,* Who conquered death and lives forevermore, go back!

The horned figure on the stallion grasped the reins, but he did not urge the horse forward. I was shouting now.

Go back where you came from. Return only when you come
to be judged by Him who lives forever and ever.

For long moments, time battled eternity. I held the cup before me.
No heavenly voices chanted or fragrant spices wafted to assure me. I
knew only the glory reflected from the cup and the stench of evil. The
cross burned on my breast while I waited, expecting to be trampled
by Death himself.

At last one of the hounds whimpered and fled back down the tunnel. The others followed, their tails between their legs, their high-
pitched yelps fading. The rider stared at me through the stag's hollow
eyes, but I stood firm. I raised the cup higher. My hands no longer
trembled. The cup's brilliant rays caught the silver cross on my breast.
Gwyn ap Nudd turned his head from its pure light.

In the name of *Jesu Christe.*

Before I had finished the cry, he had turned and was gone in a swirl
of blood-red cape. Only a faint smell of burning refuse remained.

I sank to my knees, clutching the bowl to my stomach. Did Saint
Collen's bones turn to porridge when the faery lords were gone? The
bowl faded quickly to a polished sheen, and I found I could hear the
far off chant of angels, fading in the quiet drip of water before I quite
sensed the words. And as I slipped the cup into my shirt, I caught a
whiff of cinnamon.

Father Bede lay stretched on the floor, his feet extending in the
direction of the tunnel through which the phantoms had come and
gone. His arms were extended. Blood puddled around his wounds,
but it no longer ran. His face was white. His lips were blue. I laid my
ear against his chest but heard no sound of breath or blood. He was
dead.

I closed his staring eyes and gazed at the still face. Why did I feel
such sorrow for this man who had been my enemy? I found the robe
he had abandoned. When I had covered him and folded his hands on
his breast, I made the sign of the cross and prayed for his wounded
soul. I don't know how long I knelt there, but in the end I found I was

weeping and praying, not for Father Bede or even for my friends who would die this day, but for my own father—and for myself.

I rose at last, and left him beneath the single torch that still burned.

I had not gone five strides into the passage before the ground began to tremble once more. I looked back. Perhaps I should take the body. I could carry him on my shoulders. I had before. The faint light of the single torch flickered on the white walls at the entrance to the tunnel. I stepped toward it. At that moment the earth shook violently. My courage failed me, and I fled as a large slab of ceiling fell behind me and sealed the tunnel forever.

❧

Father Aidan was kneeling in the ravine when I emerged. His face was turned upward in prayer. The storm had passed. The stars had come out, and the tree that had flamed like a torch, was a pile of red-gold embers against the black of Chalice Hill. I grasped a branch to steady myself and struggled to catch my breath.

"Colin?" Father Aidan clambered to his feet. He drew near and peered at me in the darkness. "Are you all right?"

I nodded, breathing hard, and turned back toward the tunnel. "The earthquake—"

"What earthquake?" he asked.

"You didn't feel it?"

"No." He looked at me curiously. "I followed you from the abbey," he went on. "I didn't like to think of your being alone in this. I have been praying."

"And you felt nothing?"

"Only the trembling of my own tired knees."

I sat abruptly on the cold, wet ground and closed my eyes to stop the world swirling around me.

"Is Father Bede in there?" Father Aidan asked.

I nodded. "He's dead, and the passage is blocked." Father Aidan lowered himself beside me and sat quietly while I recounted what I had seen and done in the cavern. He crossed himself several times as I talked, and when I had finished, his lips moved in silent prayers.

"And the cup?" he said at last.

I drew it from my shirt. It glowed faintly, whether from its own light or from the reflection of the fading embers on the hill, I wasn't sure. Holding it in my palms, I knew I had made a decision.

"I'm going home," I said. "Llwyd told me my father has changed, but even if he has not, I have."

I looked at Father Aidan. He nodded slowly. I studied the bowl as though I would find the words I needed written in its grain. "'Tisn't about deserving or not deserving. 'Tis about living like a citizen of the kingdom of heaven."

Father Aidan laid a hand on my arm. He turned his face toward the Tor, rising above us, and closed his eyes in prayer.

CHAPTER 32

I LEFT THE FORMER NOVICE master at his lodging near Saint John's Church. He promised to send word to Father Bede's family in Godney. My heart was heavy as I walked the soggy towpath that edged the River Brue as far as Meare. The events of the night had done nothing to change the fate of Abbot Whiting, Roger, or Brother Arthur. A thick mist hovered over the water and curled damp fingers around my tired feet.

A smoking wick burned in the dish when I entered the house to gather my few belongings. Nicholas sat, eyes closed, hands folded over the open Bible on the table before him. His eyes flew open, taking in my sodden clothes, streaked with Father Bede's blood from our struggle on the floor of the cave.

"It seemed a good night for prayer," he said at last.

I nodded slowly. "Nicholas, I'm going home."

As I began my story, Wilfrith started up from where he had fallen asleep on a stool by the fire. "Never was too good at passin' a night in prayer after a hard day's work," he mumbled. He brought cups of cider and set them before us.

"I'd like to come back," I added when I had finished, "after I have made my peace with my father." I took a deep breath. "If Alice will have me. . . ."

Wilfirth grinned. "Oh, I'd not fret on that. She'll have ye. Won't

233

GLASTONBURY TOR

hear of havin' any other, that girl, and ye know what she's like when her mind is settled."

Matilda stirred on the pallet in the corner. "Nicholas? What's happening?"

"Colin's back," he replied. "He's goin' home to Wales."

⁂

The eastern sky was beginning to pale when I took my leave of the family.

"When will ye be back?" Wil asked, rubbing sleep from his eyes.

"Not before summer." I smiled at him. "My father and I have a lot of forgiving to do. Seventy times seven. Right, Wil?"

I looked at Alice, who pressed her lips together and blinked rapidly as if to hold back tears. "But I will come back, if there's cause in your heart for me to come."

Alice laughed and two tears spilled out of the corners of her blue eyes. She took my hand, and pulled me toward the door. Outside in the darkness while Matilda prepared an early breakfast, we spoke our love and made our promises. Her face seemed to light the garden even before the day had dawned. Then we went back inside so I could speak to her father.

Wilfrith put an arm around his daughter. "Ye'll be right welcome, lad."

Alice broke the last blossom from the primrose bush that grew by the door and pressed it into my hand. I raised it to my nose and slowly drew in its scent before sliding it into my shirt over my heart and next to the cup.

"Thank you, Alice . . . , Wilfrith—all of you."

I turned and started down the path from Meare and from Glastonbury. When I looked back, the family still stood watching where the light from the house spilled into the garden. Beyond them, across the pool and the water meadows, the Tor showed dark against the dawn sky. The Tower of Saint Michael's still pointed its finger toward heaven. A line of torches wound its way up the distant hill, and at the top three gibbets stood stark against the gray of morning, waiting.

If I had more courage, I might have stood with them against the injustices of the court. If I had their holiness, I might have accepted their loss more easily. I had neither.

But I had a cup. More, I had a sure sense of God's presence—a Presence that would go with me to face my father as it would stay with my friends, both here in Meare and on the Tor this day.

> . . . From the ancient enemy: free and defend their souls, O Lord. . . .

I turned my back on Glastonbury Tor and began the long walk home.

AFTERWORD

THE EARLY SIXTEENTH CENTURY was a long and painful bridge for England between the faith-dominated High Middle Ages and the relatively secularized Elizabethan world. It likely would have been a traumatic era even without the complications of King Henry and Lord Cromwell. While religious wars raged on the continent, the line between Catholics and Protestants in England was not yet so clearly drawn. Godly men and women on both sides sought to follow Christ. Unscrupulous men bent the fragile religious framework to whatever best served their personal interests at the moment. Motives surely were mixed and confused on every side.

Glastonbury had epitomized the time of medieval faith that was ending. People firmly believed the many traditions associated with the place, including those of Joseph of Arimathea, King Arthur, the Holy Grail and the Celtic underworld of Gwyn ap Nudd.

While there is no proof that Joseph of Arimathea set foot upon Britannia or brought the Holy Grail, scholars believe that there was an historic Arthur. He was probably a fifth-century warlord, elevated to lead a coalition of tribes against the invading Saxons when the Roman presence had become too weak to offer protection. The real man would not recognize himself in the stories of medieval romance that grew up around his memory.

Arthur's Glastonbury would have been an island in the flooded

Vale of Avalon. Arthur could well have gone to this relatively safe haven for the healing of his wounds as the legends suggest. But the bones the monks found after the Great Fire are more likely those of a pre-historic, bronze age warrior of the Somerset Lake Village culture. Both the bones and the tomb disappeared in the confusion that surrounded the dissolution of the monasteries under Henry VIII.

∾

On November 15, 1539 Abbot Richard Whiting was executed on the Tor along with monks John Thorne and Roger James. The charge was robbing his own church of land and other valuables. No one actually believed him guilty of those charges. However his guilt or innocence on the charge of treason depended entirely on the viewpoint of the teller. Whiting was beatified by Pope Leo XIII in 1896.

Many shared the vision, here ascribed to the fictional novice Colin, of literate men and women who could read the Word of God and govern themselves. John Wycliffe saw that ideal as early as the thirteenth century and was the first to translate the Bible into English. Lollards suffered and died with a yearning that the Bible would one day be universally available in everyday language. William Tyndale, the son of a prosperous yeoman, translated the Bible from the original languages while in exile in the Low Countries. His inexpensively printed, mass market English editions were smuggled from Lutheran Germany into English and Irish ports for the use of ordinary people like the Thatchers. His poetic language strongly influenced both Myles Coverdale's *The Great Bible* which appeared at the time of our story (April 1539) and the 1611 edition of King James.

I have taken the liberty of incorporating the Pilgrimage of Grace, which actually occurred two years earlier in 1536. The fate of its participants was as portrayed. Also a young Colin could not legally have entered the monastery in 1538. A 1535 edict removed everyone under the age of twenty-four from the monasteries.

Hugh Latimer, Thomas Cromwell, Robert Layton, and King Henry are historic persons. Thomas Cromwell was beheaded in 1540 after the king rejected his choice of Anne of Cleaves as queen. Hugh

Latimer was burned at the stake by Henry's Catholic daughter, Queen Mary. I have used the names of actual monks of Glastonbury in its last days, although the personalities I have given them are entirely fictional, as are Colin and the Thatcher family.

A nineteenth-century water works destroyed the faery formations around the White Spring, although the waters still flow. Behind the water works a tunnel leads into the hill, long believed to be hollow. A fallen slab of roof blocks the tunnel today.

Although it has been nearly five hundred years since the buildings were destroyed, worship continues at the site of Glastonbury Abbey. Formal prayers are said every Tuesday morning in the crypt of Saint Joseph during summer and in the Chapel of Saint Patrick in winter. And visitors stand on the grassy lawn among the fallen stones where the abbey church once rose to say their prayers of praise to the God who reigns forever and ever, world without end. Amen.